reasonable
doubt
FULL
SERIES

WHITNEY G.

# Copyright

Cover designed by Najla Qambers of Najla Qambers Designs

Formatting by Erik Gevers

ISBN-13: 978-1502385512

ISBN-10: 1502385511

# CONTENTS

.

For my BFF/ultimate beta-reader/amazing assistant/shoulder to cry on whenever I'm acting crazy/ "person" like they say on 'Grey's Anatomy'... Tamisha Draper. (My books would suck without you...)

To Tiffany Neal. Thank you for being the balance. You'll always be the perfect balance...

To Natasha Gentile...How did you become my friend? LOL

And for the F.L.Y. crew: I fucking love you more than you'll ever know....

# Prologue

*Andrew*

New York City is nothing more than a shit-filled wasteland, a dump where failures are forced to drop all their broken dreams and leave them far behind. The flashing lights that shined brightly years ago have lost their luster, and that fresh feeling that once permeated the air—that *hopefulness*, is long gone.

Every person I once considered a friend is now an enemy, and the word "trust" has been ripped from my vocabulary. My name and reputation are tarnished thanks to the press, and after reading the headline that *The New York Times* ran this morning, I've decided that tonight will be the last night I ever spend here.

I can't deal with the cold sweats and nightmares that jerk me out of my sleep anymore, and as hard as I try to pretend like my heart hasn't been obliterated, I doubt that the agonizing ache in my chest will ever go away.

To properly say goodbye, I've ordered the best entrées from all my favorite restaurants, watched *Death of a Salesman* on Broadway, and smoked a Cuban cigar on the Brooklyn Bridge. I've also booked the penthouse suite at the Waldorf Astoria, where I'm now leaning back on the bed and threading my fingers through a woman's hair—groaning as she slides her mouth over my cock.

Teasingly darting her tongue around my tip, she whispers, "Do you like this?" as she looks up at me.

I don't answer. I push her head down and exhale as she presses her lips against my balls, as she covers my cock with her hands and moves them up and down.

Over the past two hours, I've fucked her against the wall, forced her to bend over a chair, and pinned her legs to the mattress

1

while I devoured her pussy.

It's been quite fulfilling—*fun*, but I know this feeling will only last for so long; it never stays. In less than a week, I'll have to find someone else.

As she takes me deeper and deeper into her mouth, I tightly tug her hair—tensing as she bobs her head up and down. Pleasure begins to course its way through me, and the muscles in my legs stiffen—forcing me to let go and warn her to pull away.

She ignores me.

She grips my knees and sucks faster, letting my cock touch the back of her throat. I give her one last chance to move away, but since her lips remain wrapped around me, she leaves me no choice but to cum in her mouth.

And then she swallows.

Every. Last. Drop.

Impressive…

Finally pulling away, she licks her lips and leans back against the floor.

"That was my first time swallowing," she says. "I did that just for you."

"You shouldn't have." I stand and zip my pants. "You should've saved it for someone else."

"Right. Well, um…Do you want to order some dinner? Maybe we could eat it over HBO and go at it again afterwards?"

I raise my eyebrow, confused.

This is always the most annoying part, the part when the woman who previously agreed to "One dinner. One night. No repeats." wants to establish some type of imaginary connection. For whatever reason, she feels like there needs to be some type of closure conversation, some bland reassurance that'll confirm that what just happened was 'more than sex,' and we'll become friends.

But it *was* just sex, and I'm not in need of any friends. Not now, not ever.

"No, thank you." I walk over to the mirror on the other side of the room. "I have someplace to be."

"At three in the morning? I mean, if you just want to skip the HBO and go for another round instead, I can…"

I tune out her irritating voice and begin to button my shirt. I've never spent the night with a woman I met online, and she isn't going to be the first.

As I adjust my tie, I look down and spot a tattered pink wallet on the dresser. Picking it up, I flip it open and run my fingers across the name that's printed onto her license: Sarah Tate.

Even though I've only known this woman for a week, she's always answered to "Samantha." She's also told me—*repeatedly*, that she works as a nurse at Grace Hospital. Judging by the Wal-Mart employee card that's hiding behind her license, I'm assuming that part isn't true either.

I look over my shoulder, where she's now sprawled across the bed's silk sheets. Her creamy colored skin is unmarred and smooth; her bow shaped lips are slightly swollen and puffy.

Her green eyes meet mine and she slowly sits up, spreading her legs further apart, whispering, "You know you want to stay. *Stay...*"

My cock starts to harden—it's definitely up for another round, but seeing her real name has ruined any chance of that for me. I can't stand to be around anyone who's lied to me, even if she does have double D tits and a mouth from heaven.

I toss the wallet into her lap. "You told me your name was Samantha."

"Okay. *And?*"

"Your name is *Sarah.*"

"So what?" She shrugs, beckoning me with her hand. "I never give my *real name* to men I meet on the internet."

"You just fuck them in five star hotel suites?"

"Why do you suddenly care about my real name?"

"*I don't.*" I glance at my watch. "Are you spending the night in this room or do I need to give you cab money to get home?"

"*What?*"

"Was my question unclear?"

"Wow...Just, wow..." She shakes her head. "How much longer do you think you'll be able to keep doing this?"

"Keep doing *what?*"

"Chatting someone up for a week, fucking her, and moving on to the next. How much longer?"

"Until my dick stops working." I put on my jacket. "Do you need cab fare or are you staying? Check out is at noon."

"Do you know that men like you—*relationship avoiders*, are the type that typically fall the hardest?"

"Did they teach you that at Wal-Mart?"

"Just because someone from your past hurt you doesn't mean that every woman after her will." She purses her lips. "That's probably why you are the way you are. Maybe if you tried to actually *date* someone you'd be a lot happier. You should take her out for dinner and actually listen, see her to her door without expecting an invitation inside, and maybe bypass the whole 'let's go fuck' in the hotel suite thing at the end."

Where are my keys? I need to go. Now.

"I can see it now…" She can't seem to shut up. "You're going to want more than sex one day, and the person you want it from is going to be someone you least expect. Someone who will force you to give in."

I pull my keys from underneath her crumpled dress and sigh. "Do you need cab money?"

"I have my own car, dick-face." She rolls her eyes. "Are you really this incapable of having a regular conversation? Would it kill you to talk to me for a few minutes after sex?"

"We have nothing more to discuss." I put my room key on the nightstand and walk toward the door. "It was very nice meeting you, Samantha, *Sarah*. Whatever the hell your name is. Have a great night."

"*Screw you!*"

"Three times was more than enough. No, thank you."

"Things are going to catch up to you one day, asshole!" She yells as I step into the hallway. "Karma is one hell of a bitch!"

"I know." I toss back. "I fucked her two weeks ago…"

# Contract (n.):
An agreement between two people that creates an obligation to do or not do a particular action.


*Six years later...*
*Durham, North Carolina*

**Andrew**

The woman who was currently sitting across from me was a fucking liar.

Dressed in an ugly ass grey sweater and a red plaid skirt, her hair looked as if it'd been dyed with a box of crayons. She looked nothing like the woman in the picture online, nothing like the smiling blonde with C-cup breasts, butterfly tattoos, and plump, pink lips.

Before I'd agreed to this date, I'd specifically asked for three separate proof of truth pictures: one of her holding a newspaper with the most recent date on it, one of her biting her lip, and one of her holding up a sign with her name on it. When I requested these things, she'd laughed and said that I was "the most paranoid person ever," but she'd done them. Or so I thought. With the exception of telling her my real name—I stopped giving out my real name years ago, I'd been completely honest and I expected that in return.

"Well, now that we're *alone*..." She suddenly smiled, revealing a mouth full of metal and rubber bands. "It's nice to finally meet you in person, *Thoreau*. How are you today?"

I didn't have time for this. "Who's the girl in your profile picture?" I asked.

"What?"

*"Who is the girl in your profile picture?"*

"Oh…Well, that isn't me."

*"No shit* it isn't you." I rolled my eyes. "Did you hire a model? Buy a bunch of stock images and use Photoshop?"

"Not exactly." She lowered her voice. "I just thought you'd be more likely to talk to me if I used that photo instead of my own."

I looked her over again, now noticing the strange unicorn tattoo across her knuckles and the "Love is blind" quote that was inked onto her wrist.

"What were you expecting to happen when we actually *met?"* This shit was boggling my mind. "Did you *think* about what would happen when that day came? When I realized that you weren't who you said you were?"

"I was kind of expecting for you to have lied about your picture too," she said. "I didn't know that you would really look like *you,* you know? This is the first time a guy on *Date-Match* has told the truth. I think it's a *sign."*

*"It's not."* I shook my head. "And the model? How did you get someone to take all those pictures?"

"It wasn't a model. It was my roommate." Her eyes widened as I stood up. "Wait a second! All the things I said to you on the phone were absolutely true. I *am* interested in politics, and I do love studying the law and keeping up with high profile cases."

"What law school did you go to?"

"Law school?" She raised her eyebrow. "No, not *law school* type of law. Law like, I've watched every episode of *SVU* and I've read all of John Grisham's books."

I sighed and pulled a few bills out of my wallet, putting them on the table. I'd wasted enough time with her.

"Goodbye, *Charlotte."* I walked away, ignoring the rest of her apology.

The moment the valet pulled my car around, I slipped inside and sped off.

This shit is getting ridiculous…

This was the sixth time this had happened to me this month, and I didn't understand why someone would willingly lie with a potential face to face meeting on the line. It didn't make any fucking sense.

Annoyed, I picked up a bottle of scotch from the store across the street, and made a mental note to block this latest liar from my page. I was starting to feel like I'd run out of available women to sleep with in Durham. I was also starting to feel like I needed to switch cities and start all over again; the cold sweats from years ago had returned, and I knew the nightmares were coming next.

As soon as I stepped into my condo, I poured myself three shots and tossed them back. Then I poured three more.

I scrolled through my phone and checked my emails for the day—client referrals, more requests to chat from *Date-Match*, and a message from the sexy blonde I was supposed to meet this Saturday.

The subject-line read,

**Honesty is Key, right?**

I tossed back another shot before opening it, hoping it was an invitation to meet tonight instead.

It wasn't. It was a goddamn essay.

> Hey, Thoreau. I know we're supposed to meet each other this Saturday and trust me, I was sooo looking forward to it, but I need to know that you're interested in me for me and not my looks. I've met a lot of creepy guys on here because they just like my picture, and when we meet, they just want to have sex. I can assure you that I am who I say I am, but I'm looking for something a little more fulfilling than casual sex. We don't have to have a full blown relationship, or engage in an intense affair, but we could at least build a friendship first, you know? I'm looking forward to seeing you, so let me know if you're still interested in meeting me
>
> —Liz.

I immediately clicked on my profile and opened the "What I'm Looking For" box, making sure that it still read the same: "Casual sex. Nothing more. Nothing Less."

That line wasn't there for decoration, and it was in bold print for a reason.

I returned to the woman's message and responded.

> I am no longer interested in meeting you. Best of luck finding whatever you're looking for
>
> —Thoreau.

She replied instantly.

> Are you for real?
>
> You can't use another friend? We can't be 'just friends'?
>
> —Liz.

> Hell no
>
> —Thoreau.

I signed off and blocked her address.

Another shot made its way down my throat, and I scrolled through the remaining emails—immediately opening the one that came from the only person I considered a friend in this city. Alyssa.

**Subject: Desert Dick**

So, I'm emailing you right now because I just thought about how much pain you're in currently...We haven't talked about you getting laid in quite a while, and that concerns me. Greatly. Like, I've CRIED about your lack of pussy...I'm very sorry that so many women have sent you fraudulent pictures and given you a severe case of blue balls. I'm attaching the links to a top of the line lotion that I think you should invest in for the weeks to come.

Your dick is in my prayers,

—Alyssa.

I smiled and typed a response.

**Subject: Re: Desert Dick**

Thank you for your concerns about my dick. Although, seeing as though you've NEVER discussed getting laid, I think having Cobweb Pussy is a far more serious illness. Yes, it is true that so many women have sent me pictures, but it's quite sad that you've never sent me yours, isn't it? I'm more than willing to send you mine, and eventually help you cure your sad and unfortunate disease.

Thank you for telling me that my dick is in your prayers.

I'd prefer if it was in your mouth.

—Thoreau.

Just like that, my night was now ten times better. Even though I'd never met Alyssa in person and our conversations were restricted to phone calls, emails, and text messages, I felt a strong connection to her.

We'd met through an anonymous and exclusive social network—LawyerChat. There were no profile pictures, no newsfeed activity, only message boards. There was a small profile box where information could be placed (first name only, age, number of years practiced, high or low profile status), and a logo on each user's profile that revealed his or her sex.

Every user was "guaranteed" to be a lawyer who'd been personally invited via email. According to the site's developers, they'd "cross-referenced every practicing lawyer in the state of North Carolina against the board's licensing records to ensure a unique and one of a kind support system."

I honestly thought the network was bullshit, and if it weren't for the fact that I'd fucked a few of the women I'd met on there, I would've cancelled my account after the first month.

Nonetheless, when I saw a new "Need Some Advice" message from an "Alyssa," I couldn't resist trying to replicate my previous results. I read through her profile first—twenty seven, one year out of law school, book lover—and decided to go for it.

My intent was to answer her legal questions, slowly steer the conversation to more personal things, and then ask her to join *Date-Match* so I could see what she looked like. But she wasn't like the other women.

She sent me constant messages, and she always kept the topic of conversation professional. Since she was such a young and inexperienced lawyer, she asked for advice on the simplest topics: legal brief editing, claim filing, and exhibition of evidence. After we'd chatted five times and I'd grown tired of having three hour long info-dump sessions, I asked for her phone number.

She said no.

"Why not?" I'd typed.

"Because it's against the rules."

"I've never met a lawyer that hasn't broken at least one."

"Then you're not a very good lawyer. I'll find someone else to chat with now. Thanks."

"You're going to lose that case tomorrow." I typed before she could end our session. "You have no idea what you're doing."

"Are you really that upset about me not giving you my phone number? What are you, twelve?"

"Thirty two, and I don't give a fuck about your phone number. I was only asking for it so I could call and tell you that the brief you sent me is littered with typos, and the closing argument reads like a first year law student wrote it. There are too many mistakes for me to sit here and type them all."

"My brief isn't that bad."

"It's not that good either." Before I could sign out of our chat, her phone number appeared on the screen, and underneath it was a short paragraph: "If you're going to call and help me, fine. If you're using my number to talk me into joining a dating site later, then forget it. I joined this network for career support, that's it."

I stared at her message long and hard—debating whether I should help her with no chance of getting anything out of it, but something made me call her anyway. I walked her through every mistake she'd made, insisted that she clear up a few sentences, and even re-formatted her brief.

Just when I was about to tell her goodbye and hang up, the strangest thing happened. She asked, "How was your day today?"

"That's not in your brief." I said. "You only want to talk about lawyer shit, remember?"

"I can't change my mind?"

"No. Hang up." I waited to hear a beep, but the only thing I heard was laughter. If it wasn't for the fact that it was such a raspy and sexy sound, I would've hung up myself, but I couldn't put the phone down.

"I'm sorry," she said, still laughing. "I didn't mean to offend you."

"You didn't. Hang up."

"I don't want to." She finally stopped laughing. "I apologize for that hostile message I sent you…You're actually the only guy I've met on here who answers all my questions. Are you busy right now? Can you talk?"

"About *what*?"

"About yourself, your life...I've been asking you boring legal questions every day, and you've been very patient so...It's only fair that we talk about something less boring for once if we're going to be friends, right?"

Friends?

I was hesitant to respond—especially since it didn't seem like the 'less boring' topics would involve sex, and she'd said the word "friends" so easily. Yet, I was in the middle of another sex-less night already, so I began to have a regular conversation with her. Until five in the morning, she and I discussed the most mundane things—our daily lives, favorite books, her dream of becoming a late, professional ballerina.

A few days later, we spoke again, and after a month, I was talking to her every other day.

Tossing back another shot, I pressed the call button on my phone and waited to hear her soft voice.

No answer. I considered sending her a text, but then I realized it was nine o' clock on a Wednesday and we wouldn't be able to talk at all tonight.

Practice...Wednesday nights are always ballet practice...

"Mr. Hamilton?" My secretary stepped into my office the next morning.

"Yes, Jessica?"

"Mr. Greenwood and Mr. Bach would like to know if you want to participate in the next round of intern interviews today."

"*I don't.*"

"Okay..." She looked down and scribbled something onto her notepad. "Did you at least look over the resumes then? They have to narrow it down to fifteen today."

I sighed and pulled out the stack of resumes she'd given me last week. I'd read through them all and written notes, mostly—"Pass" "Double Pass" and "I don't feel like reading this." All the remaining applicants were from Duke University, and to my knowledge, we were the only firm in the city who accepted pre-law *and* law school applicants for paid internships.

"I wasn't impressed with any of the applicants." I slid the papers across my desk. "Was that the entire selection pool?"

"No, sir." She walked over and placed an even larger stack in front of me. "*This* is the entire selection pool. Do you need me to do anything else for you this morning?"

"Besides getting my coffee?" I pointed to the empty mug at the edge of my desk. I hated that I always had to remind her to bring it; I couldn't function in the morning without a fresh cup.

"I'm so sorry. I'll get that right away."

I turned on my computer and scrolled through my emails, sorting them all by importance. Of course, Alyssa's latest email was pushed straight to the top.

**Subject: Get Over Yourself.**

Thank you for the childish picture text of the white dust that was outside your condo this morning. I really appreciated it, but I can assure you that that is NOT what the inside of my vagina looks like right now.

Not that it's any of your business, but I don't need to get laid every other day to satisfy my needs. They are WELL taken care of with a VARIETY of tools.

—Alyssa

**Subject: Re: Get Over Yourself.**

I sent you *two* pictures. One of the white dust and one of a dried up lake with dying animals. Was the second picture more accurate?

The only tool your pussy needs is my tongue. It's here whenever you want it, and it works in a "VARIETY" of ways.

—Thoreau

"Here you are, Mr. Hamilton." Jessica suddenly set my coffee on the desk. "Can I ask you something?"

"No, you may not."

"I thought so," she said, lowering her voice and looking into my eyes. "I know this is a bit unprofessional, but I need a date for the gala next month.

"Then *find a date* for the gala next month."

"That was my way of asking *you* to be my date..."

12

I blinked. I needed to find a way to word this "Hell no" very carefully.

Jessica was fresh out of college—way too damn young for me, working here because her grandfather started this firm, and looking for much more than I'd ever be willing to give. I'd overheard her several times on her lunch breaks, talking about how she wanted to be married before she turned twenty five. She also apparently wanted to be a stay-at-home mom with six kids, and live in a house in the suburbs.

In other words, she was completely out of her fucking mind.

"So, what do you say?" She smiled.

I tried not to roll my eyes. "Jessica..."

"Yes?" Her eyes were full of hope.

"Look, sweetheart. Not only would it be highly inappropriate for the two of us to *ever* engage in any type of relationship outside of this office, but I'm not the man you're looking for. At all. Trust me."

"Not even for *one night?*"

"The words 'one night' in my book hold certain expectations that you couldn't possibly meet. So, *no*. Go do some work."

"Is 'one night' a code for sex?"

"Why are you still in my office?"

"I wouldn't tell anyone if we had sex," she whispered. "I've actually fantasized about it since we first met. And, since you never have any calls on the books from a girlfriend, I'm assuming you're available."

"*I'm not.*"

"I walked in on you while you were in the restroom once... You're at least nine inches I think."

What the fuck?!

I was five seconds away from recording this conversation on my phone and emailing it to her grandfather.

"I'm *really good* at giving blowjobs," she said. "I've been doing it since high school. All the guys I've blown have said my mouth is *amazing.*" She bit her lip.

"Is there super-glue on my floor? Is that why you're still standing there?"

"If you were my date to the gala and we ended up having a good time, you'd be the first man I'd actually went all the way with." She blurted out, blushing. "I'm still a virgin, *down there.*"

"Then I'm *definitely* not the man for you." I rolled my eyes. "Now, leave before I call Mr. Greenwood and tell him that his precious granddaughter is offering to suck my dick over morning coffee."

Shocked, her cheeks tinged red and she quickly walked to the door. Then she looked over her shoulder and winked at me— fucking *winked* at me, before stepping out.

I immediately typed a note into my planner: *Find a new secretary—an older, married one...*

Before I could finish organizing my inbox, my cell phone rang. Alyssa.

"I'm busy," I answered.

"Then why did you pick up the phone?"

"Because the sound of my voice makes you wet."

"Funny." She laughed. "How's your morning?"

"Typical. My secretary just came onto me for the third time this month."

"She sent you another 'You and me belong together' note with chocolates?"

"No, she offered to suck my dick."

"What?" She gasped. "You're kidding!"

"Unfortunately not. After that, she told me she was willing to give me her virginity. Needless to say, I'll be posting a replacement ad pretty soon. Anyone from your office want to work for a better firm? I'll double the salary."

"How do you know that *my* firm isn't better than yours?"

"Because you call and ask me for advice on cases all the time— silly cases at that. If your firm was better, you'd never have to ask."

"Whatever." She groaned. "Have you bucked off the online dating wagon yet?"

"*Bucked? Wagon?*" I could never understand her little Southern metaphors. "What the hell does that mean?"

"Ugh, god..." She sighed. "It means you didn't update me about your date last night so I guess it was a bust, which means you haven't slept with anyone in over a month. That has to be a record for you."

"It is."

"Do you want some advice?"

"Not unless you want to come to my office and tell me *in person*." I smiled.

14

"No, thanks. Speaking of advice, I'll need your help Friday night."

"With what?"

"I just landed a pretty big case. I haven't gone through all the documents yet, but I already know I'm in over my head."

I leaned back in my chair. "If it's that big of a case, you could bring the documents to my condo tonight. I'd be happy to help you sort through them. Categorization has always been my specialty."

"Ha! Nice try, but I don't think so." She continued to talk about her case, but I was only halfway listening. It still struck me as odd that she didn't want to meet me in person, that she shut down the very thought any time I brought it up.

"Also…" She was still rambling. "I'll probably have to do some research on those changes. I'm not sure if—"

"Tell me the real reason why I can't meet you in person." I cut her off.

"*What?*"

"We've known each other for six months now. Why don't you want to meet?"

Silence.

"Do I need to repeat the question?" I stood up and walked over to my door, locking it. "Did you not understand me?"

"It's against the LawyerChat rules…"

"Fuck *LawyerChat.*" I rolled my eyes. "It's against the rules for you and me to have each other's phone numbers in the first place, for us to act like fucking teenagers and make each other cum over the phone at night, but you've never complained about that."

"You've never made me cum…"

"Don't lie to me."

"You haven't."

"So, last week when I said that I wanted you to ride my mouth so I could eat your pussy until you came all over my lips, you were *pretending* to breathe hard?"

She sucked in a breath. "No, but—"

"I thought so. Why can't we meet in person?"

"Because it would ruin our friendship and you know it."

"*I don't.*"

"You've told me that you never sleep with the same woman twice, that after you sleep with someone you're done with her."

"I've never fucked one of my *friends* before."

"That's because I'm your only one."

"I'm aware, but—" I stopped. I had no defense for that.

Silence lingered over the line, and I tried to think of another argument.

She spoke up first. "I honestly don't want to ruin our friendship over one senseless fuck."

"I guarantee we'll have more than *one* senseless fuck."

Her light, airy laugh drifted over the line, and I sighed—attempting to envision what she looked like. I wasn't sure why, but over the past few weeks, I'd been longing to experience her laughter face to face.

"You know," she went on, "for a high profile lawyer, you have a pretty dirty mouth."

"You'd be surprised how much filthier it can get."

"Filthier than what I've already experienced?"

"*Much filthier.*" I'd been treading the waters since we began this friendship—still hopeful that we'd meet in person someday, but now that we weren't, there was no point in holding back. "I guess I'll *talk to you* tonight."

"Not unless you find another date between now and then. I know you'll be searching."

"Of course I'll be searching." I scoffed. "Is Alyssa your *real* name?"

"Yes, but I'm sure *Thoreau* isn't yours. Do you care to finally give it to me?"

"I'll give it to you when you come to your fucking senses and let me see you."

"You just won't let that go, will you?" She laughed again. "What if the real reason I don't want to meet you is because I'm ugly?"

"I have a good feeling that *you're not.*"

"But if I *was?*"

"I'd fuck you with the lights off."

"I prefer the lights *on.*"

"Then I'd make you wear a paper bag over your head."

"*WHAT?!*" She burst into giggles. "You're ridiculous! Ugh, there's a client at my door right now. I have to go. Can I call you later?"

"Always." I hung up, smiling. Then it hit me.

Fuck…She always finds a way out of that line of questioning…

# Perjury (n.):
The willful giving of false testimony under oath.


### *Alyssa (Well, my real name is "Aubrey"...)*

*"Lies always catch up to people in the end. Why don't people understand that?"* That's what Thoreau's text message said this morning.

*"You don't think some lies are justifiable?"* I texted back.

"No. Never."

I hesitated. *"So, you've never lied to me?"*

"Why would I?"

"Because we barely know each other..."

*"Only because you keep me at a distance."* He sent me another text before I could respond. *"Would you like to know my real name and where I work?"*

"I prefer our anonymous arrangement."

"Of course you do, and I've never lied to you. I trust you for some strange reason."

"Some strange reason?"

"Very strange. I'll talk to you later."

I tossed my phone into my purse and sighed, letting that familiar feeling of guilt wash over me. I'd never meant to continue talking to him, to become his friend outside of LawyerChat, but I was in too deep, and I didn't want to let him go.

Months ago, when I'd spotted the invitation to the exclusive network on my mother's desk, I swore to only use it when I needed to ask questions for my pre-law classes. I'd used her access code to log in, built a fake profile, and made sure all the questions I asked were weaved in a way that no one would know that they were for homework assignments.

Unfortunately for me, the pre-law program at Duke was unlike any other program in the country. It consisted of more hands-on classes, one-on-one mentoring from practicing lawyers, and it was mandated that each student find an internship for the final four semesters. In addition to that, they expected us to read through and interpret case files like we were already lawyers.

If I had known that asking Thoreau for so much homework advice would lead to an actual friendship, I might have stopped talking to him sooner. Then again, just like I was his only friend, he was my only friend, too.

He was open and honest every time we spoke, and I only wished that I could be the same—especially since he seemed to have a habit of saying, "I hate fucking liars" whenever one of his dates deceived him.

Damnit…

Smoothing the tulle fabric of my tutu, I took several deep breaths; I could think about my friendship with Thoreau later, right now I needed to focus.

Today was audition day for a production of *Swan Lake* and I was a nervous wreck; I'd barely slept the night before, skipped breakfast, and showed up to the theater five hours early.

"Please clear the stage, ladies and gentlemen!" The director shouted from below. "The official auditions will begin in thirty minutes! Please clear the stage and make your way to the wings!"

Before heading backstage, I looked out into the audience. Most of the faces were familiar—my classmates, instructors, a few directors from the ballet company I'd worked for last summer, but the faces I needed to see weren't there.

They never were.

Hurt, I found a corner in the dressing room and called my mother.

"Hello?" she answered on the first ring.

"Why aren't you here?"

"Why aren't I *where*, Aubrey? What are you talking about *now*?" She let out an exasperated sigh.

"My open audition for *Swan Lake*. You promised that you and dad were coming."

"It's Aubrey, honey!" She yelled to my dad in the background. "Your recital was today?"

"I haven't been in a *recital* since I was thirteen." I gritted my teeth. "This is an audition, a once in a lifetime audition, and you're supposed to be here."

"I guess my secretary forgot to tell me about it this morning," she said. "Have you landed any internships for your major yet?"

"I have *two* majors."

"*Pre-law*, Aubrey."

"No." I sighed.

"Well, why not? Do you think one is just going to fall from the sky and land in your lap? Is that it?"

"I had an interview yesterday at Blaine and Associates," I said, feeling my heart grow heavier by the second, "and I have another one next week at Greenwood, Bach, and Hamilton. I'm also about to audition for the role of a lifetime if you'd like to pretend to give a fuck for five seconds."

"*Excuse me*, young lady?"

"You're not here." There were tears in my eyes. "*You're not here*...Do you know how huge this production is going to be?"

"Are you getting *paid*? Is the New York Ballet Company running it?"

"That's not the point. I've told you over and over how important this audition is to me. I called and reminded you last night, and it would be really nice if my *parents* showed up and believed in me for a change."

"Aubrey..." She sighed. "I do believe in you. I always have, but I'm in the middle of a huge hearing right now and you know that because it's all over the papers. You also know that becoming a professional ballerina is not a stable career choice, and as much as I would *love* to leave my high-paying client to watch you tiptoe around on stage—"

"It's called dancing *en pointe*."

"Same thing," she said. "Regardless, it's just an audition. I'm sure your father and I won't be the only parents who couldn't make it today. Once you graduate from college and get into law school, you'll see ballet for what it really is—*a hobby*, and you'll be grateful that we pushed you into double majoring."

"Ballet is my *dream*, mother."

"It's a phase, and you're way past the prime age for becoming a professional last time I checked. Remember how you suddenly up and quit at sixteen? You'll quit again, and it'll be for the best. As a matter of fact—"

I hung up.

I didn't want to listen to another one of her dream-killing speeches, and it angered me that she'd called ballet a "phase" when I'd been dancing since I was six years old. When she and my dad had poured countless dollars into private classes, costumes, and competitions.

The only reason why I'd "quit" at sixteen was because I'd broken my foot and couldn't audition for any of the dance schools anymore. And the only reason I started to show the faintest interest in law was because I couldn't do much outside of my rehab sessions except *read*.

My heart had always belonged in pointe slippers, and that fact would never change.

"Aubrey Everhart?" A man suddenly called my name from the theater door. "Is that you?"

"Yes."

"You're next to take the stage. Got about five minutes."

"Be right there..." I stuffed my bag into a locker. Before I could close it, my phone rang.

Knowing it was my mother calling to offer a half-assed apology, I tried my best not to scream. "Please spare me your apologies." I immediately picked up. "They don't mean anything to me anymore."

"I was calling to tell you good luck," a deep voice said.

"Two minutes!" A stagehand glared at me and motioned for me to head onto the stage.

"*Thoreau?*" I turned my back to the stagehand. "What are you telling me good luck for?"

"You mentioned having some type of audition weeks ago. It's today, right?"

"Yes, thank you..."

"You don't sound too excited about your *dream* right now."

"How can I be when my own parents don't believe in it?"

"You're *twenty seven years old*." He scoffed. "Fuck your parents."

I laughed, guiltily. "I wish it was that simple..."

"It really is. You make your own money, and despite the fact that you don't really know shit about the law, you seem to be a pretty decent lawyer. Fuck them."

"I'll keep that in mind," I said, trying to steer that subject away. "I'm shocked you remembered that my audition was today."

"*I didn't.*" He hung up, and I knew he was smiling as he did that.

"Fifteen seconds, Miss Everhart!" The stagehand grabbed my arm and practically pulled me onto the stage.

I smiled at the judges and stood in fifth position—arms over my head, and waited for the first note of Tchaikovsky's composition to play.

There was a rustling of papers, a few coughs from someone in the audience, and then the music began.

I was supposed to demonstrate an arabesque, a pirouette, and then perform the routine that I'd been rehearsing in class for the past month and a half. I didn't feel like it, though, and since this was one of my last opportunities to make an impression, I decided to dance how I wanted.

I shut my eyes and completed pirouette after pirouette, fouette turn after fouette turn. I wasn't even on beat with the music, and I could tell the pianist was confused and trying to keep up with me.

I demonstrated every jump I knew, perfectly landing each one of them, and when the pianist gave up and struck the last note, I returned to fifth position—smiling.

There was no applause, no cheers, nothing. I tried to read the judges' faces to see if they looked mildly impressed, but they were stoic.

"That will be all, Miss Everhart," one of them said. "Will Miss Leighton Reynolds please take the stage?"

I murmured "Thank you" before stepping off and rushing out of the theater. I didn't bother watching the rest of the auditions.

For the remainder of the afternoon, I walked around campus and tried not to cry. When I was sure that no tears would fall, I sent emails to Thoreau; that was the only thing that could possibly make me feel better.

**Subject: Thinking…**

"One dinner. One night. No repeats." Do you pick a cheap or expensive restaurant? Do you pay for the dinner and the hotel room? Or do you make the woman split it with you?

—Alyssa.

**Subject: Re: Thinking…**

Expensive dinner. Five star hotel suite. I pay for everything.

Would you like me to book a few reservations for us so I can show you?

—Thoreau.

**Subject: Re: Re: Thinking…**

Of course not. And a "few" reservations? What happened to just one?

**Subject: Re: Re: Re: Thinking…**

I told you I'd make an exception in your case. I invested in a box of paper bags today.

—Thoreau

I laughed and looked at my watch. It was five o' clock and I was sure the results for the production had been posted hours ago, but I was too scared to look. All I wanted was a chance to be a member of the swan corps, or even an understudy for the lead.

Why did I fuck up that routine? What the hell was I thinking?

After driving myself crazy with questions, I forced myself to make the trek back to the dance theater to look at the final cast posting. When I arrived, there was a huge crowd in front of the sign, and I could hear the usual "I'm in! I'm in!" and "How could they not pick me?" revelations.

I squeezed my way through everyone and squinted at the sheet, looking for my name on the minor cast sheet but it wasn't there.

It was on the *major* cast sheet, and right next to the lead role of Odette/Odile, the white and black swan, was my full name in bold.

I burst into tears, jumping up and down in disbelief. I wanted to call my mom and tell her the good news, but my heart suddenly sank at the thought.

I knew that at this very moment, she was probably telling my father that I'd hung up in her face, and that he needed to make sure I knew the strings behind them paying for my education: "If you drop pre-law, we'll stop writing the checks…Pre-law pays for your classes, ballet doesn't."

I lifted my aching feet out of a bucket of ice and patted them dry with a towel. I wasn't sure how I was going to juggle a leading role, classes, and a potential internship, but I didn't have a choice.

Sighing, I glanced at the calendar on my desk where I'd scribbled "Interview prep day" in today's slot.

My upcoming interview with Greenwood, Bach, and Hamilton—one of the most prestigious firms in the state, was more than just an interview. It was a *process*, and every intern-seeking student knew that landing an internship at that firm could do wonders for a resume.

The firm was so selective that they conducted four rounds of phone interviews, three online tests, and required each applicant to complete several essays before the final interview with the partners.

I'd soared through the phone interviews and the exams, but the essays— regarding hundred paged case files, were something that I hadn't expected. I'd even thought they'd sent me the wrong packet so I called to say, "I believe my packet was switched with the *law-school level* intern application." The secretary simply laughed at me.

She'd said the firm expected all of its interns—law school level *and* undergraduate level, to fill out the same packet to the best of their ability.

"Don't worry," she'd said. "We're not expecting perfection from you. We just want to see how your mind works."

I grabbed the case file that was giving me the most trouble and placed it into my lap. Then I went to the GBH firm's website and familiarized myself with the three partners who would be interviewing me.

Greenwood, the founder of the firm, was a salt and pepper haired man with wiry framed glasses. He touted Harvard as his reason for being so demanding and thorough, and boasted that in his thirty years of practicing the law, he'd attained one of the highest victory rates in the country.

Bach, partner of the firm for over ten years, was a bald man in his early forties, though he looked a bit older. He'd worked his way up through the firm, and since he was "such a hardworking individual with unparalleled passion," Greenwood had no choice but to make him his first partner. He had one of the second highest victory rates in the country.

Last was Hamilton—Andrew Hamilton, and he was…He was *sexy as fuck*. I tried to focus on his biography and ignore his picture, but I couldn't help it. His deep and piercing blue eyes were staring right at me, and his short, dark brown hair was begging my hands to run through it.

He had the face of a Greek God—evenly tanned, perfectly symmetrical, strong and chiseled jawline, and his full lips were curved into a slight smirk.

Even though the picture only showed the top part of his body, I imagined that by the way he filled out his navy blue suit that there were hard and defined muscles underneath it.

I was getting wet just looking at him.

*Focus, Aubrey…Focus…*

Strangely, his bio was the shortest one of them all. It didn't list his education, his background, or the year he became partner. It was just a bunch of filler words about how "the firm was so honored to have such an esteemed and proven lawyer" on their team. Oh, and he enjoyed eating chocolate.

How informative…

I copied and pasted all of their bios into a word document, and then I called Thoreau.

"Good evening, *Alyssa*," he answered, making me melt with his voice as usual. I swore he could talk me into doing anything—*almost* anything.

"Hey, um…"

"*Yes?*"

*God, I loved his fucking voice…* He hadn't said much of anything and I was already turned on.

"You called so I could listen to you breathe?" He had to be smiling.

"I did, actually." I rolled my eyes. "Are you enjoying my sounds?"

"I'd enjoy them a lot better if you were underneath me."

I blushed. "Um…"

"The case, Alyssa." He laughed. "Tell me about your latest case."

"Right, um…" I cleared my throat. "Long story short: My client carried a gun into a federal bank and forgot to turn on the safety lock. Someone bumped into him and his hands instinctively went to his pocket, and the gun fired—shooting him in the leg."

"Since when do you practice *criminal* law? I thought your specialty was corporate."

*Shit...* "It is, it is. I'm taking this case for a friend, pro bono."

"Hmmm. Well, your *friend* is looking at two to five years in a federal prison if he doesn't have any priors. What part of this do you need help with exactly?"

"The pleading part. He didn't hurt anyone but himself."

"Did he have a license to carry?"

"No..." I looked through my notes.

"Then I'm sure the prosecution will convince the jury that he carried that gun into the bank with the intent to harm someone other than *himself.* Take whatever deal they offer."

"Well, I..." I looked at what the assignment sheet said. "What if I already rejected that deal?"

He sighed. "Call the prosecution and try to get it back. If they say no, plead no contest."

"*No contest?* Are you out of your mind?"

"*Are you?* What type of corporate lawyer agrees to take an open and shut criminal case? A fairly inexperienced one at that..."

"For your information, it's an assign—" I coughed. "Never mind. Telling me to plead no contest is pretty much the same thing as telling me to plead guilty."

"If that was the case, I would have said *plead guilty.*" He sounded annoyed. "*No contest* is your client's best option, and any *real* lawyer would know that. Are you sure you passed the bar exam?"

"I wouldn't have been invited to join LawyerChat if I hadn't, would I?" I felt my heart ache with that lie. "I'm just trying to avoid my client being sentenced to prison."

"Then you *really* should stick to corporate law." There was a smile in his voice. "Your client is going to prison and there's nothing you can do about it. The only negotiable thing about his case is *how long* he'll spend there. Anything else I can help you with? Do I need to lecture you on the difference between *guilty* and *not guilty?*"

I rolled my eyes and put the file away. "Thank you for your condescending help as always."

"My pleasure," he said. "I need to ask you something important."

"About my case?"

"No." He let out a low laugh. "What do you look like?"

"*What?*" I could barely hear my voice. "What did you say?"

"You heard me. Since I may never get a chance to see you, I'd like to know. *What do you look like?*"

I stood up and walked over to my mirror, letting my eyes roam over my reflection. "I'm not sure how I'm supposed to answer that..." I needed to change the subject, fast. From everything he'd told me about his dates over the past few months, he definitely had a type he liked best, a type that intrigued him like no other: Blonde, slightly curvy, full lips...

Me.

I'd tried to envision what he looked like plenty of times. Dark haired, maybe? Dirty blond? A mouth made for kissing with deep green eyes? Six pack, no, *eight pack* that leads down to a lick-able V?

He does mention working out every day...

I was more than certain that he was attractive—he had to be if so many women put up with him on those dating sites, but each time my mind drew a picture, I'd convince myself that I had him all wrong.

"You know what?" I said, snapping out of my thoughts. "I've never been good at describing things. What do *you* look like?"

"I look like a man who wants to fuck you."

Tingles ran up and down my spine. "That's not a description..."

"What color is your hair?" He didn't sound amused, and I knew he wasn't going to let me direct the conversation tonight.

"Red." I yanked the band from around my bun and let the blond strands fall to my shoulders.

"How long is it?"

"It's short..."

"Hmmm. What about your eyes?"

I stared at my blue and grey irises. "Green, light green."

"Do you have freckles?"

"No." At least that part was true.

"And your lips?"

"You want to know how thin or thick they are?"

"I want to know how they'd look wrapped around my cock."

I gasped.

"Are you playing shy tonight?" Ice cubes clinked against a glass in his background. "How much of my cock do you think you could take into your mouth?"

I remained silent, and my breathing began to slow.

"Alyssa?" His voice was soft. "Are you going to answer me?"

"It's hard to make a prediction about something you've never done." I heard him inhale a deep breath, and the line went completely silent.

I thought he'd ask me how I'd managed to have sex with boyfriends in the past without ever giving a blowjob, but he didn't.

"Hmmm. Are you a natural redhead?"

"What does it matter?" I moved over to my bed. "I'm clearly not your type."

"I have a *preference*, not a type, and a smart mouthed redhead who's never had another man's cock in her mouth is more than worthy of an exception."

I hooked a thumb underneath my panties and peeled them off before slipping under the sheets. "Too bad I'm not a full blown virgin, huh?"

"I don't fuck virgins." He paused. "But considering the fact that you and I have never fucked, you might as well be one."

Wetness slipped down my thighs, and I felt my nipples hardening. "I highly doubt—"

"I'm tired of only being able to talk to you on the phone, Alyssa..."

Silence.

"I *need* to see you..." His voice was strained. "I *need* to fuck you..."

"*Thoreau*..."

"No, *listen to me*," His tone was a warning. "I need to be buried deep inside of you, feeling your pussy throb around my cock as you scream my name—my *real* name."

A hand trailed down past my stomach and between my thighs, and my fingers began to strum my clit. Slow at first, then faster, faster with every sound of his heavy breaths in my ear.

"I've been very patient with you..." His voice trailed off. "Don't you think?"

"No..."

"I have," he said. "I'm tired of imagining how wet your pussy can get, how loudly you'll scream when I suck your tits as you ride me...How hard I'll pull your hair when I bend you over my desk and fuck you until you can't breathe...*Tired*."

I shut my eyes, letting my other hand squeeze my breast, letting my thumb pinch my nipple.

"I'm giving you two weeks to come to your fucking senses..."

"*What?*"

"*Two weeks,*" he whispered. "That's when you and I are going to meet face to face, and I'm going to claim every inch of you."

"I can't...I can't agree to...that."

"*You will.*" His breathing was now in sync with mine. "And the second you do, you're going to invite me over and I'm going to remind you of everything you've teased me with over the past six months."

I was speechless. My clit was swelling with each rub of my finger, and my breaths were getting shorter and shorter.

"I'll be gentle at first," he whispered, "especially when I slide my cock into your mouth and pull on your hair, showing you exactly how I like it to be sucked."

"*Stop...*" I was panting. "*Please...Stop...*"

"Trust me, *I won't.*"

"*Thoreau...*" My legs were trembling.

"I can't just *talk* to you anymore. I need to *feel you*, I need to *taste you*. Say yes to two weeks..."

I bit my lip, knowing that if he said it again, if he asked me one more time, I would say yes.

"*Alyssa...*" He was begging.

I was seconds away from coming, seconds away from screaming "Yes! Yes! Yes!"

"Promise me you'll let me fuck you in two weeks..."

As if my mouth was under his command, it freed my bottom lip and prepared to say yes, but I hung up.

Keeping my eyes shut, I lay in bed and let the waves of an orgasm roll through me as I screamed the three yeses he couldn't hear. When I finally stopped shaking, I rolled over and grabbed a pillow, pulling it to my chest.

Before I could force myself to sleep, I heard my phone ringing beneath me.

It was a text from Thoreau. "*I'll take that as a yes. Fourteen days.*"

# Burden of Proof (n.):
The obligation to prove or disprove a disputed fact.


**Andrew**

"Did I tell you that I landed the leading role for that ballet I auditioned for?" Alyssa said to me the next morning.

I'd been talking to her since I arrived at work, but I'd made no mention of the fact that she'd hung up in my face last night; I was going to punish her for that later. Severely.

Thirteen days...

"Did I tell you about it?" she asked again.

"*No*, and if you're not going to tell me when and where the show is, then I don't care."

"Oh, wow." She laughed. "You're mad about last night, aren't you?"

"*Furious.*"

"Because I hung up?"

"Because I know you screamed yes when you came, and you hung up because you didn't want me to hear it."

She was silent, and I was about to say something else, but Jessica suddenly stepped into my office, smiling at me.

"Hold on one second." I put my phone against my chest. "Yes, Jessica?"

"The final interviews are going to start in twenty minutes. They need you in the conference room now."

"I'll get there when I get there." I acted as if the kiss she was now blowing me wasn't happening, and waited until she closed the door. "I'll have to call you back later, Alyssa. I have a meeting."

"Must be bad timing for both of us. I have a meeting, too."

"Your doomed gunshot client?"

29

"No, something much worse. An intern interview."

"Must be in the air then." I sighed as I slipped into my jacket. "I have to sit through a few of them myself, unfortunately."

"Any advice you want to share?"

"Try to look like you're actually paying attention while they answer the questions, and make sure your cell phone is fully charged so you can get on the internet."

"Not for me." She laughed. "For the interns. Something I should say if one of them is nervous."

"Oh." I shrugged. "Tell them my motto."

"And what motto would that be?"

"It is what it is."

"Why do I ever ask you anything?"

"Because I always tell you the truth." I hung up.

"Mr. Hamilton?" Jessica stepped into my office again. "They want you to look over the files before they begin."

"I'm right behind you." I followed her into the conference room, where Will Greenwood and George Bach were waiting, and I sat next to them.

"Good to see you out of your office today, Andrew." Will laughed.

"Yeah," George added. "Thank you for bestowing your presence upon us this afternoon. We know how much you *love* being sociable."

I rolled my eyes. "Why do the three of us need to conduct intern interviews? What's the purpose of having an HR department if *the partners* do their job for them?"

"This is a *family*, Andrew." Mr. Greenwood spoke sternly. "Whether it's an intern, the secretary, or the young man who stays overnight and cleans this office, I want everyone to feel like they're a part of a huge family. Don't you?"

"I'm not answering that," I said. "How many are we picking this year?"

"Not too many." Will slid me a folder. "We have our top five picks. We just need to narrow it down to three. Two from law school, one from pre-law. We'll add two more next semester."

"Hmmm." I pulled out the applications and pretended to pay attention as the two of them went over each applicant's achievements.

"Okay, Jessica!" Will pressed the intercom button. "You can

send in the first applicant!"

When the door opened, I expected to see the usual plainly dressed stiff with a wooden smile, but the woman who stepped inside was far from that. Dressed in a light grey dress that clung to her hips and a pair of nude high heels, she was one of the sexiest women I'd ever seen; I couldn't take my eyes off her.

Her eyes were a deep ocean blue that matched the sapphire necklace hanging around her neck. Her hair was pulled into a low ponytail—the loose strands slightly grazed her breasts, and her lips—her bright pink, fuck-able lips, seemed to be mouthing words of some kind.

*I have no idea what you're saying...*

As I was noticing the pink bra strap that had slipped from underneath her dress and onto her bare shoulder, her stunning eyes met mine. I raised my eyebrow and she blushed. Then she immediately turned away, looking at my partners.

"Welcome to GBH, Miss Everhart," George said. "We're happy that you're here for an interview, but as you know we can only select *one* undergraduate intern for our program at this time."

"I understand, sir." Her eyes met mine again, and my cock twitched.

I tried to stop the images that were flooding my brain, images of me bending this woman over the table, fucking her against my office wall, and tying her hands above her head and torturing her with my tongue all night, but they wouldn't stop. Each image dissolved into another one, and before I knew it, I'd visually undressed her and there was no one in this room but the two of us.

*What the hell is wrong with me? Attracted to a prospective intern? An UNDERGRADUATE intern?*

"Well, let's get started then." George interrupted my thoughts. "Mr. Hamilton, would you care to start with the first question?"

"Not particularly," I said, trying to ignore the fact that Miss Everhart was smoothing her dress over her thighs.

He nudged me under the table and whispered under his breath, "Family, Andrew...*Family.*"

I rolled my eyes. "Why do you want to be a lawyer, Miss Everhart?"

"I enjoy screwing people over," she said. "I figure I might as well get paid for it."

My lips curved into a smile, and George and Will laughed.

"In all seriousness, gentlemen," she continued, "I come from a large family of lawyers and judges; it's what I've known my whole life. I know the justice system is far from perfect, but nothing makes me happier than seeing it at its best. There's no greater feeling than working for the good of society."

"Good answer," Will said. "Now, we're going to ask you a series of questions regarding the real-world case study packets that we mailed you. Were you able to complete everything?"

"Yes, sir."

"Great. Question number one: Your client walks into a federal bank with a loaded gun in his pocket. Upon being brushed by a stranger, the gun fires—shooting him in the leg. Regarding the charges that the prosecution filed, how would you have your client plead?"

"*What?*" I looked over at him. "Could you repeat that question, Will?"

"The prompt?"

"Whatever you just asked."

He nodded and happily repeated it, putting extra emphasis on the crime of walking into a bank with a loaded firearm.

My mind immediately flashed back to the conversation I'd had with Alyssa last night.

I smiled, thinking that maybe Alyssa's "friend" was a headline story in the local news, that maybe I could figure out who she was without her telling me. I pulled out my phone and held it underneath the conference table, googling "Man shoots himself in federal bank. North Carolina."

Nothing relevant appeared.

Hmmm…

"How would you make him plead, Miss Everhart?" Will asked again.

"No contest," she said quickly.

"*No contest?*" He sounded slightly impressed. "Why so?"

"He doesn't have a license to carry, so I'm sure the prosecution will try to make it seem like he carried that gun into the bank for a reason. Regardless of if he only hurt himself, he's looking at a prison sentence, so we could bypass the trial and try to limit it to the lowest terms possible."

I blinked, refusing to believe that her answer was anything more than a coincidence. As a matter of fact, as soon as she started to further explain her logic, I knew that it was; only a student would start talking about "emotional appeal" right after a no contest plea.

As Will and George continued to pepper her with questions, I googled variations of that federal gun case. "Man fires gun in bank." "No contest plea in federal bank case." "Man injures himself in bank shooting."

Still, nothing.

"Miss Everhart, are there any lawyers that you wish to model your own career after?" Greg asked.

"Yes, actually," she said. "I've always admired the career of Liam Henderson."

"*Liam Henderson?*" I raised my eyebrow. "Who is that?" Usually, interviewees named a federal judge, a well-known prosecutor, or a familiar district attorney. But an unknown? Never.

"Well, he made history as the youngest lawyer to ever uncover a government conspiracy, and he—"

I tuned out her answer. I'd just thought of another phrase to google.

"Interesting choice, Miss Everhart," Will said. "Do you have any current mentors in the law profession besides your family members?"

"I do."

"Are you in close contact with this mentor? If so, how often?"

"We talk almost every day, so I'd like to think that we're close."

Why isn't this case popping up? If it's a "federal" bank shooting, it should be plastered all over the papers...

"Would your mentor be able to speak to us, or send a letter regarding your character?" Will was definitely impressed with this woman, and she had this job. The second set of questions he had yet to ask weren't really necessary.

"I'm sure I could ask him to do that if need be," she said just as I was starting a new web search.

"Great. So, tell us, what's the last bit of advice that your mentor gave you?"

I looked at my watch. As soon as today's interviews were over, I was going to call Alyssa about this case. Maybe she'd fudged some of the details to continue shrouding her identity.

"When I told him I was nervous about my interview today," Miss Everhart said softly, "he told me, *it is what it is.*"

My head immediately shot up.

"Did he now?" George clutched his chest, laughing. "That sounds like something our Andrew would say!" He patted me on the shoulder. "Isn't that right, Andrew?"

"*Yes.*" I narrowed my eyes at 'Miss Everhart.' "That sounds *exactly* like something I would say…"

She tucked a loose strand of hair behind her ear. "I'll be sure to tell my mentor that someone actually enjoys his odd sense of humor."

"*Please do.*" I watched as she answered the next questions with ease, as she barely blinked her big blue eyes when the questions became tougher. And the more I heard her talk, the more I heard the familiarities of her speech pattern, I had to force myself not to fucking lose it.

One coincidence was fine, but two? Damn near unfathomable.

As they asked her about her favorite inspirational quotes, I scrolled down to Alyssa's number and dialed. I knew for a fact that she *never* silenced her phone for some strange reason, and I had to know if what I was thinking was true, or if my mind was playing a cruel joke on me.

I could see the rings on my phone's screen, see the seconds as they passed, and when it rang three times, I let out a huge sigh of relief. But then the sound of bell chimes filled the room.

"I am so sorry." Miss Everhart's cheeks turned pink and she picked up her purse. "I have a weird thing about never putting this on silent…I really meant to leave it in my car." She pulled out her phone, slightly smiling once she looked at the screen, and then she hit ignore.

WHAT. THE. FUCK!

"Happens all the time." Will laughed. "We were going on and on anyway. It's a good thing it went off so we can close out with the final questions. Anything from you, Andrew?"

I glared at 'Alyssa'. I was confused, pissed, and unfortunately aroused all at once.

"Andrew?"

"*No*," I said, noticing that she was blushing again. "I have absolutely nothing to say."

Will and Greg both stood up and smiled, reaching out to shake her hand, but I remained seated.

I couldn't believe this shit.

She wasn't a green-eyed redhead like she'd said over the phone, *far* from being a licensed lawyer, and she was a *fucking liar*...

"Mr. Hamilton?" She was standing in front of me with her hand outstretched. "Thank you for interviewing me today. It was an absolute pleasure meeting you."

"The pleasure's all mine." I shook her hand, trying my best to ignore the smooth softness of her touch. "Good luck."

She nodded, said goodbye to the three of us once more, and then she left the room.

As Will and George discussed how impressed they were with her interview, I forced myself to look through her file.

Double major student at Duke: Pre-law and Ballet. Perfect 4.0 GPA. Recently cast as the lead of *Swan Lake*, recently listed in the top ten percent of her class. There were *ten* letters of recommendation in her folder—all from impeccable lawyers; there was even one from the newly appointed assistant district attorney.

As amazing as her personal accomplishments were, it was her birthdate that stood out to me the most. She was twenty two.

Twenty fucking two.

And, even though she was the most accomplished out of all the undergraduates, she wasn't even a senior.

She was a *junior*...

I ignored Alyssa's text tonight, the one that read, *"If you haven't found another unfortunate date for tonight, call me when you see this."*

I was too angry to say anything to her. After all the hours we'd spent on the phone, all the times that I'd told her that I hated liars, she'd lied to me. Repeatedly.

I'd wanted to vote no for her employment, but I couldn't bring myself to do it. Once we'd finished with the last interview of the day, the decision on the top pick was unanimous: Aubrey Everhart.

Yet, while they frenziedly weighed the pros and cons of the other applicants, I sat there in a daze—angry with myself for not seeing through all of Aubrey's lies earlier.

In the six months that we'd spoken, she'd always asked questions that were a little too simple, questions that sometimes made me wonder, but I never thought twice about it. She'd mentioned Duke University a few times, but she never talked about it for long and she always made it seem as if she'd graduated from there. But her constant talk of how she wanted her parents' approval and had conflicted feelings between choosing dance and the law should have been a dead ass giveaway.

At this point, I wasn't sure which lie to be more upset about: The fact that she wasn't a lawyer, the fact that she was still in college, or the fact that she'd lied about her physical appearance.

Pouring my sixth shot of the night, I realized that that last lie— although irrelevant in the grand scheme of things, was the one that hit me the hardest. She was definitely my 'type,' and the second she walked into that interview I wanted her, before I found out who she really was, before I found out her age.

Tossing back a shot, I heard my phone ringing. *Her.*

I rolled my eyes and let it sit on the table. I grabbed one of my last Cuban cigars and stepped out onto my balcony. I needed to think.

The sky was starless tonight—nearly pitch black, and the moon was hiding underneath a curtain of dark clouds. As much as I didn't want to admit it, tonight's sky bore a horrid resemblance to a certain night that occurred six years ago.

It was the night my life changed forever, the night that left me broken, shattered, and numb. All because of lies—a series of heartbreaking and inconceivable lies.

I tried hard to prevent myself from picturing the memories, but I could still hear that strained, ragged voice in my head: *"Andrew...You have to help me...You have to get me out of here... Please...Save me, Andrew..."*

I shook my head and blocked out the rest of that memory. Unlike six years ago, I was in control of this situation, and "Alyssa" lying to me meant that our friendship was over, done.

There was no justification for what she'd done, but before I cut her off, I needed to make her pay for lying to me, and I needed to figure out *how.*

# Conviction (n.):
A judgment of guilt against a criminal defendant.

## *Andrew*

"Mr. Hamilton?" Aubrey set my coffee down on my desk two weeks later. I'd *personally* insisted that she work as my intern, even though looking at her made me angry.

I'd made a point not to say too much around her, to refrain from staring at her too long, and I couldn't help being crueler than ever—dismissive even. I made her responsible for my daily coffee, demanded that she re-do every assignment at least three times, and whenever she asked for my help, I answered her with a detached "Figure it out yourself."

She never seemed upset or offended by my harshness, which made me even angrier. I'd thought that by having her work for me and seeing her crack under pressure that my attraction to her would fade, but it only intensified each time I saw her face.

Especially today.

As I pulled my coffee closer, I noticed that her nipples were poking through her thin, beige dress, and it was so tight that I could see the imprint of lace panties.

Fuck...

"Mr. Hamilton?" she asked again.

"Yes, Miss Everhart?"

"I have an important rehearsal for a ballet I'm a part of, so I was wondering..." She looked absolutely nervous. "Can I go home early today?"

"*No.*"

She sighed. "I really need to be at this rehearsal...It's at the Grand Hall."

"So?"

"*So*," she said, clearing her throat, "with all due respect, *Mr. Hamilton*, this is a pretty big deal for me. The Grand Hall is usually reserved for performances, so for them to open it and let us use it for a rehearsal is—"

I wasn't listening, and as much as I wanted to look at my work again and make it clear that she was being ignored, I couldn't. I was too busy staring at the contours of her mouth.

"That's a fact." She was still talking for some reason. "I think I've made very valid points, and since I'm not asking for too much, you should agree to let me go."

"Get back to work, Miss Everhart."

"Mr. Hamilton, please—"

"Get. Back. To. Work." I glared at her, daring her to let another word slip out of her seductive mouth. "I don't care about your personal life. I pay you for twenty five hours a week, so you'll work *twenty five hours a week*, and you'll work them when I say you'll work them. So, get back to your cubicle."

She stared at me for a few seconds, and I couldn't help but notice tears welling in her eyes.

"You can take that box of Kleenex with you on your way out," I said.

Shaking her head, she stepped back and headed for the door. "I'm going to ask Mr. Bach if I can leave early. No disrespect to you."

"*Excuse me?*" I stood up. "What did you just say?"

She continued to walk toward the door, the sound of her heels clicking faster and faster. Before she could turn the knob, I spun her around and slammed my hand against the door.

"I'm not a fan of insubordination, Miss Everhart."

"You won't have to worry about that anymore." Her face was red, twisted in anger. ""I'm going to ask Mr. Bach to move me with someone else because I refuse to work with you anymore."

"Good luck with that. No one else wanted you. *Only me.*"

"I highly doubt that." She tried to move away, but I grabbed her hands and pinned them above her head.

"I was the best interviewee and you fucking know it." She hissed. "And since we both know that's a fact, I don't have to put up with your shit anymore." She looked as if she wanted to spit in my face. "You are a cruel, cold, and condescending asshole, and I haven't learned shit from you; I doubt I ever will."

"Watch your goddamn mouth. I'm still your boss."

"You *were* my boss."

I tightened my grasp around her wrists and looked directly into her eyes, pressing my chest against her breasts. "Let me tell you what's about to happen, *Aubrey*. You're going to go back to your cubicle and you're going to stay there until you're done for the day—only getting up to bring me a new cup of coffee. You will tell your ballet director that you'll come after you get your work done, and you will not go to Mr. Bach and say anything, because we don't reassign interns just because they cry."

"Then I guess there's a first time for everything." She threw my glares right back at me, narrowing her eyes as her chest heaved up and down.

"Aubrey—"

"Let me go before I *scream*, Mr. Hamilton. I wasn't listening to a thing you just said so I highly suggest—"

I crashed my lips against hers, effectively making her shut the hell up. I kept my hands tightly clamped around her wrists, pressing her body against the door with my hips.

She murmured as I slipped my tongue into her mouth, as I bit her bottom lip as hard as I could. Without thinking, I let her hands go and gripped her waist—pulling her taut against me as my hand found its way underneath her skirt.

I slid my hand across the crotch of her panties, tapping my fingers against the lace, and then I slowly pushed them to the side and plunged a finger deep into her pussy.

"Ahhh…" she moaned, making me bite her lip again, making me use two fingers instead of one.

She was wet—*soaking wet*, and as much as I wanted to fuck her senseless against my door and make her forget her name, I tore my mouth away from her.

"Get the hell out of my office."

"*What?*" She asked breathlessly, her eyes widening in surprise.

"Go to your *important* rehearsal."

"Mr. Ham—"

"Hurry up before I change my mind." I reached around her and opened the door. "*Go.*"

She didn't hesitate to walk past me, and as soon as she was gone I knew damn well this arrangement wasn't going to work for too much longer. Either she was going to be reassigned or I was going to have to fire her, fast.

Hours later, when I was halfway through my work for the day, I noticed I'd received a new text from Alyssa. I rolled my eyes and changed her name to Aubrey before reading it.

*"Where have you been for the past two weeks?"* it said. *"Are you okay? I've called and texted you and you haven't said anything. I'm really concerned…If you get this, say something, anything. "*

I didn't want to respond, but with the taste of her mouth still lingering on my lips, I gave in. *"I'm fine. Just made a major discovery not too long ago and I've been trying to figure out how to deal with it. "*

"Is it something serious?"

"VERY serious."

"I'm sorry…Want to know something that will make you feel better?"

"I doubt anything you say can do that right now."

"Want to bet?"

"Try me."

"My boss just kissed the shit out of me. I think that's why he's so damn mean to me; he wants to fuck me…"

"I really don't think your 'boss' wants to fuck you…"

"He definitely does. His cock was rock hard when he was kissing me, and he was biting my lips and gripping me like he wanted to own me… I've never been so wet in my life…"

I hesitated. *"How exactly is this supposed to make me feel better?"*

"I was pretending he was you the whole time. I miss you."

I immediately turned off my phone. I didn't know what type of shit she was trying to pull, but I wasn't falling for it.

"I was pretending it was you? I miss you?" Bullshit.

I wasn't going to answer her calls or her messages for a long time. Sexy ass mouth or not.

# Cross Examination (n.):
The interrogation of a witness called by one's opponent.

## Aubrey

I couldn't stop thinking about the way Mr. Hamilton kissed me the other day, the way he pulled me against his chest and fucked my lips with his mouth.

Thoughts of him kissing me had been invading my mind all day, and even now, when I was setting down his latest cup of coffee, I was tempted to walk behind his desk and dare him to kiss me again. Ever since I'd become his intern, he'd been quite mean to me—reckless, but I thought it was a training technique, a way to see if I'd quit under pressure.

Until he kissed me that day.

There was something intangible in his kiss; unspoken words, a repressed desire. It made me think that the glances he often tossed my way, those looks of scorn that were laced with wanting, meant a little more.

I placed a plastic stirrer into his cup and cleared my throat. "Do you need anything else, Mr. Hamilton?"

No answer.

I stood my ground and waited for him to look up at me; I wanted to see his face.

The suit he was wearing today—a dark grey three piece with a silver silk tie, made him look even more devastatingly beautiful than he normally did.

"Is there a problem, Miss Everhart?" He clenched his fists above the desk, trying his best to act like my presence wasn't bothering him. But it was, I could tell.

I knew he would look up at any moment, so I stepped back,

making sure the light blue dress I wore specifically for him would be in full view, but he kept his gaze lowered.

"No, sir."

"Then get out of my office. I'll need your Brownstein report with my next cup of coffee. Four o' clock."

"You just gave me that report yesterday. You said I could take all the time I needed."

"You must've misheard me. You can take all the time you need *today*. Things change instantly around here, and that's the exact reason why some of us never leave early. Four o' clock."

I stood there completely speechless. There was no way I'd be able to read and summarize a three hundred paged report by the end of the day.

"Did you lose some of your hearing between today and yesterday?" He finally looked up, his perfect face expressionless. "I need complete silence when I work and I can't focus with your heavy breathing." He narrowed his eyes at me. "Get out, finish the report, and bring it back to me with my coffee. If you don't, you're fired."

I quickly decided that he was bipolar, and that our seemingly connected kiss was just a mistake. I turned around and left his office, rushing straight to the break room.

There was no way I was going to get that Brownstein report done by the end of the day.

I pulled out my phone and scrolled through my messages—realizing that Thoreau hadn't responded to my morning texts. Sighing, I decided to call him. I needed someone to tell me that my life wouldn't end today when I was fired.

It rang once.

It rang twice.

It went to voicemail.

He hit ignore?!

I sent him a text. *"What the hell is wrong with you lately? Is your lack of sex forcing you to act like a jerk toward me? Is the withdrawal THAT BAD? Talk to me."*

I waited for a response, but none came, so I slumped onto the couch. There was no point in even attempting to finish that report. I was just going to sit here, relax, and when it was five o' clock I was going to collect all of my things and leave.

I could find another internship in two weeks, or worst case, ask the department chair if I could shadow my mother and father around their stuffy firm for credit.

Ugh…God…

I shut my eyes and lay back against the cushion, wishing I could fall asleep.

"Aubrey?" Someone shook my shoulder just as I was drifting away.

"Yes?" I opened my eyes. It was Jessica.

"I've been looking for you forever. Mr. Hamilton wants to speak with you."

I raised my eyebrow. "More coffee?"

"Probably." She shrugged. "He's been a bit off lately. Just come on, you don't want to make him angry." She held the door open and I stood up, making my way past her.

I debated whether I should even go to his office. Then again, seeing the look on his face as I said, "Fuck you. I quit." was too good of an experience to pass up. I forced a smile and knocked on his door.

"Come in." His voice was stern.

I slipped inside, expecting to see him holding an empty coffee cup, but he was sitting at his desk–glaring at me.

"Have a seat," he said.

I sat in front of his desk, waiting for him to scold me about something, to unleash more of his seemingly bipolar tendencies, but he didn't. He just kept staring at me.

I hated the effect he was having on my body right now, and as much as I wanted to ask him what the hell he wanted, I couldn't get my mouth to say a thing.

Without addressing me, he suddenly stood up and walked around his desk, sitting on the edge of it, letting his knees touch mine.

"Lawyers are supposed to be people with integrity, are they not?" he whispered.

"Yes."

"Do you think *you* have integrity, *Miss Everhart?*" He emphasized every syllable of my name.

"Yes."

"Hmmm." He leaned forward. "So, would you ever willingly withhold the truth from someone you supposedly cared about?"

"It depends…" My breath hitched in my throat; my heart was

racing a mile a minute.

"It *depends?*" He sat back a bit. "It depends on what?"

"If the truth would damage anything or hurt someone unnecessarily, then I believe I have a right to withhold it."

"But what if someone blatantly asked you for the truth, several times? What if he said, I want you to tell me the truth no matter how much it hurts, or how angry it may make me?"

*Where is he going with this?* "Are you referring to a potential witness changing his testimony on the stand, Mr. Hamilton?"

"No..." He trailed his fingers across my collarbone, setting my nerves on fire. "This is a *personal* inquiry. I'm just in need of an outside opinion. Answer the question."

"Well, I think—" I sucked in a breath as he placed his hand on my thigh and strummed his fingers against my skirt. "I think certain lies have to be told, and certain truths have to be withheld. The ultimate conviction is up to those who can discern which is which."

"So, you believe in reasonable doubt?"

"In certain cases, yes..."

"What about in *our* case?" His hand was slowly slipping underneath my skirt, traveling further and further up my thigh.

"*Our* case?"

"Yes," he said. "I believe you and I are currently in an unfortunate web of deceit."

"No..." I said, breathless and confused. "We're not in a web of deceit..."

"We definitely are, *Alyssa*—" He pulled me forward by the strand of pearls around my neck. "It's the case of a woman who befriended me online, but she turned out to be someone completely different than who she told me she was. So, in this case—*our case*, how do you feel about reasonable doubt?"

Gasping, I could feel all the color draining from my face. My heart wasn't racing anymore; it was flailing around wildly—ready to jump out of my chest, and my eyes were as wide as they could go.

"You were very good at covering your tracks for such a long time, so I'll give you that," he said. "But I thought we thoroughly discussed how I felt about liars. Did we not?"

I murmured as he tightened his grip on my pearls, as he pulled me so close that we were lip to lip.

"Do you plan on answering me, *Aubrey?* Are you tired of this fucking charade?"

"I never thought that…" I was stuttering, trying to look away from him, but his grip prevented me from moving. "I am so sorry…"

He didn't say anything further. He stared into my eyes, searching for something that wasn't there. Then he lowered his voice, and leaned back. "Once someone lies to me they're dead to me forever. Do you remember me saying that?"

"Yes…"

"So, you've always been willing to lose our friendship over lies?"

"I never wanted to meet you in person…"

"I can see that." He hissed.

"If I had known who you really were…" I was breaking down in front of him. This was too much for one day. "I would've never—"

"Save it." He cut me off. "I've heard enough about your thoughts on *lying*. Seeing as though we don't share the same views, you're not worthy of being my intern. You'll be serving as my secretary's assistant until further notice."

"You're *demoting* me?"

"It's not a demotion. It's a way to keep you out of my sight."

My heart dropped.

"Our online relationship—whatever the hell that was anyway," he said, "is over. I don't want to hear from you outside of these walls again."

"*Thoreau*…"

"It's Mr. Hamilton, *Miss Everhart*." He glared at me. "Mr. fucking Hamilton."

"You have to believe that I'm sorry…I never thought that this would happen."

"Take however much time you need on the Brownstein account." He disregarded my apology and released his hold on my necklace. "You have until the end of next week. And from now on, you can just set my coffee on my bookcase. I don't need you coming anywhere near my desk."

"Andrew—"

"We are definitely *not* on a first name basis. Do not ever call me that."

"Just let me explain…"

"There's nothing *to* explain. You lied to me and you no longer exist. Get out. Now."

45

I felt tears welling in my eyes. "I was serious about you being my only friend...Friends are supposed to give each other a chance to make things right. Just let me tell you why I had to lie to you..."

"I don't deal with liars. *Ever.* And seeing that that's exactly what you are, I don't care why you felt the need to deceive me. Get out of my office, stay out of my sight as much as possible, and do your damn job."

I stood up and looked into his eyes, pleading for him to simply hear me out, to let me explain, but he turned away from me. Then he picked up his phone.

"Jessica?" he said. "Could you help Miss Everhart find her way out of my office? And could you please have the janitor check my floors for fucking superglue?"

I stood underneath the scalding hot streams of my shower, crying. Right after I'd left Andrew's office, I'd told HR that I wasn't feeling well and needed to leave for the rest of the day.

I'd driven straight for the dance hall—locking myself into a private room and dancing until I couldn't feel my feet anymore. I knew I must've looked crazy to my classmates, sobbing in between every twirl, but I didn't care; I needed to clear my mind of all thoughts of Andrew, Thoreau, and Alyssa.

As the water continued to lash against my skin, I shut my eyes and murmured, "How long has he known?" I thought about the past couple weeks, how "Thoreau" had been less talkative than normal, how he'd ignored me, and then it hit me.

My interview...

I still remembered it because seeing Andrew in person made me realize that no picture could ever accurately capture how sexy he really looked, and I'd blushed the second his eyes met mine. He didn't seem to act any differently throughout the questioning, but then I remembered that random phone call...

I wasn't sure why I was just remembering it now, but while Mr. Bach and Mr. Greenwood had simply laughed that intrusive phone call away, Andrew had stared at me. As if he was in complete and utter shock. And at the end of the interview, when I'd reached for his hand, his gaze wasn't intrigued anymore, it was heated.

Wiping away my tears, I turned off the water and stepped out. I wrapped myself in a towel and did what I always did when I felt sad: ordered a sandwich and made myself a couple of stiff martinis.

Just as I was downing the first one, there was a knock on my door. I noticed the pink Barbie keys on the counter—courtesy of my forgetful and "never here" roommate and knew it was her.

She always leaves something…

"Would it kill you to double check for these before you—" I stopped when I opened the door.

It was Andrew, and the look on his face was one of pure anger. He wasn't dressed in a suit anymore, just a simple, thin white T-shirt that slightly clung to his chiseled abs and a pair of faded blue jeans.

I tried to slam the door in his face, but he held it open and forced himself inside my apartment. I started to step backwards and he matched me step for step, backing me against my living room wall.

"We need to talk." His voice was flat, emotionless.

"No, we don't. You said plenty earlier." I looked down at the floor. "Don't worry, I'll be resigning in the morning. Please leave."

He tilted my chin up and looked into my eyes. "You're not quitting."

"*Watch me.*" I swallowed. "I want you to leave…"

"I would believe that, but you say things you don't mean all the time."

The tension between us was damn near palpable, and I could feel my blood heating every second he stood there staring at me. I tried to move away, but he gripped my hips.

"You told me you were a lawyer, Aubrey…" he said, his voice dripping with malice. "You told me you were twenty seven years old."

"I never *said* I was twenty seven. You assumed."

"It was on your fucking profile!" He pushed my back against the wall. "You never thought to correct me whenever I said I was only five years older than you…I'm *ten years* older than you."

"I didn't think I would ever meet you in person," I barely managed to say as he pressed his chest against mine.

"That excuses your *lies?*"

"I said I was sorry, and it was clearly a huge mistake to ever befriend you. You didn't even give me a chance to completely explain."

"Do you not understand how *fucked up* this situation is?"

"No..." I murmured as our lips touched.

"I've been looking forward to fucking the woman who teased me every night for nearly six months," he whispered, sliding his fingers underneath my towel. "I wanted her to ride me." He trailed his hand up my thigh and rubbed his thumb against my clit. "On my cock and my mouth. And I wanted to teach her how to taste me...Don't you think this woman fucked all of that up?"

I shook my head in response; I couldn't handle the way he was looking at me.

"You said you weren't my type when I asked what you looked like." He pulled away from my mouth, but he kept his thumb against my clit. "But you clearly *are*. Why did you lie about something as simple as that?'"

"You didn't tell me what you looked like, so—"

"Stop *deflecting*." He hissed, and took a step back. "Tell me the reasoning. I've already figured out your reasoning for the other bullshit lies. By the way, no self-respecting lawyer would *ever* let another lawyer do their work for them."

"Only a self-absorbed asshole who wants to seem deeper than he really is would call himself *Thoreau*."

"Good to finally see the version of you that I remember." He took another step back and crossed his arms. "Answer my question."

"*Fuck you*." I scoffed. "I told you I was sorry, begged you to listen to me, and now when *you* feel like talking, you think you can barge into my apartment and *make me*?"

"I haven't *made you* do anything." He smirked. "*Yet*."

Silence.

He leaned against the wall, waiting for me to speak, but I couldn't get a word out.

Look away from him...Look away from him...

As if he knew the power his gaze was having on me, he grinned and picked up one of my makeshift martinis.

Lifting one of the cherries from the liquor, he placed it against his lips. "Do you plan on standing there all night and looking at me, or are you going to answer my question?"

"No," I said, finally looking away from him. "After the way you treated me in your office today, I don't owe you a goddamn thing. You can stand there all night for all I care." I walked towards my

room. "There's even a sandwich delivery coming if you decide to—
"

My breath caught in my throat as he grabbed me from behind and pulled me against his chest. He quickly spun me around so we were face to face, and then he ripped my towel from around my body, letting it fall to the floor.

The cherry he'd picked up was in his mouth, and he was pressing it on my lips—silently commanding me to open up and eat it.

I stuck out my tongue to take it, but before sliding it to me, he whispered, "Don't chew...I want to see how capable you are of *swallowing.*"

My gasping did all the swallowing for me.

"Good girl," he said, loosening his grip around my waist. "Now, step back and hold the wall."

"*What?*"

He pushed me against the wall before I could take another breath, grabbing my hands and lifting them above my head. "*Hold the wall...*"

I nodded, pressing my hands against the cool surface.

With a 'don't-fuck-with-me' look on his face, he sucked my bottom lip into his mouth, and spoke softly, "I'll make you regret it if you let go."

"Yes..."

"That wasn't a question." The look on his face softened, and I was sure he could hear the loud beating in my chest.

I shut my eyes as he ran his hands up and down my sides.

I could feel his cock hardening through his pants as he lowered his kisses to my breasts and swirled his tongue around my nipples.

His mouth trailed down my stomach, and his hands caressed every inch of me as he made his way down.

"*Thoreau...*" I gasped as his tongue skimmed the inside of my thighs.

"My name is *Andrew.*" He got down on his knees. "We're done playing that game." He trapped my legs with his hands and pressed his mouth against my pussy. Licking me gently, he massaged my clit with his thumb.

I tried not to moan too loudly, tried to keep it all in, but each time he swirled his tongue, my mouth let another sound escape.

"You're so fucking wet..." He groaned. "*So fucking wet...*" He slipped two thick fingers inside of me, pushing them as far as they could go.

My eyes fluttered open as he added a third finger, as he whispered, "*So tight...*"

"*Ahhh...Andrew...*" I gave up trying to be quiet.

"*Yes?*" He slowly pulled his fingers out of me and looked up, waiting for me to say something, but I couldn't focus when he looked at me liked that.

With no lead-in kisses whatsoever, he buried his head in my pussy and fucking devoured me.

"*Ohhh...*" I cried out in indescribable pleasure. "Ohhh godddd, Andrewww....Waitttt...Slow down..."

He ignored me, plunging his tongue deeper and deeper.

I couldn't help but let go of the wall. I dropped my hands to his head, grabbing fistfuls of his hair to keep my balance. The harder I pulled his hair, the more his tongue lashed against me with no mercy.

Suddenly, there was a loud knock at the door, but Andrew didn't bother stopping. Instead, he lifted my right leg up and draped it over his shoulder. He grasped my thigh so I couldn't move, and then he slid his tongue into me a little deeper—licking every corner of my walls.

On the verge of coming, I grabbed his shoulders as my pussy throbbed against his mouth. But he stopped abruptly.

He moved my leg and kissed his way back up my body, stopping when he reached my breasts. He palmed them with one hand and roughly twisted my nipples.

"I told you not to let go of that wall," he said, looking down at me as he unzipped his pants.

I stared back into his eyes, nearly breathless.

"I did tell you that, *didn't I?*" He clasped my hand and pressed it against his chest, slowly moving it lower and lower.

When my hand finally reached his dick, I looked down in utter shock. He was huge, massively thick, and my jaw was hanging wide open.

"You don't like it?" He tilted my chin up and smirked.

I was utterly speechless, but I couldn't deny how horny I felt right now. Remembering what he'd said on the phone, I lowered my head to taste him, but he stopped me.

"*Not tonight.*" He pulled a condom out of his pocket, and kept his eyes on me as he put it on.

Leading me to the couch, he sat down and pulled me into his lap.

I leaned forward to kiss his lips, but he quickly repositioned me so I was facing away from him. Then he teased me with the head of his cock—rubbing it against my slit. Again and again.

"Remember how you said you wanted to ride me until I came inside of you?" he whispered into my ear. "How you wanted to grind on me until I begged you to stop?"

"*Yes...*" I moaned.

He pushed me down by my shoulders and sank me onto his cock, burying himself to the hilt inch by inch. The further I slipped onto him, the more he groaned. The more he said my name.

When he was completely inside of me, he held me still and pressed his lips against the back of my neck, letting me adjust to his length.

The feel of him was like nothing I'd ever felt before. It was intense, powerful, *addictive*.

"*Ride me, Aubrey...*" He pushed me forward. "Fucking ride me..."

I took a deep breath and rocked against him, slowly stretching my insides further and further. I could barely maintain a rhythm; the fullness of him was almost too much, and he was rubbing my clit with his thumb—driving me insane.

"You feel so fucking good right now.." He yanked me back by my hair. "Don't fucking stop."

I held onto his legs to steady myself, slightly lifting my body up and down. I tried to finally establish a tempo, to finally take control.

"*Andrewww...*" I couldn't handle his cock anymore. "I'm...I'm about to cum..."

"No." He gripped my hips harder than ever. "*Not yet.*"

He suddenly stood up, with me still impaled on his cock, and bent me over. "Grab that table and don't let go."

My fingers clutched the edge of the coffee table and he pounded into me again and again, smacking my ass each time I cried out.

"I told you I was going to *own* your pussy," he whispered harshly. "Don't cum until I tell you to fucking cum..." His cock was throbbing inside of me, and my muscles were clenching with his every stroke.

"Fuck....Fuckkkk!" My legs were starting to give out as an intense pressure built inside of me, as he fucked me relentlessly. "Andrewwwww…"

"*Don't let go.*" He warned, but I couldn't help it.

My orgasm took ahold of me in a rush and I collapsed, falling forward. Before I could land face first onto the coffee table, he pulled me back and continued pounding into me until he reached his own release.

I shut my eyes and leaned back against him, panting heavily as we both tried to catch our breath. Several minutes later, Andrew gently lifted my hips and pulled out of me.

He stood up, and I watched him as he walked into the kitchen and threw the condom away. He picked my fallen towel up from the floor and walked back over to me.

I made no move to get up, but I re-wrapped the towel around myself.

"Is there anything you *didn't* lie to me about?" His voice was a whisper.

"Yes…"

"And what would that be?"

"I did miss you…"

He raised his eyebrow, keeping the rest of his face stoic. Expressionless. He started to buckle his pants, not taking his eyes off mine.

I was hoping that he would say something, *anything*, but he didn't.

He smoothed his shirt with his hands and walked to the door. All of a sudden, he stopped and glanced over his shoulder. Then he walked over to me and lightly kissed my lips—brushing his thumb against my cheek.

I wanted to speak, to ask what he was thinking, but he pulled away and left.

This time he was gone.

# Recess (n.):
Temporary withdrawal or cessation from the usual
work or activity.


*Andrew*

I'd broken a lot of rules in my life, but sleeping with an intern was probably one of the worst ones. There was no precedent for this, and that terrified me.

The second I left Aubrey's apartment, I did what I normally did after fucking someone I met online: I went home, showered, poured a glass of my favorite scotch, and pulled out my laptop—preparing to search for the next.

Except this time, I didn't want to search for a next. I wanted to fuck Aubrey, again and again. I wanted to hear her scream a little louder, feel her body wrapped against mine, and see her face as I buried myself deep inside of her.

Damn...

I couldn't believe this. I could count on one hand the number of women I'd thought about after I left a hotel, and it wasn't because any of them were memorable in a *good* way. And the ones that *were* good, were just "good"—never amazing, like Aubrey.

A part of me felt bad for leaving her right after we finished, for not saying a word, but I *had* to leave.

I didn't do pillow talk conversations after sex. Ever.

Even though I was more than tempted to drive back over there right now and claim her again, I had to make myself accept a very harsh fact: I was never going to sleep with her again. It was against my rules.

"Where is my coffee, Jessica?" I called her desk. "Why hasn't Miss Everhart brought it to me yet? Is she late today?"

"No, sir." She sounded confused. "It's only seven thirty..."

I looked at the clock on my wall and sighed before ending the call. I was on edge for some reason, and I didn't like it.

I'd failed to get any sleep the night before and I'd purposely ignored Aubrey's midnight text. It'd read, *"Can't sleep...Can we talk about what just happened between us?"*

The answer was *no*.

Our conversations were long over. There was nothing more we had to discuss.

We talked. We fucked. That was the end of us.

I pulled up the Dating-Match website, determined to get her out of my mind. All I needed to do was find someone else, and she would become a drop in the sea of other endless women—a fleeting memory that I would halfway remember whenever I saw her gorgeous face.

There were hundreds of new women on the site now, but very few of them caught my eye. The ones that did seemed too good to be true, so I didn't bother clicking on their full profiles.

Just as I was reading about a math professor, a cup of coffee was set on my desk.

"Good morning," Aubrey whispered.

I didn't answer. I continued to scroll through online profiles; she'd get the point eventually.

She sighed. "Andrew—"

"It's *Mr. Hamilton*." I looked up, immediately wishing that I hadn't. She looked even more stunning today than she did yesterday. She was wearing the same grey dress she'd worn to her interview, and it was tighter today than it was on that day. Her hair was falling in soft curls that fell past her shoulders, and her blue eyes were bright, hopeful.

"Can I talk to you for a second?" she asked.

"Is it about your work?"

"No..."

"Is it about *my* work?"

"No..."

"Then no. Get out."

"It's about yesterday." She stood still, making my cock stiffen as

54

she bit her lip.

"Yesterday was a *mistake*, a regrettable moment in both of our careers, and I assure you that it won't be happening again."

"That's not what I was going to say."

"Miss Everhart," I said, standing up from my desk and walking over to her, "you and I work together professionally. If I had known the truth behind all of your ridiculous lies earlier, I would've immediately stopped talking to you. And then I would've reported you for stealing someone else's information and using it as your own. The fact that you are a *liar* remains, and unfortunately—given those circumstances and the fact that I've already fucked you, there's nothing more that needs to be said between us."

She opened her mouth to say something, but I pressed my finger against her lips.

"Nothing more," I whispered, bringing my face close to hers. "Understood?"

"You are..." Her bottom lip quivered as she jerked away from me. "You are such an *asshole*! I can't believe that I slept with you!"

"Believe it. I'm sure it'll be a very good memory for you since you hardly ever have sex."

She shook her head. "Were you pretending on the phone, too? You're nothing like the man I talked to at night, nothing like—"

"Please spare me the emotional appeal bullshit, Miss Everhart. I'll have my next cup of coffee at noon. Thanks."

"You'll be waiting." She rolled her eyes. "I'll get it when I *feel* like it."

"You're going to make me fire you over a cup of coffee?"

"To be honest, you might not want me to make your coffee, *Mr. Hamilton*." She narrowed her eyes at me. "There's no telling what I'll put in it."

"I fucking *dare you*..." I stepped closer.

"Is that a threat?" She shrugged.

"It's a fucking *promise*." I pushed her against the wall and pressed my lips against hers, lifting her leg around my waist.

My cock had been hard ever since she set down my coffee, and she was rubbing her hand against it through my pants right now, murmuring.

I pulled a condom out of my pocket and pressed it into her hand as I devoured her mouth—biting her soft lips, teasing her tongue with mine. If I could, I would fuck her mouth all day.

As she unzipped my pants, I slipped a hand underneath her dress and pushed her panties to the side, groaning once I felt how wet she was.

"*Andrew...*" She was taking too long with the condom, so I did it myself. The second I had it on, I slid into her deeply, biting her lips so she wouldn't scream.

I grabbed her hands and placed them around my neck. "*Always wet...*" I felt her trying to move her leg from around my waist but I held it still. "Say my name again..."

"*Yes...*" She gasped as I pounded into her, over and over and over. "*Yes...*"

"*Say it.*" I squeezed her ass.

Her murmurs were becoming louder and louder.

"My name, Aubrey..." I kissed her mouth. "Say my name..."

Her pussy was gripping my cock tighter and tighter, and her nails were clawing my neck. "I...I'm about to..."

I immediately stopped mid thrust and whispered harshly into her ear. "Say my fucking name, Aubrey..."

Her nails dug into my skin. "*Andrew...*"

At the sound of my name on her lips, I slid into her again and she came, so perfectly. I felt my own release seconds later, and could feel her burying her head in my chest to stifle her moans, but I tilted her head up.

"Stop that..."

Panting, she kept her eyes on mine. "Stop, what?"

"Hiding your voice from me..." I kissed her lips again, making no move to slide out of her, and we stood there entwined in each other for what felt like forever.

As much as I wanted to tell her to leave and get the hell out of my office, I couldn't bring myself to do it. Instead, I kissed her forehead and slowly pulled out, readjusting her dress.

After throwing away the condom, I picked up one of her heels that had fallen off and held it out for her.

Her curls were tousled all over her head, so I smoothed them back into place. As if she was returning the favor, she refastened my zipper and fixed the collar of my shirt.

Then the two of us stood staring at one another. I had no idea what the fuck just happened, and only a part of me liked it. The other half loved it.

"You need to get back to work." I tugged at the ballet slipper charm around her neck. "You still owe me that Brownstein report, demotion or not."

"You told me it wasn't a demotion."

"I took a page out of your book and *lied*." I rolled my eyes and stepped back. "Get back to work."

"Fine, *Mr. Hamilton*." She smiled and headed for the door.

"And when you come back," I added, "just leave my afternoon coffee on that bookshelf and walk out. Don't come anywhere near my desk and don't say anything to me."

"Why not?"

"Because I'll fuck you again if you do."

She blushed and stepped out of the room.

The second she was gone, I fell back into my chair and shook my head.

Twice in less than twenty four hours? Jesus...

I pulled up my latest case file, but I couldn't bring myself to read it. All I could think about was Aubrey.

I'd felt something like this before, and I knew it would lead to nothing but despair. What I felt was nothing deep, nothing all-encompassing—*yet*, but it was real, and there was nothing I could do to stop it.

I'd built the last six years of my life detaching myself from any chance of having feelings for someone else, *refusing* to build any friendships, but Aubrey had snuck by my impenetrable doors somehow. And not only had she snuck by, she'd done it with lies, something I would never allow from anyone else. Something that would make me immediately discard her and never think of her again.

I had absolutely no idea how to handle this. This was uncharted territory and I had no idea where to sail next.

Sighing, I picked up my case file and forced myself to read the first few pages so I could get a grip on myself. Before I knew it, I was lost in my work, and the only thing on my mind was how I was going to convince a jury to believe my latest client's bullshit.

Before I could call the lead prosecutor and ask what he was offering in exchange for a plea deal, I felt something hot splashing into my lap.

My goddamn coffee.

"What the hell do you think you're doing?" I dropped my papers to the desk, glaring at a red-faced Aubrey. "Did you just throw that into my lap *on purpose?*"

"I did." She nodded, and I realized there were tears in her eyes. "Bringing you your coffee is my job, right?"

"Are you fucking bipolar?"

"No, I'm just a *liar* like you said. I'm actually just like you, but at least I can admit when I haven't told you the truth, at least I have a *reason.*"

"*Excuse me?*"

Tears fell down her cheeks. "You have a visitor at the front desk."

"Is it your replacement?" I asked dryly. "Because I swear to God, if these stains don't come out of my pants—"

"It's *your wife.*"

reasonable
doubt

VOLUME
TWO

WHITNEY G.

# Prologue

*New York City*
*Six years ago...*

**Andrew**

For the third week in a row, I woke up to a relentless rain falling over this repulsive city. The clouds above were coated in an ugly hue of grey, and the streaks of lightning that flashed across the sky every few seconds were no longer marvels; they were predictable.

Holding up my umbrella, I walked to a newspaper stand and picked up *The New York Times*—bracing myself for what lay between its pages.

"How many women do you think a man could possibly screw in his lifetime?" The vendor asked as he handed me my change.

"I don't know," I said. "I've stopped counting."

"Stopped counting, eh? What did you do, get to ten and decide that was enough before settling down?" He pointed to the gold band on my left hand.

"No. I settled down first, then I started fucking."

He raised his eyebrow—looking stunned, and then he turned around to organize his cigar display.

A couple of months ago, I would've entertained his attempt to make conversation, would've answered his question with a lighthearted laugh and a "More than we'll ever admit to," but I didn't have the ability to laugh anymore.

My life was now a depressing reel of repeated frames—hotel nights, cold sweats, marred memories, and rain.

Goddamn rain.

I tucked the newspaper underneath my arm and turned away,

glancing at the ring on my hand.

I hadn't worn it in a long time, and I had no idea what possessed me to put it on today. Twisting it off my finger, I looked at it one last time—shaking my head at its uselessness.

For a split second, I considered keeping it, maybe locking it away as a reminder of the man I used to be. But that version of me was pathetic—*gullible*, and I wanted to forget him as fast as I could.

I crossed the street as the light turned green, and as I stepped onto the sidewalk, I tossed the band where I should've thrown it months ago.

Down the drain.

# Exculpatory Evidence (n.):
Evidence indicating that a defendant did not commit
the crime.

*Present Day*

**Andrew**

The hot coffee that was currently seeping through my pants and
stinging my skin was the exact reason why I never fucked the same
woman twice.

Wincing, I took a deep breath. *"Aubrey..."*

"You're fucking *married.*"

I ignored her comment and leaned back in my chair. "In the
interest of your future short-lived and mediocre law career, I'm
going to do two huge favors for you: One, I'm going to apologize
for fucking you a second time and let you know that it will *never*
happen again. Two, I'm going to pretend like you didn't just assault
me with some goddamn coffee."

"*Don't.*" She threw my coffee mug onto the floor, shattering it
to pieces. "I definitely did, and I'm tempted to do it again."

"Miss Everhart—"

"*Fuck you.*" She narrowed her eyes at me, adding, "I hope your
dick falls off" as she stormed out of my office.

"Jessica!" I stood up and grabbed a roll of paper towels.
*"Jessica?"*

No answer.

I picked up my phone to call her desk, but she suddenly stepped
into my office. "Yes, Mr. Hamilton?"

"Call Luxury Dry Cleaning and have them deliver one of my
suits to the office. I also need a new cup of coffee, Miss Everhart's

file from HR, and you need to tell Mr. Bach that I'll be late to that four o'clock meeting today."

I waited to hear her usual "Right away, sir" or "I'm on it, Mr. Hamilton," but she said nothing. She was silent—blushing, and her eyes were glued to the crotch of my pants.

"Don't you need some help cleaning that up?" Her lips curved into a smile. "I have a really thick towel in my desk drawer. It's very soft...and *gentle.*"

"Jessica..."

"It *is* huge, isn't it?" Her eyes finally met mine. "I really wouldn't tell a soul. It would be our little secret."

"My fucking dry cleaning, a new cup of coffee, Miss Everhart's file, and a message to Mr. Bach about me being late. *Now.*"

"I really love the way you resist..." She stole another glance of my pants before leaving the room.

I sighed and started to soak up as much of the coffee as I could. I should've known that Aubrey was the emotional type, should've known that she was unstable and incapable of behaving normally the second I realized she'd made up a fake identity just for LawyerChat.

I regretted ever telling her that I wanted to own her pussy, and I was cursing myself for driving to her apartment yesterday.

Never again...

Just as I was tearing off a new paper towel, a familiar voice cleared the air.

"Why, hello...It's good to see you again," she said.

I lifted my head up, hoping that this was a hallucination—that the woman at my door wasn't really standing there smiling. That she wasn't stepping forward with her hand outstretched as if she wasn't the very reason that my life was heartlessly altered six years ago.

"Are you going to shake my hand, *Mr. Hamilton?*" She raised her eyebrow. "That is the name you're going by these days, isn't it?"

I stared at her long and hard—noticing that her once silky black hair was now cut short into a bob. Her light green eyes were still as soft and alluring as I remembered them, but they weren't having the same effect.

All the memories I'd tried to suppress were suddenly playing right in front of me, and my blood was starting to boil.

"*Mr. Hamilton?*" she asked again.

I picked up my phone. "Security?"

"Are you fucking kidding me?" She slammed the phone down. "You're not going to ask why I'm here? Why I came to see you?"

"Doing so would imply that I *care*."

"Did you know that when most people get sentenced to prison, they get care packages, money orders, even a phone call on their first day?" She clenched her jaw. "I got divorce papers."

"I told you I'd write."

"You told me you'd *stay*. You told me you forgave me, you said that we could start over when I got out, that you would be right there—"

"You fucking ruined me, Ava." I glared at her. "*Ruined me*, and the only reason I said those dumb ass things to you was because my lawyer told me to."

"So, you don't love me anymore?"

"I don't answer rhetorical questions," I said. "And I'm not a geography expert, but I know damn well that North Carolina is outside of New York and a direct violation of your parole. What do you think will happen when they find out you're here? Do you think they'll make you serve out the sentence that you more than fucking deserve?"

She gasped. "You would snitch on me?"

"I would *run my car* over you."

She opened her mouth to say something else, but the door opened and the security team walked in.

"Miss?" The lead guard, Paul, cleared his throat. "We're going to need you to vacate the premises now."

Ava scowled at me. "Really? You're really going to let them haul me off like I'm some kind of animal?"

"Once again, *rhetorical*." I sat down in my chair, signaling for Paul to get rid of her.

She said something else, but I tuned it out. She didn't mean shit to me, and I needed to find someone online tonight so I could fuck her random and unwanted appearance out of my mind.

# Evasion (n.):
A subtle device to set aside the truth, or escape the
punishment of the law.

## Aubrey

Andrew was the epitome of what it meant to be an asshole, a
shining example of what that word stood for, but no matter how
pissed I was, I hadn't been able to stop thinking about him.

In the six months that we'd spoken, he'd never mentioned a
wife. And the one time I'd asked if he'd ever done anything more
than "One dinner. One night. No repeats." –he'd said "Once," and
quickly changed the subject.

I'd been replaying that conversation in my mind all night, telling
myself to accept that he was a liar, and that I needed to move on

"Ladies and gentlemen of La Monte Art Gallery…" My ballet
instructor spoke into a mic, cutting through my thoughts. "May I
have your attention, please?"

I shook my head and looked out into the full audience. Tonight
was supposed to be one of the highlights of my dance career. It
was an exhibition for the city's college dancers. All of the leading
performers for spring productions were supposed to dance a two
minute solo in honor of their school, in celebration of what was to
come months later.

"This next performer you're about to see is Miss Aubrey
Everhart." There was pride in his voice. "She is playing the role of
Odette/Odile in Duke's production of *Swan Lake*, and when I tell
you that she is one of the most talented dancers I've ever seen…"
He paused as the crowd's chatter dissolved into silence. "I need
you to take my word for it."

One of the photographers in the front row snapped a picture of me, temporarily rendering me blind by the flash.

"As most of you know," he continued, "I've worked with the best of the best, spent countless years in Russia studying under the greats, and after a long and illustrious career with the New York Ballet Company, I've retired to teach those with untapped potential."

There was a loud applause. Everyone in the room knew who Paul Petrova was, and even though most in the field were confused as to why he'd ever want to teach in Durham, no one dared to question his decision.

"I hope you'll come out and see the first transformation of the Duke ballet program in the spring," he said as he slowly walked to the other side of the stage. "But for now, Miss Everhart will perform a short duet from Balanchine's *Serenade*, with her partner Eric Lofton!"

The audience clapped again, and the lights above them dimmed. A soft spotlight shone on me and Eric, and the violinists began to play.

Short, soft notes filled the room, and I stood on my toes—trying to dance as delicately as the music demanded. Yet, with each step, all I could picture was Andrew kissing me, fucking me, and ultimately *lying* to me.

"I've never lied to you, Aubrey. I trust you for some strange reason..."

I pushed Eric away when he held out his hands, and twirled across the stage until he came after me. He held my face in his hands—as if he was begging me to stay, but I spun away again, launching myself into a full set of nonstop pirouettes.

I was angry, I was hurt, and I wasn't holding anything back as I showed off just how well I could dance en pointe.

The second the violinists struck the last note, the audience let out a collective gasp and applauded the loudest they had all night.

"Wow..." Eric whispered as he took a bow next to me. "I don't think anyone will talk shit about you getting the swan role after that..."

"People have been talking shit about me?" I raised my eyebrow, but I already knew the answer to that. A junior landing the top role over all the seniors was unheard of.

"Bravo, Miss Everhart." Mr. Petrova walked over to me. "She's going to blow you all away in the spring, I'm sure of it!"

Another round of applause began to build and he moved the mic away from his mouth. "Where are your parents? I'd like for them to come up for a picture."

"They're out of town." I lied. I hadn't wasted my time even attempting to invite them to this.

"Well, that's too bad," he said. "I'm sure they're very proud of you. You can exit the stage now."

"Thank you." I headed into the dressing room and changed into a short white silk dress and a grey feathered headband. As I looked myself over in the mirror, I smiled. There was no way anyone could tell that I was an emotional wreck inside.

I pulled out my phone and noticed a new voicemail from GBH. I knew it was about me missing my internship for the fourth day in a row, so I deleted it. Then something came over me and I googled "Andrew Hamilton" for the umpteenth time this week—hoping something would pop up.

Nothing. Again.

With the exception of his perfectly poised photo on GBH's website and that less than telling bio, there was no information about him anywhere.

I'd even tried "Andrew Hamilton: New York, lawyer," but the results were just as dismal. It was as if he hadn't come into existence until starting at GBH.

"Great performance, Aubrey…" Jennifer, one of Duke's top seniors, suddenly stepped into the bathroom. "It really is an honor watching someone so young and underdeveloped get unnecessary credit."

I rolled my eyes and zipped my purse.

"Tell me something," she said. "Do you honestly think you're going to last until the spring performance?"

"Do you honestly think I'm going to stand here and continue this dumbass conversation?"

"You should." She smirked. "Because between you and me, four years ago—back before your time…There was a certain dancer picked to be the lead in *Sleeping Beauty*, a double major. She was quite talented—a natural really, but she caved under pressure because she couldn't devote as many hours to the craft as the dancers who only wanted to dance."

"Is there a point to this story?"

"I took her spot and I was only a freshman." She smiled. "Now

I'm a senior, and a certain someone is dancing in the role that belongs to me. So, just like back then, I'm going to do everything in my power to make sure I get what's rightfully mine."

I shook my head and moved past her, ignoring the fact that she'd whispered "stupid bitch" under her breath. I was supposed to return to the gallery room and watch the other performers, but I needed a break.

I slipped past the sliding doors on the other side of the room and stepped into the gallery's bistro. It was much quieter on this side, and the people sitting at the tables seemed to be preoccupied with conversations not centered on ballet.

"Miss?" A tuxedoed waiter stepped in front of me with a tray. "Would you be interested in a complimentary glass of champagne?"

"Two, please."

He raised his eyebrow, but handed me two glasses anyway.

With no grace whatsoever, I tossed one back, then the other— licking the rims to make sure I didn't miss a drop.

"Where's your bar?" I asked.

"Our *bar*? I don't think the patrons of the art gallery are permitted to—"

"Please don't make me ask again."

He pointed to the other side of the room where a few smokers were sitting, and I walked toward them.

"What can I get for you tonight, Miss?" The bartender smiled as I approached. "Would you like to try one of our house specials?"

"Can any of those help me forget about sleeping with a married man?"

The smile on his face faded and he set out three shot glasses, filling them with what I could only hope was the strongest liquor in the house.

I slid my credit card across the counter and downed the first one in seconds—shutting my eyes as the burning sensation crawled down my throat. I held the next one against my lips, and I suddenly heard a familiar laugh.

It was low and gravelly, and I'd heard it a million times before.

I turned around and spotted Andrew sitting at a table with a woman who was *not* his wife. I didn't want to admit it, but she was pretty. Very, very pretty: Auburn hair with blond highlights, deep green eyes, and perky breasts that were too perfect to be natural.

She was rubbing him on his shoulder and giggling every ten seconds.

Andrew seemed undaunted by her affection, and as he signaled for the check, I could only assume how their night would end.

I tried to turn away—to act like seeing him with someone else wasn't affecting me, but I couldn't help it.

His date was now leaning over the table—purposely putting more of her cleavage on display, and whispering words that were hard to read. As she playfully licked her lips and stroked his chin with her fingertips, I realized I couldn't take it anymore.

**Subject: SERIOUSLY?!**

Are you really on a date right now with someone who isn't your wife?! It's bad enough that you're a cheating and lying philanderer, but are you really that much of a sex addict?

—Aubrey

His response came within seconds.

**Subject: Re: SERIOUSLY?!**

I'm really on a date right now with someone who's not going to leave third degree burns on my dick. And I'm not a sex addict, I'm a pussy addict. There's a difference.

—Andrew

**Subject: Re: Re: SERIOUSLY?!**

You are a disgusting and vile asshole, and I honestly regret ever sleeping with you.

—Aubrey

No response.

I watched as he looked down at his phone and raised his eyebrow. He turned around in his chair—slowly scanning the room until he found me.

His eyes widened the second they met mine, and his lips slowly parted. His gaze traveled up and down my body, and I could feel

71

him undressing me.

There was suddenly no one else in the room but the two of us and I could tell that he wanted me to come to him—right here, right now. I felt my body responding to his stares, felt my nipples hardening as he dragged his tongue against his lips.

I swallowed as I looked him over, realizing that I'd pictured his hair entirely wrong in my dreams this week. I'd finger fucked myself for hours on end last night—using his face and the memories of his voice for inspiration, and seeing him in person only made me want to feel his cock inside of me again.

I leaned forward, wanting to go to him, but my tunnel vision quickly cleared and I saw that we weren't alone in this room.

Far from it.

His date's perfectly manicured hand found its way to his chin, and turned his head away.

I followed suit and asked for two more drinks. I downed them both and when I looked over my shoulder, I saw that Andrew was staring in my direction with undeniable want in his eyes.

I forced a smile and opened my mouth very slowly, mouthing, "Fuck. You." before leaving. I snatched a handful of mints from a random waiter's tray and rushed back toward the gallery.

I was halfway there when I felt my phone vibrating. An email.

**Subject: Meet me in the bathroom.**

NOW.

—Andrew

I turned off my phone and continued walking toward the gallery doors—damn near running. I reached the lobby, but someone grabbed my arm and pulled me across the room.

Andrew.

I tried to jerk away, but he tightened his hold and looked back at me—giving me a 'Don't Fuck with Me' look as the people around us whispered.

He pulled me into a bathroom and locked the door, narrowing his eyes at me. "You think I'm disgusting?"

"Extremely." I stepped back. "I've lost what little respect I had for you and if you even *try* to put your hands on me, I'll scream."

"I don't doubt that." A trace of a smile grazed his lips, but it didn't stay. "You haven't shown up to work for four straight days. You think just because I fucked you that I won't fire you?"

"I don't give a fuck whether you fire me or not! Have you ever thought about why I haven't shown up to work?"

"Incompetence?"

"You're fucking married! *Married!* How could you—" I shook my head as he closed the gap between us. "How could you leave that part out?"

"I didn't," he said. "And for the record…I'm not technically married, Aubrey."

"I'm not technically *stupid*, Andrew."

"You're making it very difficult to talk to you right now…" His lips were brushing against mine.

"That's because you're not making any fucking sense." I freed myself from his grasp and headed for the door, but he grabbed me and slammed me against the wall.

"It's a *contested divorce*," he hissed. "If you were a *real* lawyer I'm sure I wouldn't have to explain what the hell that term means, but since you're not—"

"It means that you're still legally married. It means that if you die before the papers go through, that your wife—which is what she is, will still be entitled to everything you ever owned. It means that you're a LIAR! A *fucking liar*, who is apparently exempt from his own stupid and ineffectual rules!"

"I filed." He gritted through his teeth "She refused to sign, and there's a lot of complicated shit that I'll never feel like discussing, but we've been separated and out of touch for over six years. Six. Years."

I shrugged and tried to put on my best poker face, ignoring the fact that my heart was skipping every other beat as he wiped my tears away with his thumb.

"I've never lied to you, Aubrey," he said sternly. "You asked me before if I'd ever lied to you and that answer is still the same. I don't talk about my life before Durham with anyone, but yes, I did once have a wife and she showed up to my office on her own. I didn't call her, I never will, and I haven't called her since I left New York. Our case is extremely complicated and I prefer not to think about it."

"I don't care," I said. "You're still *wrong*. You still neglected to tell me about her for six months. Six. *Months!*"

"At what point was I supposed to bring that shit up?" His face turned red. "In between fucking you over the phone? When I was begging your lying ass to meet me in person? When I was unknowingly helping you with your fucking *homework*?"

"How about before you fucked me?" I hated that being around him pulled emotions out of me. I couldn't pretend to act unaffected if I tried. "How about then?"

He clenched his jaw, but he didn't say a word.

"That's what I thought," I said, knowing that I'd won this. "Now, I'm sure you and your lovely D-cup date have a room reserved across the street, so if you don't mind—"

"There's nothing going on between me and my soon to be *ex-wife*," he said harshly. "Nothing. And I *do* have a room reserved across the street. I've had the same one reserved for the past four nights with four different women, but I've been unable to fuck any of them because I can't seem to stop thinking about my incompetent-ass-intern and how I only want to fuck her."

Silence.

"Do you..." I shook my head. "Do you honestly think saying shit like that is a turn-on?"

"Yes..." He trailed his fingers underneath my dress, slightly brushing his thumb against the crotch of my soaked panties. "And apparently you do, too..."

"Me being wet just means that I can't control my body's reaction to you. It doesn't mean that I want to have sex with you. I *hate* you."

"I'm pretty sure that you don't." He slipped his hand around my waist and pulled me close—making my breathing slow.

"Get your hands off me..."

"Say it more convincingly and I will." He waited for my request, raising his eyebrow, but I couldn't bring myself to say those words.

We stood staring at each other for several minutes, letting that raw, palpable tension build between us before I finally broke the silence.

"I think you should get back to your date..." My voice was a whisper. "You've said all you had to say so...What more could you possibly want from me?"

"In this moment?" He trailed his finger against my collarbone.

"In general." I turned my cheek before he could kiss me. "I'm never sleeping with you again, I'll be formally resigning by the end of the week, and I think we need to end our so-called friendship for good."

"You mean that?" he whispered.

"Yes, I mean that." I ignored the feel of his hand squeezing my ass. "I want to be friends with someone who's interested in more than my pussy."

"I'm interested in *your mouth*, too."

I had no response for that, and he must've sensed it because he tightened his grip on my waist.

"I know how hard it is for you to tell the truth," he said softly, "so I need you to be completely honest when I ask you these next few questions. Can you do that?"

I nodded, breathlessly, and he leaned closer to my lips. "You don't enjoy fucking me?"

"That's not the issue."

"That's not the *answer*. Tell me."

I ignored the loud beating in my chest. "I do enjoy it…"

"Are you really resigning?" He kissed me.

"No…I just—" I sucked in a breath as his hand cupped my right breast, as he squeezed it. Hard.

"You just *what*?"

"I want to be reassigned to another lawyer, and I don't want to see you any more than I have to."

He stared into my eyes for a long time, not saying a word as he let me go. "That's how you truly feel?"

"Seeing as I'm the only one between us who actually *feels* anything, yes. Yes, that is how I really feel about you."

He blinked. Then he suddenly pulled me back into his arms and crushed his lips onto mine.

"Why are you such a fucking liar, Aubrey?" He hissed. Pushing me against the vanity, he bit down on my bottom lip and snatched the feathered headband out of my hair.

Keeping his lips on mine, he pushed my dress above my waist—ripping off my panties with one pull.

"Andrew…" I tried to catch my breath as he picked me up and set me on the sink. "Andrew, wait…"

"For what?" He grabbed my hand and placed it over his belt, telling me to unbuckle it.

I didn't answer him. I slipped my fingers underneath the metal clip and unclasped it as he pressed his mouth against my neck.

WHITNEY G.

Trailing his tongue against my skin, he whispered, "You haven't missed me fucking you?"

"It was only twice." I sucked in a breath as his hands caressed my thighs. "Not enough to miss anything..."

He bit me harshly and leaned back, glaring at me.

My breath caught in my throat as he slipped two fingers inside my pussy and teasingly moved them in and out.

"It *feels* like you've missed fucking me..." He pushed his fingers as deep as they could go, making me moan.

I arched my back as he stroked my clit with his thumb.

He suddenly pulled his fingers out of me and brought them up to his lips, slowly licking them. "It *tastes* like you've missed fucking me, too." He pressed another finger against my throbbing wet clit and then he brought it up to my face—placing it against my lips. "Open your mouth."

I slowly parted my lips, and he narrowed his eyes as he slid his finger against my tongue. I felt his cock rub against my thigh, felt him using his other hand to wrap my leg around his waist.

"Tell me that you don't want to fuck me," he said. "That you don't want me to bury my cock deep inside of you *right now.*"

He grabbed my face and pressed his lips against mine, drawing my bottom lip into his mouth with his teeth.

I was sliding off the edge of the counter, about to fall, but he pressed me back against the mirror.

I kept my eyes locked on his as he unwrapped a condom, as he put it on and stared at me with that same angry expression he'd been wearing all night.

He grabbed me by my ankles and pulled me forward, sliding his cock into me as my legs gripped his waist.

My hands clawed at his neck as he pounded into me again and again.

"*I've* missed fucking you," he rasped, threading his fingers into my hair and pulling my head back. "But you haven't thought about me at all?"

"Ahhh!" I screamed as he sped up his thrusts. I squeezed my legs around him even tighter, trying my best not to give in.

I shut my eyes and heard him saying my name—panting, "Fuck, Aubrey...Fuck..."

"Put your hands on the counter..." he commanded, but I ignored him and tightened my grip around his neck.

76

"Aubrey…" He bit my shoulder again, still fucking me harder than ever. "Put your hands on the counter. Now."

I slowly unclasped my hands from around him and lowered them to my sides—gripping onto the cold counter. The next thing I felt was his tongue swirling around my nipples, roughly sucking my breasts.

I gripped the tile harder as his kisses became more ravenous—more possessive, and as he fucked me harder and harder, I felt myself on the verge of losing control.

"*Andrew….*" I moaned. "*Andrew….*"

He released my nipple from his mouth and slid his hands underneath my thighs, picking me up and pinning my back against the wall.

"I know you love the way I fuck you, Aubrey…" He looked into my eyes, forcing his cock even deeper into my pussy. "And I know you've touched yourself every night this week, wishing it was my cock inside of you instead of your fingers."

My clit throbbed with his every word, and I was wetter than I'd ever been in my life.

"Tell me it's true…" He pressed his lips against mine and slipped his tongue into my mouth—muffling my moans with an angry, unrelenting kiss. "Finally tell me something that's fucking true…"

Tremors traveled up and down my spine, and I was seconds away from coming, but he wouldn't let my mouth go.

He was still kissing me—glaring at me, begging me to tell him the truth.

I nodded, hoping that he could read my eyes and see that I needed him to let go of me, I needed to be able to breathe.

He slammed into me one last time—hitting my spot, and I managed to tear my mouth away from his.

"Yessssss!" My head fell forward into his shoulder and I gasped for air.

"*Aubrey…*" He gripped my waist until he stopped shaking.

As we both came back down, there were a few random knocks at the door, a few "Is anybody in there?" taps, but both of us remained silent and breathless.

Minutes later, when his breathing seemed to be under control, he pulled out of me—staring into my eyes. He tossed the condom away in the trashcan behind him and pulled up his pants.

I watched as he fixed himself in the mirror, as he smoothed everything so well that no one would ever know that he'd just fucked the shit out of me.

I slid off the sink and looked at my own face—flushed cheeks, wild hair, runny mascara—and pulled my bra straps back over my shoulder. Before I could pull up my dress straps, Andrew moved my hand away and pulled them up for me.

Our eyes met in the mirror as he smoothed my hair, and for a split second he turned away—to pick up my headband. He gently held it over my head and slid it into place, and then he walked away.

"You know, it's rude to just leave someone after sex without saying anything," I muttered.

"What?" His hand was on the doorknob.

"Nothing."

"What did you say?" He cocked his head to the side. "I'm not a mind reader."

"I said it's rude to just leave after you fuck me. You could at least say something, *anything*."

"I don't do pillow talk."

"It's not pillow talk." I scoffed. "It's part of being a gentleman."

"I never said I was a gentleman."

I sighed and turned around. I waited to hear the door close, but his hands were suddenly on my waist and he was spinning me around to face him.

"What am I supposed to say after I fuck you, Aubrey?"

"You could ask if it was good for me or not..."

"I don't believe in asking pointless questions." He looked at his watch. "How long do you have to stay here?"

"Another hour or so."

"Hmmm." He was quiet. "And while you were stalking me and my date how many shots did you have?"

"I wasn't stalking you and your date. I've been avoiding you all week, or haven't you noticed?"

"*How many?*"

"Five."

"Okay." He tucked a strand of hair behind my ear. "I'll take you home whenever you're ready and have someone deliver your car to your apartment tomorrow." He planted a kiss on my forehead before heading to the door. "Just call me."

"Wait," I said as he opened it. "What about your date?"
"What about her?"

An hour later, I slipped inside of Andrew's car—a sleek black Jaguar. He held the door open until I was comfortable, and waited until I put on my seatbelt before shutting it.

On his dashboard, I spotted a red folder with a New York State seal on its center. I picked it up, but he immediately took it from me and locked it inside his glove box.

He looked offended that I'd touched it, but he quickly turned away from me and revved up the car.

"Can I ask you something, Andrew?"

"Depends on what it is."

"I googled you this week and nothing came up…"

"That's not a question."

"Why didn't anything come up?" I looked over at him.

"Because I'm thirty-two years old and I don't waste my time on Facebook and Twitter."

I sighed. "And you really haven't spoken to her in six years?"

"Excuse me?" He looked over at me as we approached a red light. "I thought we just sorted this out in the bathroom."

"We did, but—" I cleared my throat. "You filed for a divorce, and it couldn't go through?"

"It takes two people to complete a divorce, Aubrey. Surely you know that."

"Yes, but…" I ignored the fact that he was clenching his jaw. "Wouldn't it be easier for someone like you to make it happen? Six years is a pretty long time to stay married to someone you claim you don't love anymore, so—"

"You'd be surprised at how well some people can spin a fucking lie to get what they want," he said, his voice cold. "My past isn't up for discussion."

"Ever?"

"Ever. It has nothing to do with you."

I leaned back in my seat, crossing my arms. "Are you ever going to tell me the reason why you left New York and moved to Durham?"

"No."

"Why not?"

"Because I don't have to." He steered the car into my apartment complex. "Because like I told you an hour ago, that part of my life never happened."

"I'm not going to tell anyone. I just—"

"Stop it." He faced me as he stopped the car, and I could see a world of hurt in his eyes. It was the most vulnerable I'd ever seen him.

"I lost something very special in New York six years ago." There was regret in his voice. "Something I'll never fucking get back, something I've spent the last six years trying to forget, and if it's okay with you I'd like to make it to year seven."

I opened my mouth to say sorry, but he continued talking.

"I'm not sure if I've made this apparent over the past six months or not," he said, "but I'm not the 'sit up and talk about my feelings' type. I'm not interested in deep conversations and just because I've fucked you more than once and can't seem to get you or your mouth off my mind, that doesn't entitle you to things I haven't told anyone else."

I immediately unbuckled my seatbelt and flung the door open, but he grabbed my wrist before I could get out.

"I meant what I said a few months ago, Aubrey..." He cupped my chin and tilted my head toward him. "You are my only friend in this city, but you have to understand that I'm not used to having friends. I'm not used to talking about personal shit, and I'm not going to start now."

Silence.

"If you're not going to open up to me, what incentive do I have to continue being your so-called friend?"

He said nothing for a few seconds, but then he smirked. "Get in my lap and let me show you."

"Is this a joke?"

"Am I laughing?"

"Do you really think you can just demand for me to have sex with you whenever you want?" I raised my eyebrow. "Especially since you just said you'll never be that open about your personal life?"

"Yes." He unbuckled his seat belt. "Get in my lap."

"You know..." I looked down, noticing his cock slowly stiffening through his pants. "I've let a few things slide the past few times we've had sex, but I have to tell you..." I bit my lip as I slipped out of the car. "I'm really not into the possessive caveman shit."

He narrowed his eyes at me as I grabbed my purse and stepped back.

"I think we need to give your cock a rest, don't you think?" I crossed my arms. "You have a pretty big hearing coming up next week. Don't you need to save all your energy so you can be better prepared?"

"Get back in the damn car, Aubrey..." His voice was strained.

"Are you begging me?"

"I'm commanding you."

"Did you not hear what I just said?"

He didn't answer. He reached for my hand, but I shut the door.

"I'll see you tomorrow, Mr. Hamilton." I smiled and walked away.

# Liability (n.):

Legal responsibilities for one's acts or omissions.

*A week later...*

## Andrew

There was only one thing in Durham that held no comparison to New York: Court. The lawyers in New York actually took their jobs seriously. They pored over their research all night, polished their defenses to perfection, and presented their cases with pride.

In Durham, "lawyers" didn't do shit, and in a moment like this—when I was listening to a young and inexperienced prosecutor embarrass herself, I almost missed those days.

Then again, I wasn't paying too much attention to the proceedings today. I was too busy thinking about Aubrey and how many times we'd fucked in my office this morning.

We'd said our usual, "Good morning Mr. Hamilton," "Hello, Miss Everhart" greetings and locked eyes as she set my coffee down. She'd opened her mouth to say something else, but the next thing I knew, my hands were in her hair and I was pulling her against my desk.

I was ruthlessly pounding into her from behind as I massaged her clit, and when she collapsed on my carpet, I'd spread her legs and devoured her pussy.

I was completely insatiable when it came to Aubrey, and being around her for more than five seconds was enough to send me over the edge.

There's no point in even counting how many times we've fucked anymore...

"As you can see..." The prosecutor's voice cut through my

thoughts. "Ladies and gentlemen of the jury, all of the evidence that I've presented will prove—"

"Objection!" I'd had enough of this. "Your Honor, last time I checked, this was an *evidentiary hearing*, not a trial. Why is Ms. Kline being allowed to address a nonexistent jury?"

The judge took off her glasses. "Ms. Kline, as hesitant as I am to agree with Mr. Hamilton, he does have a point. Have you concluded with your presentation of evidence? Barring a closing statement to the jury?"

"I have, Your Honor," she said, puffing out her chest as if she'd just presented the case of the century.

"Mr. Hamilton…" The judge looked my way. "Do you care to surprise me today by refuting any of the evidence presented?"

"No, Your Honor." This hearing was a waste of time, and she knew it as well as I did.

"I see." She put on her glasses again. "Let the record show that while the prosecution has presented a compelling and rather large collection of evidence, it's this court's ruling that it is not enough to warrant a trial." She banged her gavel and stood up.

Ms. Kline walked over to me and held out her hand. "So, I'll file an appeal, get more evidence, and see you on this matter again soon, right?"

"Are you *asking* me or are you *telling* me?"

"Your client committed the highest degree of fraud, Mr. Hamilton." She crossed her arms. "Someone has to pay for that."

"No one ever will if you remain on top of it, will they?" I put my files in my briefcase. "I'll be waiting for your next move. And yes, you should get more evidence since the judge clearly ruled that what you had was not enough."

"So, that means I should appeal? Do you think I could win this thing?"

"I think you could go back to law school and fucking pay attention." I scoffed. "Either that, or do your clients a favor and find them a better lawyer."

"You mean someone like you?"

"There's *no one* like me." I slid a pair of shades over my eyes. "But anyone would be better than you."

"Are you always this rude to your opponents, Mr. Hamilton?" She cracked a smile. "I mean, I've heard stories, but you are really—"

"Really, what?"

"Intriguing." She stepped closer. "You are really intriguing."

I blinked and looked her over. If I'd met her on Date-Match she might've been worthy of one night, but I never mixed business with pleasure.

At least, I didn't used to.

"I'm not sure if you're seeing anyone or not," she said, lowering her voice, "but I think you and I have a lot in common."

"What exactly do we have in common, Miss Kline?"

"Well..." She stepped even closer and rubbed my shoulder. "We were both staring at each other during the hearing, we both have high profile careers, and we both have a passion for the law— a passion that could be transferred to *other things*." She licked her lips. "Right?"

I stepped back. "Miss Kline, I was staring at you during the hearing because I was trying to comprehend how someone could show up to court and be so unprepared, unprofessional, and utterly annoying. We do both have high profile careers, but if you continue presenting cases like the one you presented today, I'll be interviewing you for a secretary position at my firm within the next six months." I ignored her gasp. "And if your passion for the law is *anything* like the way you fuck, then you and I have absolutely nothing in common."

"Did you..." She shook her head, stepping back as her face reddened. "Did you really just say that to me?"

"Did you really just proposition me for sex?"

"I was simply *probing*—seeing if you were interested in going out."

"I'm not," I said—noticing that I wasn't even the slightest bit aroused. "Am I free to leave the courtroom now or would you like to probe me for something else?"

"You are an asshole!" She spun around and grabbed her briefcase off the floor. "You know, for your clients' sake, I hope you're a lot nicer," she spat out as she left the room.

I wanted to tell her that I actually wasn't nicer to my clients. I didn't put up with bullshit from anyone, and since I hadn't lost a single case since moving to Durham, I didn't have to.

Looking at my watch, I figured I'd wait a few minutes before leaving. I didn't want to run into her in the parking lot, and since the remaining courts were adjourning for lunch, I figured I'd wait a while.

I stuffed my hands into my pocket and smiled at the feel of the lacy fabric that grazed my left hand. Pulling it out, I smiled at Aubrey's black thong from this morning.

I took my phone out of my briefcase to text her about it, but she'd emailed me first.

### Subject: Wet Panty Fetish

I'm not sure if you've realized that I left my thong in your pocket yet, but I want you to know that I did it for your own good, and that your secret is safe with me.

Ever since you fucked me in the bathroom at the art gallery, I've noticed that you have a tendency to stare at my panties before taking them off.

You run your fingers across them, pull them off with your teeth, and then you stare at them again. I have no problem continuing to appease your panty fetish. I'm sure you place them over your face at night, so if you ever need more, feel free to let me know.

—Aubrey


### Subject: Re: Wet Panty Fetish

I did realize that you slipped your thong into my pocket this morning. I've noticed that you've done this all week.

Contrary to your unfounded and silly assumptions, I do not have a panty fetish and I do not sleep with them over my face at night. I do, however, have a new fetish for your pussy, and if you're interested in letting me sleep with THAT over my face at night, feel free to let me know.

—Andrew

I waited for a  response—watched my screen for several minutes, but then I realized it was Wednesday and she wouldn't see my email until later.

I made my way outside and slipped into my car. I didn't feel like going back to the firm—my case files were all up to date, and it was too early to go home.

Revving up my engine, I coasted down the street in search of a decent bar. As I was turning past the law school, I noticed Duke's dance hall across the street.

I wasn't sure what came over me, but I made a right turn and pulled into the parking lot. I followed the signs that read "Dance Studio" and parked in front.

There was a sign on the double doors of the auditorium that read "Private Rehearsals: Dancers Only," but I ignored it. I followed the faint sound of piano keys and opened the door to a colossal theater.

Bright lights shone directly on the stage, and dancers dressed in all white were spinning. Before I could come to my senses and make myself leave, I spotted Aubrey in the front.

Wearing the same feathered headband she'd worn at the art gallery, she was smiling wider than I'd ever seen her smile before—dancing as if no one else was in the room. There was a gleam in her eyes that I never saw while she was at GBH, and although I didn't know shit about ballet, it was clear that she was the best dancer onstage.

"Extend, Miss Everhart! *Extend!*" A grey haired man walked onto the stage, yelling. "More! More!"

She continued dancing—stretching her arms out further, extending her hands.

"No! No! NO!" The man stomped his foot. "Stop the music!"

The pianist immediately stopped and the director stepped in front of Aubrey.

"Do you know what the characteristics of the *white swan* are, Miss Everhart?" he asked.

"Yes."

"*Yes?*" He looked offended.

"Yes, Mr. Petrova." She stood still.

"If that's so, why don't you enlighten us all as to what those special characteristics are?"

"Light, airy, elegant—"

"Elegant!" He stomped his foot again. "The white swan is all about smooth, gentle movements... Her arms are well poised, graceful." He grabbed her elbow and pulled her forward. "Your arms are erratic, rough, and you're dancing like a pigeon on crack!"

Her cheeks reddened, but he continued.

"I want a swan, Miss Everhart, and if you're not up to the part—if your heart is elsewhere, like that other major you have, do me a favor and let me know so I can groom someone else for the role."

Silence.

"Let's try this again!" He stepped back. "On my count, start the song from the second stanza…"

I leaned back against the wall, watching Aubrey effortlessly dance again, as she made everyone else look like amateurs. I watched until I couldn't anymore, until her old director spotted my shadow and yelled at "the goddamn intruder" to leave.

Later that night, I walked into the kitchen and pulled out a bottle of bourbon—pouring myself a shot. It was two in the morning and I was beyond restless.

I hadn't been able to sleep since I came home and spotted a note from Ava on my door: "I'm not leaving until we talk—Ava."

I'd crumpled it and thrown it into the trash, wondering which person at GBH had been stupid enough to give out my address.

As I tossed back a shot, my phone rang.

"It's two in the morning," I hissed, holding it up to my ear.

"Um…" There was a slight pause. "May I speak to a…A Mr. Hamilton, please?"

"This is he. Did you not hear me say what time it is?"

"I'm sorry, Mr. Hamilton." She cleared her throat. "I'm Gloria Matter from the parole board in New York City. I'm sorry to call you so late, but I didn't want to turn in until I returned your inquiry from last week," she said. "The inmate you called about is no longer an inmate. She was released recently and is now on parole."

"I'm aware that she's on parole." I poured another drink. "However, I'm pretty sure leaving the state is a direct violation of those terms. Is New York soft on crime now? Do you let previous offenders roam the world as they please?"

"No sir, but she checked in with her officer this morning. We also checked her monitor the second we received your phone call so she's still in the state. I must warn you that we don't take too kindly to false reporting, Mr. Hamilton. If this was some type of—"

"I know what the fuck I saw." I seethed. "She was here." I hung up. I didn't care enough to think about Ava right now.

I headed into my bedroom and lay against the sheets, hoping this second round of alcohol would work better than the first.

I lay there for an hour, watching the seconds on my clock tick by, yet no sleep came and thoughts of Aubrey began to fill my mind. I was thinking about the things she'd told me when we we'd first met, things she'd told me about her sex life, and I had the sudden urge to hear her voice.

I rolled over and scrolled down to her name.

"Hello?" She answered on the first ring. "Andrew?"

"Why haven't you sucked a cock before?"

"What?" She gasped. "How about 'Good morning, Aubrey'? Are you awake?' How about asking those things first?"

"Hello, Aubrey." I rolled my eyes. "You're clearly awake, so I'll bypass that unnecessary question. Why haven't you sucked a cock before?"

She was silent.

"Do I need to drive to your apartment and make you answer the question in person?"

"Are you really in need of this information at three in the morning?"

"Desperately," I said. "Answer the question."

"It's just something I ever wanted to do." There were papers shuffling in the background. "One of the guys I used to date would ask me to do it to him from time to time—to reciprocate, but I just...I didn't like him enough to do it."

"Hmmm."

Silence.

We hadn't had an actual phone conversation since the last time we had phone sex, right before I found out her real name was Aubrey and not Alyssa.

"Were you thinking about me?" she asked.

"What?"

"Were you thinking about me?" she repeated. "You've never called me this late before. Are you lonely?"

"I'm horny."

She let out a soft laugh. "Would you like me to tell you what I'm wearing?"

"I already know what you're wearing."

"Oh, really?"

"Yes, really." I put a hand behind my head. "It's Wednesday, which means you had practice until midnight, which means you went home and showered and immediately put your feet in an ice tub without putting on any pajamas."

She sucked in a breath.

"And from the way you're breathing right now I take it you're still naked, and the reason you picked up my call on the first ring is because you want to touch yourself to the sound of my voice."

Another gap of silence.

"Am I wrong?" I asked.

"No..." Her voice was low. "I don't think you're horny right now though."

"Trust me. I am."

"Maybe, but I think you called me because you like me— because you want to hear my voice since we haven't talked on the phone in a while."

"I called you because my dick is hard and I want to make you cum over the phone."

She laughed again. "So, you don't like me?"

"I like your pussy."

"So, the white roses and the "He's just yelling at you because he knows you're the best. Don't let him get to you," note that was on the hood of my car today wasn't from you?"

I hung up.

# Retraction (n.):
The legal withdrawal of a promise or offer of contract.


## Andrew

"How do you think we should proceed with the client, Harriet?" I leaned back in my chair the next night, dreading my "Let the Interns Help with One Case per Month" required hours.

"Um, Mr. Hamilton…" She twirled a strand of hair around her finger. "My name is Hannah."

"Same thing," I said. "How do you think we should proceed with this case?"

"We could put his ex-wife on the stand. She could vouch for his character."

"They were married for thirty days." I rolled my eyes and looked at the intern sitting next to her. "And that was ten years ago. Bob, what do you have?"

"It's…It's actually Bryan."

"It's whatever I say it is. What. Do. You. Have?"

"I was doing some research on his background and he apparently was reprimanded for breaking his university's firewall his senior year. We could start there and build a case around his past of anarchy…"

I sighed. "He's our client, Bryan. Why would we intentionally make him look bad?"

He blinked.

I turned toward the last intern in the room, a petite brunette. "What do you suggest?"

"You're not going to try and guess my name?" She smiled.

"I just realized that you weren't my janitor today. What do you have?"

"This." She slid a folder across the table. "If we're trying to prove that he wasn't in breach of his company's policies when he took out his initial shares, we could use this case as a reference."

I opened the folder, reading the first line of a case that was not only over a hundred years old, but it had been overturned by the Supreme Court decades ago.

"Did you all smoke the same drugs before your interviews?" I shook my head. "You're in *law school*. A few years away from potentially having someone's future in your hands and this is the type of shit you come up with?"

"With all due respect, Mr. Hamilton..." Bryan spoke up. "Is there even a right answer to this question? I mean...Is this one of those 'Ha-ha this was just a test to see how our minds work' things? Is there really an answer?"

"Yes." I stood up.

"Really? What is it?"

"It's go the fuck home." I started stacking my papers. "All of you. Right now."

"But—"

"Now." I glared at them, waiting until they all left the room.

The second I was alone I let out a sigh and sat down again. I was better off letting Jessica help me on this case. She didn't know shit about the law but I was sure that she would at least try.

"Mr. Hamilton, I—" Aubrey stepped into the room with a cup of coffee. "Where did everyone go?"

"Home." I took the cup from her, frustrated. "You're free to go, too."

"Are you ever going to formally give me my intern position back or am I forever stuck being your coffee and file organizer?"

"You're also in charge of taking phone calls. That's a responsibility you shouldn't take lightly."

"I'm serious..." She rolled her eyes. "As much as I enjoy having sex with you every morning with your coffee, I would like to go back to feeling like I actually have a purpose here."

"Fine." I took a sip from my cup. "Have you been keeping up with my current case?"

She nodded.

"Great," I said dryly. "How do you think I should proceed?"

"I think you need to first find the man who erased your client's identity."

"What? What are you talking about?"

She took a folder from her purse and set it in front of me. "My parents taught me how to research someone's background very, very well. That's the one thing I can credit them for." She flipped a few pages. "Your client has school records from his childhood— test scores, address changes, et cetera. There's a record of where he attended college, grad school—even a record of the time he broke into his school's firewall and got suspended for an entire semester. After that, there's a short failed marriage to some woman he met in Cabo, and a few founding records for his company. But after that—with the exception of these recent allegations, there's nothing."

I glanced at the pages.

"Don't you think that's odd?" She looked at me. "How you can google someone and nothing about them pops up? How you can search several databases for information and find entire decades are missing?"

I shut the folder. "It's slightly odd."

"Slightly?"

"Yes. Slightly. Is this all the evidence you have?"

"It's all the evidence you need." She stared into my eyes. "Find the guy who erased him, or find the guy who erased *you* and you might have yourself another win under your belt. If not—"

"Aubrey…"

"People don't just come out of nowhere, Andrew," she said. "You know that, I know that, and I'm pretty sure your client knows that."

"Now we're talking about *the client?*"

"There is no record of Andrew Hamilton in any of the state's registered lawyer databases."

"I'm not facing a trial."

"I called every law school in the state and pretended to be an alumna searching for a fellow alum and there was no record of an Andrew Hamilton getting his degree from any of them."

"Are you that obsessed with me?" He smirked.

"I did the same thing for the law schools in New York. That was a bit trickier, but the results were just the same. There was no record of you going to school during the years you would've been in attendance."

"And this affects you *how?*"

"You humiliated me when you found out I lied to you."

"I apologize."

"Don't." She shook her head. "You made me cry because you told me that I was a liar for hiding the truth and pretending to be someone I wasn't."

"I'm pretty sure I wouldn't be the only person to classify you as *a liar* after what you did."

"Yet, every day that I see you, every night that I talk to you on the phone, I'm no closer to getting to know anything about you." There was concern in her eyes. "It's always me talking about me, or you talking about abstract things that make up a blurry picture."

"It doesn't matter. I told you that I—"

"That you've never lied to me," she said. "I believe that, and for a moment I thought that you were always completely honest with me, but when I look back, you're only honest about what *you* want to talk about. Hence, the random appearance of *Mrs.* Hamilton, and—"

"I've told you about that already." I grabbed her hand and pulled her close to me. "So, I'm not going to waste my time rehashing shit I've already gone over with you."

"Just..."

"Look." I pressed my finger against her lips. "You're the only woman I've fucked regularly in six years."

"Am I supposed to be proud of that?"

I pulled her into my lap. "You're the only woman—only person actually, that I talk to outside of my hours at this office, the only woman I've ever fucked over the phone, the only woman who's been in my car, and the only woman who's lied to me and still gotten me to stay..."

She sighed, staring back at me.

"Now," I said, "if you don't mind, I'm going to fuck you in this chair. And when we're done, I'll kindly show you how to research someone the right way, because contrary to what you think, my client does have a background."

"No, I double checked everything and I—"

I pressed my lips against hers. "*After* I fuck you."

# Consent (n.):

A voluntary agreement to another's proposition.

*Aubrey*

### Subject: New York /Your Panties

For the record, I did go to law school in NYC. I was the valedictorian of my class.

—Andrew

PS—If you stash one more pair of your wet panties/"For your fetish" notes in my desk drawer, I'm going to assume that you *do* want me to sleep with your pussy over my face. My tongue has been aching to do that since I first "met" you so there's no need for unnecessary hints...

"Aubrey?" My mother's voice took the smile right off of my face. "Aubrey, were you listening to your father just now?"

"No, I'm sorry." I sighed, dreading that I was still sitting at a dinner with them.

They'd called me the second my rehearsal was over and demanded that I drive home so we could all ride to our "favorite" restaurant together. It was where all their country club friends ate regularly, and I knew they just wanted to come here to assert our seemingly perfect family image.

"Are you listening now?" My father raised his eyebrow.

"Yes..."

"We brought you here so we could tell you that I'm running for governor in the next election," he said.

"Do you want my vote?"

"Ugh, Aubrey." My mother huffed and snapped her fingers for the waiter. "This is one of the happiest moments of your life."

"No..." I shook my head. "I'm pretty sure it *isn't.*"

"All those years of hard work, building our firm to be one of the most impeccable in the city," she said as she looked into my father's eyes, "it's about to payoff in a huge way. We already have a few verbal commitments for the campaign's budget, and since we're going in on the same side as the incumbent—"

"You have a really good chance of being governor." I cut her off. "Congratulations, Dad."

He reached over the table and squeezed my hand.

My mother couldn't seem to shut up. "We'll have to take new family photos—stocks, you know? Photos we can give to the press for their write-ups, so you'll have to wear your hair in something other than that ballerina thing."

"It's a *bun.*"

"It's an eyesore."

"*Margaret...*" My father chided. "It's not an eyesore. It's just—"

"It's just *what?*" I looked back and forth between them.

"It's important for us to look like a cohesive All-American unit on the campaign trail." My mother took a glass of wine from the waiter and waited for him to step away. "We may have to make some stops together as a family."

"You're running for *governor,* not President, and what twenty-something do you know travels with her parents during a campaign just for photo-ops?"

"Our opponent has twenty year old twins who are homeschooled," she said. "They travel to third world countries every summer to help the poor and I'm pretty sure they're going to be at every stop on the campaign trail."

I snorted. "Why are you trying to compete with genuine people? Don't you think they're the type that deserve to win?"

"Aubrey, this is serious." My dad looked upset. "This has been a dream of mine for a very long time and we want to make sure that nothing stands in the way."

The two of them exchanged glances and I raised my eyebrow.

"Nothing like *what?*" I asked.

"Okay..." My mother lowered her voice and looked over her shoulder before speaking. "We need to know if there are any skeletons in your closet—any pictures on social media that make you look like a party girl, any ex-boyfriends or sexual partners that you may have dealt with, or *anything* that would make us look like bad parents."

"You *are* bad parents."

"Stop it, Aubrey." My father gripped my hand and squeezed it hard. "The two of us have given you everything you could've ever wanted growing up and all we're asking for is a small sacrifice from you."

"I don't have any skeletons in my closet." I gritted my teeth.

"Good." My mother put on her fake smile. "Then, when you pull out of school for your senior year to help us on the trail, it won't look suspicious. We've already spoken to your department chair about online classes and they are, in fact, offered. For the ones that aren't, you'll have to show up to campus to take those, but they make special considerations for students with circumstances such as yours so—"

"No." I cut her off. "No, thank you."

"This isn't up for discussion, Aubrey. This is for the benefit of—"

"Dad's *dream*, right?" I tried not to lose it. "Because he's the only person in this family who has a dream?"

"Yes," my mother said through smiling teeth. "We're talking about *real* dreams, Aubrey. Not 'no-chance-in-hell' and failed ones."

"Excuse me?!" I stood up. "You want to talk about *failed dreams* when the two of you have failed more than anyone I know at the expense of your own daughter?" There were tears in my eyes.

"Aubrey, sit back down." She grabbed my hand. "Let's not make a scene."

"*Let's!*" I snatched my hand away. "Let's discuss how I'm twenty fucking two and I'm *a junior* in college when I should already be a graduate! Shall we? Can you explain why that is?"

My father's face reddened and he motioned for me to sit down, but I stood my ground.

My mother clutched her pearls. "Aubrey…We did what was best at the time, and even though switching school systems twice in two years was unfortunate, it made you who you are today. Now, the campaign won't start until—"

"I don't care when the hell it starts. I'm not going on a pointless campaign trail, and I'm not taking any of my classes online because guess what?" I could feel my blood boiling. "You can't learn fucking ballet *online!*"

The restaurant was now silent.

"You two are beyond selfish and you don't even know it." I shook my head. "I'm voting for the other guy." I stormed off amidst gasps and whispers from the other tables—slightly content that my parents' picture perfect image had been publicly scratched a bit.

"Your number, Miss?" The valet said to me as I stepped outside.

"My what?"

"Your number?" He tilted his head to the side. "For your car?"

*Shit...* I sighed and looked over my shoulder.

Patrons were pointing in my direction and I couldn't bear to go back inside just because I didn't have a ride home.

I considered calling a cab, but I knew that was pointless. It would take forever to get here, and I could probably walk to my apartment faster than they would arrive.

There was a bus stop a mile or so down, but I only had a credit card. I doubted Andrew would come get me, but I decided to give it a try.

**Subject: A Ride.**

I really need a favor...

—Aubrey


**Subject: Re: A Ride**

Wanting to take a ride on my cock in the middle of the day shouldn't be considered a "favor" at this point.

—Andrew


**Subject: Re: Re: A Ride**

I'm not talking about your dick. I'm talking about your car...Would you be able to pick me up right now? I was at a dinner with my parents but it didn't end well…and I don't have my car.

If you can't, I'll understand.

—Aubrey

**Subject: Re: Re: Re: A Ride**

Where are you?

—Andrew

Half an hour later, he pulled into the country club's driveway.

I slipped into his car before he could even park—not looking back at the snooty members who were probably whispering and wondering about what had happened between me and my parents.

"I'm taking you home, right?" he asked as he pulled off.

"No…"

He looked over at me. "Am I taking you to GBH?"

"If you want. Just not to my apartment." I paused. "I'm sure my parents will stop by there after dinner and try to talk to me so…"

"Have you eaten?"

"Lost my appetite…" I said softly, then I smiled. "But if you're interested in taking me on a date right now, I'm not opposed to that."

"Why would I take you on *a date*?"

"Because you owe me one."

"Since when?"

"You once said that you would take me out if we ever met in person, and you haven't done it yet."

We approached a stoplight and he turned to face me.

"If I was even vaguely interested in taking you out right now—which *I'm not*, where the hell would I take you if you've already eaten dinner?"

"Surprise me." I shrugged and leaned against the glass—shutting my eyes. I could picture him staring at me, giving me that "You're out of your damn mind" look, and as he steered the car back onto the street, I smiled—hoping that this would be the start of us going out regularly.

I was dreaming of him kissing me in the gallery room again when I felt him gently shaking my shoulder.

"Aubrey..." he whispered. "Aubrey, wake up."

I lifted my head and looked outside my window. There were lush plants and a massive glass paned building—an executive condo. My heart skipped a beat because I knew he'd never taken a woman to his place before, and I was happy that I would be the first.

I looked over at him, ready to say something, but then I saw him fiddling with a green parking pass and I looked out the front window—seeing where we really were.

Outside of a Hilton hotel.

"Your idea of taking me on a date is bringing me to *a hotel?*"

"It's more about fucking you in the hotel."

"Andrew, this is where you take all your other dates..."

"And?"

My heart sank. "Do you not see why bringing me here would hurt my feelings?"

"Would you prefer the *Marriott?*"

I blinked.

"They don't have the same standard of room service," he said, "but if that's what you prefer—"

"Just take me home—*right now.*" My voice cracked and I leaned against the window, shutting my eyes again. "I'll deal with my parents..."

I woke up on a plush leather couch, tucked underneath a soft black blanket.

Sitting up, I saw that my shoes had been taken off and placed in a rack on the other side of the room. A tray of fresh fruit and chocolates were sitting on the small table in front of me, and there was a bottle of wine sitting next to two stemmed glasses.

The room looked as if it'd been plucked from a magazine: silk white draperies, taupe walls, and portraits framed in silver. One of those portraits was of a fucking hotel, making it clear exactly where I was.

I immediately tossed the blanket off—ready to find Andrew and yell at him for bringing me here against my wishes. I walked down the hallway, slowly noticing that the pictures hanging on the wall were of him.

In one picture, he was standing on a beach, looking off into the distance. In another he was standing in front of a NYC cab, and in another he was lying against a city park bench.

He was young in all of these photos—his eyes held a more boyish charm, and if I wasn't mistaken, he looked happy. Extremely happy.

In between all of the larger photos, were small wooden blocks in the shape of an entwined "E" and "H." At first I thought that the "A" for Andrew's first name was simply missing, that one of the pieces would bear it, but that wasn't the case: In the last frame at the end of the hall there was a photo of a huge "E" and "H" that were solely compiled of pictures of New York.

"E" and "H"?

I continued walking down the hallway, smiling at the more "esteemed" photos he'd hung of himself. I stopped when I heard the sound of running water and followed it into a massive bedroom.

Everything was cloaked in black—the sheets that covered the king sized bed, the long silk curtains that hung over the balcony's French doors, and the plush rug that sat atop his polished wooden floors.

I walked over to his armoire and pulled out the first drawer.

"What are you doing?" Andrew was standing right behind me.

"I was…" I stalled as he wrapped an arm around my waist. "I was looking through your stuff."

"Looking for anything *particular*?" He kissed the shell of my ear from behind.

"I'm looking for where you keep all my panties."

He let out a low laugh. "They're all next to my bed." He slid his hand underneath my skirt and stalled once his fingers reached my bare pussy. "Since you're not wearing any, do I need to give them back to you?"

I rolled my eyes and he let me go.

"Is this better than a hotel room?" he asked.

"Depends." I turned around. "How many other women have you had here?"

"None."

"None?" I couldn't believe that. "In *six years*?"

"I like to keep my fucking life separate from my home life." He clasped my hand.

"So, I'm the exception to the rule?"

He didn't answer. He simply led me across the bedroom and into an all-white en-suite where the water from the shower was still running.

"I've been waiting for you to wake up…" He looked down at me.

"Because you want to watch movies together?"

"Because I want to fuck you in the shower." He pushed my back against the wall and looked into my eyes. "Because I want to fuck you all night."

I moaned as he wedged his knee between my thighs and pulled my shirt over my head. He slipped his hand behind my back to unclasp my bra, and as it fell to the floor he trailed his tongue across my nipples.

"Take off your skirt…" He backed away from me.

My hands went to my zipper, but my eyes stayed glued on him as he started to undress himself.

I'd fucked him numerous times in his office, recklessly rode his cock time and time again, but I'd never seen him completely naked.

He pulled his white V-neck shirt over his head and tossed it into the corner—exposing a set of chiseled abs and a small cursive tattoo that was etched onto his chest.

I tried to read what the words said, but then he unfastened the drawstring of his black lounge pants and let them fall to the floor.

I could see that his cock was hard through his briefs, and I waited for him to take them off, but he walked back over to me.

Grabbing my hand, he placed it against his waistline. "Take them off of me."

I slipped my thumb underneath the elastic, but he stopped me.

"With *your mouth.*"

My eyes widened as I looked up at him, seeing the sexy smirk on his face.

I bent down slightly and trailed kisses across his waist—hearing him take in a sharp breath as his hands slipped into my hair.

I gripped his thighs for balance and tugged at the hem of his briefs with my teeth. Pulling the fabric down a few inches, I used my fingers to move them further, but he pulled me back by my hair.

"Only your mouth." He warned.

I gave him a look of understanding and he let me go. I once again grabbed the briefs with my teeth and slowly slid them down his legs.

I looked up and saw that his cock was standing at attention, rock hard and ready for my pussy like always, and from the look in his eyes, I knew he was going to pull me up and fuck me against the wall.

Before he could get the chance, I sat up on my knees and gripped his cock with my hand. I pressed my lips against it—trailing my tongue across every thick inch. I wrapped my mouth around his tip and slowly massaged it with my tongue.

"Aubrey..." He threaded his fingers through my hair and looked down at me. "What are you doing?"

"I'm..." I felt my cheeks heating. "I'm sucking your cock."

He blinked, letting a slow smile spread across his face. "You're not sucking my cock...You're *kissing* it."

"I was getting to that part. I was trying to do it like..." I shook my head and stood up, completely embarrassed. "Never mind."

"You were trying to do it like *what?*" he whispered against my lips.

I shook my head again and he looked into my eyes. "You don't need to watch anybody else to learn. *I'll* teach you..."

Still smiling, he grabbed my hand and pulled me into the shower. He pressed his chest against mine and slipped a finger into my mouth as the water ran over us. "Is this as wide as you can open for me?"

I blinked, nodding.

"You're going to have to open a lot wider than that if my cock is going to fit into your mouth..." He sat down on the small wet bench behind him and motioned for me to bend low.

The water streams from above lashed against my back as I got down on my knees.

"Lick your lips," he commanded, and I obliged—feeling completely out of my zone.

I leaned forward, assuming that I was supposed to take him into my mouth now, but he stopped me.

"Make it wet."

"What?"

"Put your mouth on my cock and *wet it.*"

Hesitant, I pressed my lips against his dick and slid my tongue across his shaft. I was swirling it against him slowly, but then he pulled my head up.

"You're being too gentle," he said. "I don't need you to be a fucking lady right now…"

"I—"

"I need you to be aggressive, greedy, and *sloppy* because I'm not going to be gentle when I'm devouring you." He gently pushed my head down and spread his legs a little further. "Massage my balls with your hand…"

I immediately cupped them, rubbing them against each other.

"A little harder…" His breathing slowed and I picked up the pace of my fingers.

"Now," he whispered. "Open your mouth as wide as it can go, and take my cock as deep as you can…"

I opened my mouth and took in the first few inches easily as he threaded a few fingers through my hair.

"*Keep your eyes on me.*" He looked somewhat impressed. "You don't have to take all of it right now…" He used my shoulders to push me back and then forward. "Keep easing it in and out of your mouth just like this…"

Groaning, he stared at me with pure lust in his eyes, and then he whispered. "Suck me deeper…"

I followed his command and he groaned even louder. I could see the muscles in his legs tensing as my mouth covered over half of his cock. I was starting to feel a little bolder, slightly more confident, so I took in a little bit more of him.

"*Fuck*…" He breathed.

I used my free hand to cover the part of his cock that wasn't in my mouth, and massaged it the same way I was massaging his balls—soft but aggressive.

He started to tug at my hair, begging me to take more of him into my mouth. "Take all of it…"

Feeling as if I was now in control, I denied his request, and sped up my rhythm—bobbing my head up and down.

"*Aubrey*…" His words were strained.

I took him a little deeper—wrapping my lips around him a little tighter, but I didn't go all the way.

"*Aubrey*…" he said again, sounding desperate.

I wasn't paying his words any attention. I was loving the way his cock felt inside my mouth, loving the way my tongue was commanding him and making him react.

"*Stop.*" He yanked me back by my hair and glared at me. "Take all of my cock into your fucking mouth right now."

I slid my mouth over him and leaned forward all the way—not stopping until it touched the back of my throat.

Andrew briefly shut his eyes and sighed. Then he opened them again and spoke firmly. "I need you to let me cum in your mouth..." His voice was raspy. "And I need you to swallow every fucking drop..."

I gripped his knees and sucked him faster and faster, and his cock began to throb in my mouth. I could feel it pulsating, constricting, and as he leaned back and finally let go I felt spurts of warmness slipping down my throat.

His cum was salty and thick, and I honestly loved the taste of it. As the last drop landed into my mouth, I looked into his eyes and he looked back at me. The expression on his face was one of pure satisfaction and awe, and I was more turned on than I'd ever been in my life.

He stood—pulling me with him, and pressed his lips against mine. "That was fucking perfect." He turned off the water and led me out of the shower and back into his bedroom—not bothering to dry me off.

He grabbed me by my waist and tossed me onto the bed. "Spread your legs."

I let my legs fall apart and he climbed on top of me. Crashing his lips against mine, he sucked my bottom lip into his mouth.

I could feel the tip of his cock rubbing against my pussy and I lifted my hips—encouraging him to fuck me.

After being with him in the shower, I didn't want to do much foreplay and I didn't want to talk.

I just wanted to be fucked. Now.

His hands caressed my breasts and I pushed them away. "Fuck me, Andrew."

"I am."

"Now."

He smiled at me, looking as if he wanted to say something smart, but he leaned over and reached into his nightstand for a condom.

He quickly slipped it on and entered me in one full stroke,

causing me to moan in pleasure.

"Ahhhh…" I reached up and grabbed his hair as his cock pounded into me relentlessly. I was sure I'd never get tired of him fucking me, each time was better than the last.

I shut my eyes as he buried his head in my neck, as he whispered how "fucking good" I felt. Small tremors started building inside of me, and as much as I wanted this to last a little longer, I wouldn't be able to hold on.

"Andrewww…" I said his name as my hips started to jerk and my orgasm took over me. I screamed, falling back onto the pillows, and he collapsed on top of me seconds later.

We both lay there, entwined in each other for a long time—not saying a word. When I finally found the energy to speak, I cleared my throat. "Are you going to sleep inside of me all night?"

"Of course not." He pulled out of me, immediately making me miss the feel of him. He walked over to his closet, tossing the condom away.

"What are you doing?" I sat up.

"Getting dressed."

"For what?"

"So I can take you home." He slipped into a pair of pants. "And so I can go to sleep." He put on a shirt, and then he looked over at me. "How long do you think it'll take you to get ready?"

"I don't need you to take me home." I shook my head. "I want to stay here."

"Here?" he looked utterly confused.

"Yes, *here.*"

"As in *overnight?*"

I nodded, and he stood there staring at me as if I'd just asked him to do the unthinkable. The look he was giving me was one of anguish, regret, and for a second I almost felt bad about suggesting it.

"Aubrey, I don't…" He sighed. "I've never let someone spend the night."

"Then let me be your first…"

He continued staring at me, tapping his chin, and then he walked over to his closet and grabbed a set of white pajamas.

"You can sleep in these…" He held them out for me.

I reached out to take them but he shook his head.

"Stand up."

I slid off the bed and stood in front of him.

He took his time helping me into the button up shirt—kissing every inch of my exposed skin until he reached the top button, and when he was finished he kissed my lips.

I expected him to hold out the pants next, but he tossed them across the room. "Get in the bed."

Smiling, I slipped underneath the sheets as he hit the lights.

He joined me in bed seconds later, pulling me against his chest.

"Are you happy?" he whispered.

"Yes…"

"Are you sure? Is there anything else outside of my comfort zone that you'd like me to do for you tonight?"

"Not tonight, but you could make me breakfast in the morning."

"You're pushing it…"

"Just in case you change your mind, I would like Belgian waffles, bacon, sliced strawberries, and orange juice."

"Unless you want to eat all of those things off of my cock, it's not happening." He pinched my ass. "Go to sleep, Aubrey."

In the morning, I opened my eyes and realized I was alone in Andrew's bed. I looked over at where he'd been sleeping and spotted a note on GBH stationery:

> Had to run to the office to meet a new client. I'll be back to take you home.
> PS—Feel free to take your panty collection home with you.
> —Andrew

I slipped out of bed, ready to explore more of his condo, but there was a sudden loud knock at the door. I rushed over and twisted the knob, expecting to see Andrew, but it was a man dressed in all black.

"Um hello?" I tried not to look too confused.

"Are you Aubrey Everhart?"

"Yes…"

"Great." He handed me a white bag. "Gourmet waffles, bacon, sliced strawberries, and orange juice, right?"

# Denial (n.):

A statement in the defendant's answer to a complaint in a lawsuit that an allegation (claim of fact) is not true.

*A few days later…*

**Andrew**

I was officially out of my damn mind.

I was in my bathtub, and Aubrey was sitting on top of me— panting as she came down from another orgasm.

She was spending the night at my condo for the third time this week, and it was pointless to even pretend like I minded.

I wasn't sure what the hell was happening, but she'd definitely gotten to me. She was infiltrating my every thought, and no matter what I did to try and come back to my senses—to remind myself that this could only be temporary, she slipped deeper into my life.

"Why are you so quiet tonight?" she asked.

"I'm not allowed to think?"

"Not when a naked woman is in your lap."

"I was giving her a chance to relax." I slid my hands underneath her thighs. "What unnecessary bullshit do you want to talk about today?"

"It's not *unnecessary*," she said. "It's about your family."

"What about my family?"

"Are they still in New York?"

I prevented myself from clenching my jaw. "I don't know."

"You *don't know*?" She raised her eyebrow. "What do you mean you don't know? Are you estranged from them?"

"No…" I sighed. "I just don't have any parents."

She tilted her head to the side. "Then why do I remember you telling me a story about your mom the first month that we met?"

"What *story?*"

"The story about Central Park and ice cream." She looked into my eyes, as if she were expecting me to say something. "You said she took you to some children's fair, I think? It was something that happened every Saturday. But the one you remembered most happened when it was raining and she still took you, and you stood in line for an hour just to get a scoop of vanilla."

I blinked.

"Is that story not right? Am I mixing it up with something else?"

"No," I said. "That's right…But I haven't seen her since."

"Oh…" She looked down. "I'm sorry."

"Don't be." I trailed a finger across her lips. "I turned out just fine."

"Can I ask you a few more things?"

"You have a daily question quota starting today."

She rolled her eyes. "What do all the "E" and "H" pictures in your hallway stand for?"

I felt a sudden ache in my chest. "*Nothing.*"

"If you hate New York so much and you don't like talking about your past or *what you lost* six years ago, why do you have so many mementos hanging on your walls?"

"Aubrey…"

"Okay, forget that question. And the Latin quote across your heart? What does it mean?"

"Lie about one thing, lie about it all." I kissed her lips before she could ask me anything else. I was starting to wonder why she hadn't wanted to be a damn journalist instead of a ballerina.

"It's your turn," she said softly. "You can ask *me* questions now."

"I'd rather fuck you again." I lifted her with me as I stood up and helped her out of the bath tub.

We both dried off and went into my bedroom. Just as I was pulling her against me, my doorbell rang.

I sighed. "Dinner's early." I slipped into a pair of lounge pants and a T-shirt and headed to the door with my credit card.

The second I opened it, I was confronted with the sight of the last person on earth I wanted to see. *Ava.*

"Don't you dare fucking slam it on me this time," she hissed.

"We need to talk."

"We don't need to talk about shit." I stepped outside and shut the door behind me. "How many times do I have to tell you that you're not wanted here?"

"As many times as it'll take you to actually believe it, which you don't." She scoffed. "Ask me why I came to Durham to see you, *Mr. Hamilton*. Appease me and I'll finally go the hell away."

"You're going the hell away regardless," I said flatly. "I really don't give a fuck why you came here."

"Not even if it's to sign the divorce papers?"

"You could've sent that shit in the mail." I gritted my teeth. "And since I'm sure you're running out of loopholes for contesting it, I'm willing to wait until all your options run out. I'm sure your lawyers will drop you as soon as they find out what *type* of client you are."

"All I'm asking for is ten thousand a month."

"Go ask the man who was fucking you in our bedroom while I was at work." I glared at her, livid. "Or better yet, ask the judge you only "fucked for a favor," or hey, if you're up to it, fuck my former best friend. Sleeping with him always seemed to make you feel better, right?"

"You weren't *Mr. Perfect* either."

"I never fucking *cheated* on you, and I never *lied* to you."

Silence.

"Five thousand a month," she said.

"Go fuck yourself, Ava."

"You know I *never* give up," she said, her eyes widened as I stepped back inside my apartment. "I *always* get what I want."

"*So do I.*" I slammed the door in her face, feeling my heart palpitating, feeling the onset of ugly memories all over again.

Rain. New York. Heartbreak.

Complete and utter heartbreak.

Seeing Ava in person again—hearing her manipulative voice and feeling those familiar pangs in my chest, immediately made me realize that I couldn't make the same mistake again.

Aubrey was already asking questions, trying to dig her way into my life as much as she could—thinking that if she stayed around long enough that we would work out together. But I knew that would never happen, not after seeing Ava and knowing just how far she would go to ruin me all over again.

I was officially done with this monogamous game we'd been playing for the past couple weeks. It was quite fun—*different*, but since Aubrey could never be mine and I could never be hers, it was quite fucking pointless, too.

I headed back into my bedroom and saw Aubrey smiling as she settled into the bed.

"Where's the dinner?" she asked tilting her head to the side. "Did you leave it at the door?"

"*No.*" I shook my head and started packing up her things, stuffing them all into her purse.

"What are you doing?" she asked.

"You can't stay the night."

"Okay…" She stood up. "Did something just happen? Do you want to talk about—"

"I don't want to talk about anything else with you." I hissed. "I just want to take you the hell home."

"What?" She looked confused. "What's wrong with you? Why are you—"

"Make sure you get all of your shit out of my bathroom. You won't be coming back here again."

"Why not?"

"Because I need to start fucking someone else." I picked up her headband. "I think I've spent more than enough time with you, don't you think?"

"*Andrew…*" Her face fell. "Where is all of this coming from?"

"The same place it was always coming from. You lied to me once, you'll lie again."

"I thought we were over that."

"Maybe *you* were, but I wasn't."

"What are you saying?"

"I'm saying that you need to get all of your things so I can take you home, and from here on out, you are my intern and I am your boss. You will forever be Miss Everhart to me, and to you I'll be Mr. Hamilton."

"Andrew…"

"Mr. Fucking. Hamilton."

She rushed over to me and snatched her things, letting a few tears escape her eyes. "Fuck you. FUCK. YOU. This is the last time you'll ever pull this hot and cold shit on me." She stormed out of my apartment, slamming the door behind her.

I sighed and felt an immediate pang of guilt in my chest, but I knew it was the right thing to do. It was either cut this bullshit off now, or be responsible for breaking her heart later.

I stepped onto the balcony and lit a cigar—looking up at the moonless sky. Even though I felt bad for ending things so abruptly, for putting her out with no explanation, I needed to get back to who the hell I was and fast before I fucked up and put my heart on the line again…

# Closing Argument (n.):

The final argument by an attorney on behalf of his/her client after all evidence has been produced for both sides.

*Six years ago*
*New York*

## Andrew (Well... Back then, you would've called me "Liam A. Henderson")

There's something about this city that makes me believe again. It's the hopefulness in the air, the flashing lights that shine brighter than anywhere else, and the dreamers who fill the streets day after day—unwilling to give up on their failures until they finally win. There's no other city like it, and there's nothing more alluring outside these state lines—nothing that will ever make me leave.

As the sun sets in the distance, I wrap my arm around my wife's waist. We're standing against the railing of the Brooklyn Bridge—smiling because I just added another high profile client to my firm.

"You think one day the papers will actually tell the truth about your first case?" She looked up at me with her light green eyes. "Or do you think they'll keep brushing it under the rug?"

"Brushing it under the rug." I sigh. "I highly doubt the government wants people knowing that a kid straight out of law school uncovered a conspiracy. It's an insult to their organization."

"So, you're fine being reduced to a random Jeopardy question that'll happen ten years from now? 'I'll take lawyers who never got credit for two hundred, Alex.' You're fine with that?"

"Why shouldn't I be?" I kiss her forehead. "I didn't need the papers to print my name to get clients. People knew, that's how they found me."

"You should be so much bigger than what you are..." She shakes her head, whispering, "Your name should be plastered across every billboard in the city. Fucking assholes..."

Smiling, I tighten my grip around her waist and start the walk back to our car. Out of all the people that have come in and out of my life, Ava Sanchez has been the one constant.

She's the only woman I've ever loved, and ever since the day I made her mine at our wedding three years ago, I swore that would never change.

"I was also thinking," she says as she slips into the passenger seat, "that maybe me, you, and your partner Kevin could go out to a singles' mixer next weekend."

"Why would we go to a singles mixer?"

"It's more so for Kevin...He needs to get his own life. I'm tired of him hanging around us all the time. It's bad enough that we all work at your firm together, but do we *have* to spend our every waking moment together, too?"

Laughing, I drive down the city streets and home to the colossal brownstone we share. (It was the first purchase I'd made after winning the "case that never was," and Ava had insisted that I buy the most expensive one.)

"Because you fucking deserve it," she'd said. "And you never treat yourself to anything nice...That's what I don't understand about you, Liam. You're such a nice guy to everyone but yourself..."

I park our car in front of our home and immediately step out to open her door. As usual, Ava whispers, "I bet she'll scream for you first," as I walk her up the steps.

The second we walk inside, that familiar sweet voice rings out across the room.

"Daddyyyyy!"

I let go of Ava's hand and stoop low so my daughter—*Emma Henderson*, can run into my arms. She's the best part of my day, the best part of my life, and seeing her always brings an unbreakable smile to my face.

I kiss her forehead as she incoherently babbles about her day with the babysitter, and I smile as her blue eyes stare into mine.

I'm unaware of it now—I'm too blind and happy to see it, but in the months to come, my life will unravel so rapidly and unexpectedly that I'll wish I never existed. The lies that come to the light will be so devastating and crushing that my entire life will crumble around me. But the worst part, the part that will break me, is not knowing that this present moment with my 'daughter' will be the last good memory of New York I'll ever have...

reasonable
doubt
VOLUME
THREE
WHITNEY G.

# Prologue

*Several months ago…*

**Andrew**

It was all there in black and white, front and center, no filler.

Although the facts were skewed and *The New York Times* had once again neglected to post my photo, the damage to my firm—Henderson & Hart, was now done. And I knew exactly what was about to occur, step by step.

I'd seen it happen in this city too many times before.

First, the top clients who'd sworn to always stay by my side would call and say that they "suddenly" found new representation. Then the employees would file letters of resignation—knowing that having a tainted firm on their resumes would hinder their careers. Next, the investors would call—pretending to sympathize as they publicly denounced me in the media and promptly pulled all funding.

Last, and most unfortunately, I was sure to become another hotshot lawyer who ruined his career before it could even begin.

"How much longer do you think you'll be able to get away with stalking Emma?" The private investigator I hired stepped beside me.

"She's my fucking daughter. I'm not stalking her."

"Five hundred feet." He lit a cigarette. "That's how far you're supposed to be."

"Are they treating her right during the week?"

He sighed and handed me a stack of photos. "Private preschool, early tap-dance lessons, and weekends at the park as you can clearly see. She's fine."

121

"Does she still cry at night?"

"Sometimes."

"Does she still beg to see me? Does she—"

I stopped talking once Emma's blue eyes met mine from the swings. Squealing, she jumped off her seat and ran towards me.

"Daddyyyy! Dadddyyy!" She shouted, but she was picked up before she made it any closer. She was taken away and put inside a car just as she started to cry.

Fuck…

I immediately sat up in bed, realizing that I wasn't in New York City's Central Park. I was in Durham, North Carolina, and I was having another nightmare.

Glancing at the clock on my wall, I saw that it was just past one o'clock. The calendar hanging directly above it only confirmed that I'd been living here for far too long.

All the research I'd done six years ago—weighing the pros and cons, checking the records of all the top firms, and scouring the make-up of women on Date-Match, was now seemingly invalid: The condo I purchased was a mere remnant of what had been advertised, there was only one firm worthy of my time, and the pool of fuck-worthy women was dwindling by the day.

Just hours ago, I'd gone on a date with a woman who told me she was a kindergarten teacher with a penchant for the color red and history books. In reality, she was twice my age, color blind, and she just wanted to "remember what some good cock felt like."

Frustrated, I slipped out of bed and walked down the hallway—straightening the "E" and "H" frames that hung on the wall while trying not to look too hard.

I was going to need more than my usual few shots to get through tonight, and I was starting to become extremely annoyed that I hadn't fucked someone in what felt like forever.

I poured two shots of bourbon and tossed them down back to back. Before I could pour another, my phone vibrated. An email. Alyssa.

**Subject: Performance Quality.**

Dear Thoreau,

I'm sure that right now you're in the middle of fucking yet another conquest, and are seconds away from giving her your infamous "One dinner. One night. No repeats." line, but I was just thinking about something and HAD to email you...

If you enjoy sex as much as you claim you do, why do you only insist on one night? Why not a strictly friends with benefits relationship so you won't have so many dry spells? (I mean, this is day thirty of "Operation: Still No Pussy" for you, correct?)

I'm actually starting to wonder if the only reason you give one night is because you already know that your performance won't be good enough to warrant another...

Having a subpar dick isn't the end of the world.

—Alyssa.

I shook my head and typed a response.

**Subject: Re: Performance Quality.**

Dear Alyssa,

Unfortunately, I am not in the middle of fucking another conquest. Instead I'm busy typing a response to your latest ridiculous email.

This is indeed day thirty of your appropriately named, "Operation: Still No Pussy," but since I've fucked you over the phone and made you cum, it hasn't been a complete failure...

I do in fact enjoy sex—my cock has an insatiable appetite for it, but I've told you countless times that I don't do relationships. Ever.

I refuse to even address your last paragraph, as I've never received a single complaint about my "performance" and my cock is *far* from being subpar.

You are quite correct in your closing statement though: Having a subpar dick really isn't the end of the world.

Having an un-fucked pussy is.

—Thoreau.

My phone rang immediately.

"Seriously?" Alyssa blurted out when I answered. "Does your message really say what I think it says?"

"Have you suddenly forgotten how to read?"

"You are *ridiculous*!" She laughed. "What happened to your date tonight?"

"It was another fucking liar..."

"Aww. Poor Thoreau. I was really hoping the thirtieth day would be the charm."

I rolled my eyes and made another drink. "Is living vicariously through my sex life your newfound hobby?"

"Of course not." Her light laughter drifted over the line, and I could hear the sound of papers shuffling in the background. "I've been meaning to ask you: Where are you from?"

"What do you mean, *where am I from*?"

"Exactly what I asked," she said. "You can't be from the South. There's no drawl or even a hint of an accent in your voice."

I hesitated. "I'm from New York City."

"New York?" Her voice rose an octave. "Why would you ever leave there to come to Durham?"

"It's personal."

"I can't imagine ever wanting to leave New York. It seems so perfect. And there's just something about the lights and the lives of people who stay there, how they all must have these huge dreams and..."

I tuned her out and tossed back my shot. Her poetical waxing about that desolate place needed to be put to a stop. Fast.

"And wouldn't the law firms in New York be far more alluring than the ones here?" She was still talking. "Like, one of my favorite—"

"What's the name of that ballet you're auditioning for this year?" I cut her off.

"*Swan Lake*." She always dropped the subject if I said anything about ballet. "Why?"

"Just wondering. When is the audition?"

"A few months from now. I'm trying as hard as I can to balance my classes—" She cleared her throat. "I mean, I'm trying really hard to balance my case loads with my practice time."

"Why don't you just ask your boss if you can work weekends in exchange for a couple weekdays off?"

"I'm pretty sure that won't work."

"Of course it would work," I said. "There's a lawyer at my firm who works Saturdays through Wednesdays so he can pursue music. If the firm you work for is worth a damn, they'll be flexible with you."

"Yeah, um, I guess I'll have to look into that..."

Silence.

"What firm do you work for?" I asked.

"I can't tell you that."

"What's one of the partners' names?"

"I can't tell you that either."

"But you can tell me how deep you want my cock to be buried inside of you later tonight?"

She sucked in a short breath, a sexy sound that drove me insane the more I heard it.

"How much longer do you think I'm going to put up with just talking to you on the phone, Alyssa?"

"For as long as I want you to." Her voice sounded more confident now.

"You think I'm going to talk to you for another month without being able to fuck you? Without being able to see you in person?"

"I think you'll talk to me for several months without fucking me. As a matter of fact, I think you'll talk to me for *years* without fucking me because I'm your friend, and friends—"

"If I haven't fucked you within the next month or two, we won't be *friends* anymore."

"You want to bet?"

"I don't have to." I hung up and grabbed my laptop, ready to give Date-Match another try. The second I clicked the prettiest woman on the page, an email from Alyssa popped onto my screen.

**Subject: Trust Me.**

You and I will still be friends a few months from now, and you'll be completely okay with not seeing my face.

Watch.

—Alyssa.

**Subject: Re: Trust Me.**

You and I will be *fucking* a few months from now, and the only reason I'll be okay with not seeing your face is because you'll be riding my cock as I bend your ass over a table.

Watch.

—Thoreau.

# Testimony (n.):
Oral evidence given under oath by a witness in answer to questions posed by attorneys at trial or at a deposition.

## Andrew

"Miss Everhart, you can take the floor and question Mr. Hamilton now," Mr. Greenwood said from across the courtroom.

It was the last day of the month, which meant that we were finally getting use out of the million dollar courtroom that sat on the top floor of GBH. There was no need for this room, but since the firm had more money than it knew what to do with, the space was being used for the interns' mock cases.

Today's "trial" was about some idiot who defrauded his own company's employees—leaving them without insurance and health care, and unfortunately, I was playing the accused.

Standing up from the defense table, Aubrey grabbed her notebook and took the floor. She and I hadn't spoken since I kicked her out of my condo two weeks ago, but from what I could tell, she seemed unfazed.

She'd been smiling quite often, being extremely nice, and each time she delivered my coffee she did it with a smirk and an, "I really hope you enjoy this coffee, *Mr. Hamilton.*"

I'd been stopping at the coffee shop up the street ever since...

"Mr. Hamilton," she said, smoothing her tight blue dress, "is it true that you previously cheated on your wife?"

"I've *never* cheated."

"Stick to the character, Andrew." Mr. Bach whispered from the judge's seat.

I rolled my eyes. "Yes. There was a time when I cheated on my wife."

"Why?"

"Objection!" One of the interns shouted. "Your Honor, do we really need to know the specifics about my client's love life? This mock trial is about his involvement in a conspiracy."

"If I may, Your Honor," Aubrey spoke before the "judge" could say anything. "I think assessing how Mr. Hamilton behaved in his previous affairs is a good assessment of his character. If we were trying a client who abandoned his company due to incompetence, it wouldn't be out of line for me to ask about his previous personal relationships—especially if our mock client is a high profile one."

"Overruled."

Aubrey smiled and looked at her notebook. "Do you have commitment problems, Mr. Hamilton?"

"How can I have a problem with something I don't believe in?"

"So, you believe in engaging in one night stands for the rest of your life?"

"*Your Honor...*" The opposing intern stood up, but I raised my hand.

"No need," I said, narrowing my eyes at Aubrey. "I'll entertain Miss Everhart's inappropriate line of questioning...I believe in living my life however the hell I want and dealing with women whenever I want to deal with them. I'm not sure how who I sleep with has anything to do with this mock conspiracy case, but since we're discussing my sex life, you should know that I'm happy and satisfied. I have a date later tonight actually. Would you like me to report the details to you and the jury tomorrow?"

The interns in the jury box laughed as Aubrey's smile faded. Even as she forced it again, I could see a hint of hurt in her eyes.

"So..." She took a deep breath. "Regarding the case—"

"So happy you're finally getting on topic."

The jurors laughed again.

"Do you believe in morals, Mr. Hamilton?" she asked.

"Yes."

"Do you think you possess them?"

"I think everyone does to a certain extent."

"Permission to approach the witness?" She looked at Mr. Bach and he nodded.

"Mr. Hamilton, can you read the highlighted portion of this document please?" She placed a sheet of paper in front of me, and I noticed a small handwritten note at the very top of the page:

*I fucking hate you and I wish I'd never met you.*

"Yes," I said, taking a pen out of my pocket. "It says that my company was unaware of insurance policy changes at the time."

As she handed a copy of the document to the jury panel, I wrote a response to her note:

*Sorry to see that you regret meeting me, as I don't regret meeting you—only that I fucked you more than once.*

She asked me to read another section to the court, and then she took the paper away—glaring at me once she read my words.

I tried to look away from her, to focus on something else, but the way she looked today prevented that from happening. Her hair wasn't up in her signature bun—it was falling past her shoulders in long curls that grazed her breasts. And the dress she was wearing, a highly inappropriate one that hugged her thighs a little too tightly, rose up an inch every time she took a step.

"I have three more questions for Mr. Hamilton, Your Honor," she said.

"There's no limit, Miss Everhart." He smiled.

"Right..." She stepped forward and looked into my eyes. "Mr. Hamilton, you and your company led your employees to believe that you cared about them, that you had their best interests at heart, and that you would literally communicate the actual changes you would make before termination. Are those promises not directly from your company's brochure?"

"They are."

"So, do you believe that you deserve to be fined or punished for giving your employees false hope? For dragging them into a situation you knew you would end all along?"

"I think I did what was in my *company's* best interest," I said—ignoring the fact that my heart was pounding against my chest. "And in the future, as those *employees* move on like they should, they'll perhaps realize that my company wasn't the best fit for them anyway."

"Don't you think you owe them a simple apology? Don't you think you should at least give them that?"

"An apology implies that I did something *wrong*." I gritted my teeth. "Just because they don't agree with what I did, doesn't mean that I wasn't right."

"Do you believe in reasonable doubt, Mr. Hamilton?"

"You said you only had three questions left. Has elementary mathematics changed recently?"

"Do you believe in reasonable doubt, *Mr. Hamilton?*" Her face reddened. "Yes or no?"

"*Yes.*" I clenched my jaw. "Yes, I believe that's a common requirement for every single lawyer in this country."

"So, given the current case that we're discussing…Do you think that someone like you, someone who treated his employees so terribly, could ever change in the future, now that you know how badly you've hurt others' livelihood?"

"Reasonable doubt is not about *feelings*, Miss Everhart, and I suggest you consult the closest legal dictionary you can find because I'm pretty sure we've had this discussion once before…"

"I don't recall that, Mr. Hamilton, but—"

"In your own ill-fated yet correct words, didn't you once tell me—post your first interview here at GBH, that certain lies have to be told and certain truths have to be withheld? And that the ultimate conviction is up to those who can discern which is which?" I looked her up and down. "Is that not the exact definition that you provided for reasonable doubt?"

She stared at me a long time—giving me that same look of hurt she had when I kicked her out of my place.

"No further questions, Your Honor." She mumbled.

Mr. Greenwood clapped loudly from the back of the room. Mr. Bach and the other interns followed suit.

"Very good job, Miss Everhart!" Mr. Bach shouted. "That was a very direct yet compelling line of questioning."

"Thank you sir." She avoided looking at me.

"You are officially the first intern to get our Andrew all riled up." He smiled, seemingly impressed. "We definitely need to keep you around. Hell, we may call you in when we need to be reminded that he's capable of showing emotion."

More laughter.

"Great job today, everyone!" He leaned back in the judge's

chair. "We'll go over your presentations later this week and email you the scores next Thursday." He banged his gavel. "Court adjourned."

The interns filed out of the room and Aubrey looked over her shoulder one last time, shooting me an angry look.

I shot one right back, grateful that I had a date tonight so I could fuck her and her stupid questions out of my mind.

Seven o'clock can't get here soon enough…

I waited a few minutes before heading to the elevator and attempted to remember my schedule for the rest of the day. I had two consultations with small business owners this afternoon, and I needed to make a Starbucks run before Aubrey could bring me my next cup of coffee.

I unlocked the door to my office and hit the lights, prepared to call for Jessica, but Ava was standing in front of my bookshelf.

"Is the homeless shelter not open today?" I asked.

"I came here to finally give you what you asked for."

"It's a little too early to jump off a bridge."

"I'm being serious."

"As am I." I walked past her and sent a quick text on my phone. "If you jump before noon, the news crew won't be able to run the story during primetime."

She stepped in front of my desk and set down a manila folder. "I won't drag your name through the courts anymore, I won't file anymore stays or injunctions, and I won't make any false claims about your character either…I'm done lying now."

"I'm sure." I picked up the papers. "In other words, there's a new guy you're anxious to fuck over. Does he know the real you?"

"Seriously? You're getting your precious divorce. Why do you even care?"

"I don't." I put on my reading glasses and looked over the documents. "No alimony requests, abuse claims, or demands for property? Am I missing a page?"

"I'm telling you. I'm done lying."

I didn't believe her for one second, but I picked up my phone and called the notary, telling her it was an emergency.

"You know…" Ava leaned against my desk. "I remember the cake you bought me for our wedding anniversary. It was white and light blue, and it had all these pretty little NYC decorations on it. It had flavored layers, too. One for every year that we were together.

Do you remember that?"

"I remember you fucking my best friend."

"We can't have one nice moment before we end things for good?"

"You and I ended a long time ago, Ava." I tried to keep my voice flat, monotonous. "When something is over, the final words—good or bad, don't make much of a fucking difference."

She sighed and I noticed how terrible she looked today. Her eyes were bloodshot, her hair was frizzy and tied into a loose ponytail, and even though the blue dress she was wearing fit perfectly, she hadn't made an attempt to iron it.

"What's this so called emergency you have, Mr. Hamilton?" The notary walked into the room, smiling. "Are you requesting that we purchase another thousand dollar coffee maker?" She stopped talking once she saw Ava.

"Miss Kannan, this is Ava Sanchez, my soon to be ex-wife. I need you to witness the signing of the divorce papers and make three copies—sealing one of them for mailing purposes."

She nodded and pulled a stamper out of her pocket.

"Did you notice that I willingly gave up our condo on the West End to you?" Ava asked.

"The condo that *I* bought?" I signed my name. "How generous."

"We made a lot of memories in that house."

"Signing papers doesn't require conversation," I said.

She snatched the pen away from me and placed her signature above mine—taking extra time to add a double swirl to the last letter.

"I'll be right back with your copies." Miss Kannan avoided looking at either of us as she shuffled out of the room.

"So, that's it, I guess," Ava said. "I'm officially out of your life."

"No." I shook my head. "Unfortunately, you're still in my sight."

"Would it kill you to wish me the best? To at least tell me good luck?"

"Seeing as though you're going back to prison, I guess that would be appropriate." I shrugged. "Good luck. The authorities are outside waiting for you, so take all the time you need. There's even a vending machine down the hall if you want to taste freedom one last time...Although, since you'll be locked up with plenty of women, I'm sure eating pussy after the lights go out will taste just as good."

"You fucking snitched on me?" Her face went white as I held up my phone, showing her the text I sent the second I saw her in my office. "How could you do that to me?"

"How could I *not*?"

"Did I really hurt you that badly, Liam? Did I—"

"Don't you ever fucking call me that."

"Did I hurt you that badly?" She repeated, shaking her head.

I didn't answer.

"This is...This is about *Emma* isn't it?" She hissed. "Is that what this is? You're still holding that shit over my head?"

"Get the fuck out. *Now.*"

"It's been six years, Liam. Six. Fucking. Years. You need to let that go." She opened the door and a sly smile spread across her face. "Things like that happen all the time...As unfortunate as it was, it helped make you the man you are today, didn't it?"

It took everything in me to stay seated, to not lunge after her.

Seething, I waited for her to leave and walked over to my window—watching as she stepped into the parking lot, as she raised her hands in the air as the officers shouted at her.

Then, just like six years ago, she smiled through the handcuffing process, and laughed when they tossed her into the back of the car.

The black fleet slowly drove away, and a familiar pang hit my chest.

Grabbing my keys, I rushed to the parking lot and slipped into my car—subconsciously telling myself to go home, consciously driving toward the nearest beach.

I put my phone on silent as I hit the highway, and as the seconds dissolved into hours, the city disappeared in the rearview mirror. The buildings appeared farther and farther apart, and eventually the only thing outside my window were trees and sand.

When I finally reached a secluded bay, I parked my car in front of a rock. I opened my glove compartment and took out the red folder Aubrey once tried to open. Then I stepped out and sat on the closest bench.

Taking a deep breath, I pulled out the photos and promised myself that this would be the last time I looked at them: Me and my daughter walking along the shore of New Jersey's beach as the sun set. Her smiling as I picked up a seashell and held it against her ear. Me carrying her on my shoulders and pointing to a starry night sky.

Even though I knew doing this would lead to cold sweats and an inevitable nightmare later, I continued flipping through the photos.

Even the ones without me: The ones of her looking sad and lonely at the park, the ones of her looking off into the distance for something—or *someone*, that wasn't there.

Emma...

My heart clenched at the final frame in the set. It was a shot of her fiddling with her umbrella, crying. She was upset because they were forcing her to go inside, because they didn't understand that although she liked being at the park in broad sunlight, she preferred to play outside in the rain.

# Emotional Distress (n.):

A negative emotional reaction—which may include fear, anger, anxiety, and suffering for which monetary damages may be awarded

## *Aubrey*

I looked terrible. Absolutely terrible.

Today was the first full costume rehearsal for *Swan Lake* and I didn't look fit for the part at all. My eyes were swollen and puffy—ruined from randomly crying about Andrew, my lips were dry and cracked, and my skin was so pale that Mr. Petrova walked by and asked, "Are you playing a white swan or are you playing a *white ghost?*"

As much as I tried to force myself to smile through my heartache, I was crying every moment I was alone, eating an exorbitant amount of ice cream and chocolate each night, and I couldn't sleep for shit.

I still couldn't believe Andrew kicked me out of his condo so cruelly. One minute he was holding me against his chest and kissing me, and the next he was telling me that he and I had fucked enough—that he didn't want me anymore, and that he was going to fuck someone else.

What was worse, was that when we returned to work that following Monday, he'd been twice as rude to me. He reassigned me to a case that would take me months to sort, scolded me in front of everyone for being ten seconds late, and then he had the audacity to complain about me smiling as I brought him his daily coffee.

At least I spit in it...

"Are you crying right now?" The make-up assistant tilted my chin up. "Do you know how expensive this stage mascara is?"

"I'm sorry." I froze my eyeballs to their sockets and held back tears.

"I didn't see your parents' names on the guest list for today. Are they coming to the second run through on Saturday?"

"No."

"I guess they just want to see the full on show with no stops then, huh?" She laughed. "My parents are the same way. I told them about the number of run-throughs we have to do and they said they'll see it when it's finished. They're all about perfection."

"Unfortunately, I can relate..."

She laughed and blabbered on and on, making me silently count the seconds until she was done.

When she pressed my face with the last puff of powder, she spun me around to face the mirror on the other side of the room.

"Wow..." I whispered. "Seriously, wow..."

I didn't look like I'd been crying at all. Although my eyelids were covered in dark eye shadow, and she'd dabbed a fake tear trail past my right eye, I looked as if I was the happiest woman on earth.

"Miss Everhart?" Mr. Petrova asked, stepping behind me. "May I borrow you for a second?"

"Yes, sir." I followed him through the backstage doors and outside to the empty stretching area.

"Have a seat on the bench, Miss Everhart." He took a cigarette out of his pocket and lit it.

The smoke unfurled in spirals between us and he looked me up and down. For some odd reason, he looked more upset than usual, like he was about to yell at me.

"Mr. Petrova..." I said softly. "Did I do something wrong?"

"No." He shook his head. "I brought you out here alone because I want you to know that you looked fat during practice yesterday. *Too fat.*"

"What?"

"Even though you danced the part of the black swan beautifully, capturing the right degree of anger and sadness, you failed—*fucking failed*, with the white swan." He coughed. "You looked like your mind was elsewhere. Like it was killing you to be happy for five minutes, and to top it off, you've gotten fat."

I rolled my eyes and tuned him out, focusing on the cars whirring down the street. I wasn't disturbed by his insults anymore. Him calling me fat was nothing compared to the things he said to me last week.

"*Miss Everhart?*" His voice snapped me out of my thoughts.

"Yes?"

"I need you to open that later," he said, patting me on my shoulder. "It's very important."

"Open what?"

"Do you not see the envelope I just placed on your lap?" He put out his cigarette. "Do I need to tell your understudy that she needs to get ready to dance?"

"No." I picked up the envelope, running my fingers along the crease. "You don't need to do that, sir."

"Good." He walked toward the building and held the door open. "Now, make me believe that I picked the right girl to be my swan."

"The Walters will be over for dinner next Sunday at six and we need you to make an appearance," my mother said to me over the phone that night. "I think they're going to write us a very nice check for the campaign."

"How exciting."

"It is exciting, isn't it?" She practically squealed. "Everything is happening so fast and falling into place quite perfectly. We're gathering funding, planning the advertising, and..."

I set my phone on the table and made myself a bucket of ice water, wincing with every step I took. I was sure that I would have a new set of blisters at the end of this week, but after the way I danced at today's run-through, they would be well-worth it.

I completed every jump with ease, matched my peers step for step, and at the end—when the final number called for ten pirouettes, I did fifteen. Everyone in the audience gave me a standing ovation, but Mr. Petrova sat silently rubbing his chin.

He stared at me, tilted his head to the side, and simply said, "Today's practice is over." That was the biggest compliment he'd ever given.

Smiling at the memory, I carried the ice bucket over to the couch and set it down. I slipped my feet inside and held the phone up to my ear again.

"Oh, and the Yarboroughs..." My mother was still talking.

"They're considering throwing a small benefit in your father's honor next month at the country club. You'll need to be present for that and it won't be casual, so I'd really prefer if you wore your hair in curls please. There will be a photographer from the local paper there."

"Are you going to ask how my day went?"

"In a minute. Did you receive the dress I sent yesterday?"

I looked at the plastic bag draped over my door. "There was a rough run through of *Swan Lake* today. It was for the costume designers, to see if everything looked right under the new lights. It was the best run through we've had so far."

"Have you tried on that dress yet? Do you think you'll be able to do it tonight?"

"Mom…"

"I need to have it tailored for Sunday's dinner ASAP if it doesn't fit."

"Could you just say, I honestly don't give a fuck about your life, Aubrey?" I groaned as my toes finally felt the effect of the ice. "That would make me feel ten times better right now."

"*Aubrey Nicole Everhart…*" She enunciated every syllable of my name. "Have you lost your mind?"

"No, but I'm starting to lose my tolerance for talking to you on the phone. Why bother calling if you only want to hear yourself talk?"

She didn't get a chance to answer.

There was a call on my other line, so I clicked over without mentioning it.

"Hello?" I answered.

"Is this Aubrey Everhart?" It was a male's voice.

"Yes. This is she."

"Great! This is Greg Houston. I'm the student enrollment chair, and I was just calling to let you know that your withdrawal from the university has been approved! It'll be official once you come in and personally sign off on the forms. I personally think it's great that you're taking time off to help out with your father's campaign."

"WHAT?!"

"That's a very selfless thing of you to do, Miss Everhart," he said. "I'm sure whenever you decide to come back, the academic committee will offer you credit for your real world experience.

Anyway, I noticed you filled out the electronic forms, but since you live within a fifty mile radius of the school, its policy that you have to sign them manually as well. Also, regarding the credits you've earned at the university thus far..."

Everything around me went black.

I couldn't believe this shit.

I wanted to click over and shout at my mother, to ask how dare she and my father pull me out of college without even telling me, but I couldn't. I simply hung up and sat still—stone-faced and lost.

There were tears falling down my face, but I couldn't feel them. I couldn't feel a damn thing.

I pressed the power button on my phone to prevent anyone else from calling me and pulled out the envelope Mr. Petrova gave me earlier. I assumed it was a long list of insults, or a new diet, but it was a letter:

*Miss Everhart,*

*I just received notice that you were leaving the university at the end of this term. While I am disappointed in your failure to alert me to this news in advance, I am impressed with the growth you have shown while being in my program.*

*You are still an average dancer, but considering the fact that your peers are all terrible dancers, I guess you can be somewhat proud of that status*

*Behind this letter is a recommendation for the New York City Ballet Company. Due to a few unfortunate circumstances, several spots have opened for their current class. This does not happen often, and you would be quite stupid not to audition.*

*However, if you do audition and are not accepted, it will only mean that you didn't dance your best. (Or that you gained another unfortunate pound.)*

*—Petrova.*

I flipped to the attached page and noticed that the deadline to audition was in three weeks, that if I auditioned and was accepted, I would be leaving my current leading role behind and would have to start all over again.

Dancing for the NYC Ballet Company had once been a dream

of mine, but after I broke my foot at sixteen, I readjusted my version of a dream career; the competition at such a place would be far too fierce for someone who sat out a complete year, full recovery or not.

Nonetheless, I couldn't fathom going away to New York City, not alone anyway. And I didn't think I could leave Andrew without at least getting a much deserved apology.

Sighing, I turned on my laptop and logged into my email, shocked to see his name at the very top of my inbox.

**Subject: Mock Trials.**

Miss Everhart,

For the third time this week, you've alluded to our former affairs in the court room. Although I am not surprised by this, I am quite disappointed.

You may regret the aftermath of fucking me, but I know damn well that you loved every single second that my cock was inside of you. (And before you lie and say that you didn't, think about the numerous times you screamed my name as my mouth devoured your pussy.)

Maybe if you thought about those things instead of your uncontrollable and erratic "feelings," your defenses in court wouldn't be so laughable.

—Andrew

I deleted his email and read Petrova's letter again.

I needed to research the New York City Ballet auditions *tonight*.

# Malfeasance (n.):
Intentionally doing something either legally or morally wrong which one had no right to do.

## *Andrew*

I opened my left drawer, searching for a bottle of aspirin. I hadn't slept well in over a week, and I was certain that most of that had to do with the half-assed reports the interns were giving me. That, or Aubrey was poisoning my lunch.

I flipped through her most recent report and groaned as I read her handwritten remarks:

> *I find it very ironic that you can give us an assignment on the importance of trust and relationships, when you have no idea what either of those words mean.*
>
> *PS—You did not "devour" my pussy.*

I tore off her note and tossed it into the trash, reading the next one:

> *A case that deals with a boss fucking his employee? At least this boss had the balls to come clean and admit that he actually liked her, instead of tossing her away like trash.*
>
> *PS—Yesterday's extra ingredient in your coffee was flakes of melted super glue. I hope you enjoyed it."*

"Mr. Hamilton?" Jessica stepped into my office.
    "Yes?"

"Would you like me to send your Armani suit to another dry cleaning company?" she asked. "This is the third time you've sent them those pants. I don't think that brown stain is coming out."

"No, thank you." I sighed. "Just order me some new ones please."

"Will do!" She batted her eyes at me as she left, and I immediately emailed Aubrey.

**Subject: Super Glue.**

I no longer drink your fucking coffee, but since you've once again proven how much of a novice you are when it comes to the law, I'll be saving your handwritten note so my friends will know who to charge with my murder.

Grow up.

—Andrew

**Subject: Re: Super Glue.**

You don't have any friends. I was your only one. And I don't care if you save my handwritten note because I've saved all of your EMAILS—especially the ones that say, "Come to my office so I can eat your pussy on my lunch break," or "I love the way your mouth looks when you wrap it around my cock."

You first.

—Aubrey.

I started typing my response—not willing to give her the last word, but I heard Jessica clearing her throat.

"Something else I can help you with today?" I looked up. "I could've sworn you just left my office."

"Word around the firm is that today is your birthday."

"Today is *not* my birthday."

"That's not what HR said."

"HR is full of shit." I looked at the coffee mug on the edge of my desk, noticing that the coffee wasn't even brown. It was orange. "But speaking of HR, could you have them ban Miss Everhart from touching the coffee machines?"

"Doubt it." She stepped closer. "Between you and me, we're throwing you a surprise party in the break room. Like, right now. We've been waiting for you to take a break but you haven't, so...Can you step in for a second?"

"Did you just tell me no about my coffee machine request?"

"I'll handle it after you come to your party." She smiled and reached for my hand, but I stood on my own.

"I've told your grandfather on multiple occasions that I don't appreciate his employee birthday parties."

She shrugged and led me down the hall. "Make sure you look surprised. I put a lot of work into this...I always go the extra mile for you."

I ignored the way she was licking her lips.

She pushed the door open, and all of the staff tossed confetti into the air and shouted, "Happy Birthday, Mr. Hamilton!" Then they began to sing the birthday song—out of tune and terribly off key.

I walked over to the windows where they'd placed a small white cake with blue candles, and blew them out before the song ended.

"Happy Birthday, Andrew!" Mr. Greenwood handed me a blue envelope. "How old are you today?"

"Seeing as though today is not my birthday, I'm the same age as I was yesterday."

He laughed, still incapable of catching when I was being short with him. Holding his stomach in jest, he motioned for one of the interns to take our photo.

As the camera flashed, I spotted Aubrey standing in a corner with her arms crossed. She was shaking her head at everyone, and when her eyes finally met mine, she scowled.

"I got you something..." Jessica pressed a small black box into my hand. "But I think you need to open it behind closed doors, when you're alone and thinking about me." She blushed and walked away.

I made a mental note to toss whatever it was into the trash. And instead of immediately leaving the party, I walked around the room and said thank you to everyone—reminding each intern that "birthday" or not, the assignments were still due at the end of the day.

I approached Aubrey with my hand outstretched, but she

WHITNEY G.

recoiled and walked into the adjoining ante-room.

"Are you seriously this immature, Miss Everhart?" I followed her, spinning her around to face me as the door shut.

"Are you seriously this cruel?" She glared at me. "You gave me more work than anyone else this morning just so you could berate me in front of them later, just because you think I embarrassed you in court again."

"You'd actually have to know what the fuck you were doing if you wanted to embarrass me in court." I unintentionally grabbed her hands, rubbing my fingers against her skin. "And I gave you more work so you wouldn't have time to make my coffee, which up until this morning, I only *assumed* you were poisoning."

"Since when is 'spit' poison?"

"You owe me another fucking suit..." I lowered my voice. "Do you have any idea how much—"

"*No.*" She cut me off. "Do you have any idea how much you've changed? I actually miss when I was Alyssa and you were Thoreau."

"Back when you were a *fucking liar*?"

"Back when you treated me better..." She stared into my eyes—giving a look of longing, and my hands went around her waist, pulling her against me.

My mouth was on hers in seconds and we were kissing like we hadn't seen each other in years—fighting each other for control. I trailed my fingers against the zipper at the back of her dress, feeling my cock hardening against her thigh.

She pressed herself against my chest and let me slip my tongue deeper into her mouth, but she eventually tore away and pushed me.

Looking absolutely disgusted, she turned away and stormed out of the room.

I straightened my tie before following her into the party room, but she was no longer there.

"Are you going to cut the cake, Andrew?" Mr. Bach called out. "Or do you want Jessica to do it for another year in a row?"

Jessica held up the knife and winked at me.

"Jessica can cut it," I said. "I'll be right back." I stepped out and headed for the interns' offices—walking straight toward Aubrey's cubicle.

Her face was beet red and she was stuffing folders into her bag.

144

"I didn't give you permission to leave early." I stepped in front of her.

"I didn't give you permission to treat me like shit, but you've done one hell of a job, haven't you?"

"You just said that I wasn't treating you like shit when I thought your name was *Alyssa*, when I thought you were a fucking lawyer."

"That makes your current treatment of me acceptable?"

"It makes it *justifiable.*"

Silence.

"I can't do this anymore, Andrew…" She shook her head.

"Does that mean you'll stop acting like a child in court? Does it mean—"

"Here." She cut me off and pressed a silver box against my chest. "I bought this for you a few weeks ago, back when Jessica was planning your birthday party."

"Did you spit in it?"

"I should have." She picked up her bag and rushed past me, heading for the exit.

A part of me actually wanted to go after her and make her explain what the hell she meant about "not doing this anymore," but I knew doing so would be pointless. Talking to her for less than three minutes aroused me, and I needed to remember why I ended "us" in the first place.

I returned to the break-room and said thank you to the last of the interns, glancing at the photo HR had pinned on the wall. It was a collage of my professional photos with a birthday hat sticker attached to my head. And they'd written "Happy Birthday, Andrew! GBH Loves You!" in bright blue.

In all actuality, my birthday was months from now—in December, a day I hadn't celebrated in a very long time. And even though I'd never publicly admit it, I somewhat liked the fact that the people at GBH were willing to celebrate my birthday—real or not.

"How many slices of cake would you like me to wrap up for you, Mr. Hamilton?" Jessica tapped my shoulder.

"Three," I said. "And I'll take a cup of lemonade, too."

"You're not going to stay for the "Who Knows Mr. Hamilton the Best" game?"

"None of you know me." I returned to my office and locked

the door, setting the new birthday gifts on top of my bookshelf.

The envelope from Mr. Greenwood contained a note that said he appreciated my hard work and dedication to the firm. Beneath his written words was a gift card to his family's other multimillion dollar entity: A golf course.

The gifts from the interns were all "I.O.U." letters that begged for extra time on their assignments. I held all of those over my shredder.

Jessica's black box was next, and as much as I wanted to throw it away and never think of it again, I couldn't resist knowing what she bought me. I took the top off and removed the paper, pulling out a soft piece of silk and a note:

> *I overheard that you like to keep these in your pocket... Here are mine.*
>
> *PS—I took them off in the bathroom five minutes ago :-)*

Jesus...

I buried her panties at the bottom of my trashcan and crumpled that note.

I stared at Aubrey's silver box for a while, wondering if I should wait until later to unwrap it, but I couldn't help peeling off the paper.

Inside of the box was a small black photo frame. It was handcrafted—bordered with iron pressed images of pointe slippers, law scales, and the words "Alyssa" and "Thoreau" in smooth white letters.

The picture in it was one of us, one of her laying against my chest in my bed and smiling at the camera. Her cheeks were flushed red—like they always were after sex, and she was dressed in one of my T-shirts.

I remembered her forcing me to take that photo—insisting that she "wouldn't share it with anyone" and only wanted it for herself. She even forced me to smile...

I set the frame down and took out the other object in the box—a sparkling silver watch with an inscription etched across its back:

**Subject: You.**

I liked you as "Thoreau," but I love you as Andrew.

—Aubrey (Alyssa)

My glass of wine sat untouched at Arbors Restaurant, and the candles in the centerpiece were shedding sheets of their wax onto the table.

I was expecting a date any moment now, but I couldn't stop staring at the watch Aubrey gave me. She'd clearly thought about each and every part of the design; no element was by mistake.

I noticed two interlocking A's in the corner of its screen, and earlier, in the sunlight, I'd noticed that my name was etched on the edge of its frame.

"Are you Thoreau?" A woman's voice interrupted my thoughts, making me look up.

"I am."

She smiled and took the seat across from me. "I hope you don't mind, but I'm a regular here and the waitress asked if I'd be having my usual when I arrived. I told her you would have the same."

"I don't mind at all." A small feeling of guilt welled inside my chest, but it wasn't enough to distract me from pursuing what I needed tonight: Pussy. ASAP.

The waitress placed two steamed dishes in front of us, and I checked the time. I was only giving this woman one hour.

"So, what type of cases do you normally handle?" she asked.

"Corporate for the most part, but I've done government and tax as well."

"Interesting. Have you lived in Durham long?"

"Too long."

"And is this your normal M.O.?" She leaned back in her chair, dragging her nails against her see-through top. "One night stands?"

"Is that a problem for you?"

"It never is."

I raised my eyebrow and looked her over. She was actually quite appealing—long blond hair, curvy figure, and perky breasts.

Physical attributes aside, we seemed to have a lot in common.

She was a real lawyer in the next county over, she read most of the same books, and from what she'd told me over the phone, we shared a comparable sexual appetite.

Our entrees came and went, the conversation plodded along, but Aubrey's watch still had a part of my attention.

"Is something bothering you?" My date waved her hand in front of my face. "I remember you being a lot more talkative over the phone."

"I'm fine." I waved the waiter over for the check. "Just tired."

"Too tired to fuck?"

"I'm *never* too tired to fuck."

Blushing, she crossed her legs and leaned over the table. "I've been looking forward to this all week."

I didn't respond. I simply signed the check and stood up, holding out my hand for her.

We walked through the hotel lobby and straight for the elevators.

The second the doors closed, she pressed her lips against mine and threaded her fingers through my hair.

"Fuck…" I groaned as one of her hands slid down to my belt.

She moved her mouth down my neck as we ascended to the top floor, grazing her teeth against my skin. Moaning, she gasped as I gripped her waist and kissed her back—controlling her tongue with mine.

I pulled the band away from her ponytail and tossed it to the floor. I closed my eyes and deepened our kiss—torturously biting her lip as she tried to pull away.

Sliding her knee between my legs, she unfastened my belt and tugged at my zipper. "How long are we going to fuck tonight?"

"As long as you want." I palmed her breasts through her shirt, slipping a hand underneath her bra.

"*Ahhhh*…" She murmured as I caressed her nipple.

The elevator doors slid open quickly, but our bodies remained entwined as we found our way to the suite. Her lips latched onto mine again as we stumbled into the room—bumping into the lamps and the dressers.

She was moaning louder now, barely controlling herself as I unzipped her dress and unclasped her bra.

I felt her hands at my waist—pushing my pants to the floor, and when my back hit the wall, I realized she was on her knees in front of me.

Leaning forward, she rubbed her hands up and down my cock, asking me to tell her how badly I wanted her mouth on me.

"I don't..." I shook my head as I realized I had been fantasizing about Aubrey the entire time.

"You're not even going to beg for it?" She smiled, bringing her head closer.

"Stop." I grabbed her by her hair and gently pushed her away.

"Is something wrong, Thoreau? Did you want to do me first instead? Should I get on the bed or the chair?"

I couldn't make out the rest of her questions; images of Aubrey were clouding my brain, invading all my senses. And the more I stared at this woman, a woman who was nowhere near as beautiful as Aubrey, the more I felt my cock softening.

Fuck...

I pulled my pants up and zipped the fly. "I no longer feel like fucking you. You can leave."

"*Excuse me?*" She sucked in a breath and crossed her arms. "What did you just say?"

"I said that I don't feel like fucking you." I spoke slowly. "And that you can leave. Enjoy the rest of your night."

"You're going to put me out? Just like that?"

"Would you like me to reserve another room for you?"

"What happened to the man I met online?" She stood up. "Was that all a front? Is this some type of game where you take out women, say sexy things you've probably read off the internet, and then make them get naked knowing damn well that you don't know how to fuck?"

"I definitely know how to fuck." I narrowed my eyes at her. "I just don't feel like fucking *you.*"

"I can't...I can't believe..." Her jaw dropped. "You're a fucking asshole!"

"Asshole? Yes. Fucking? Unfortunately not. Can you make sure that the door is completely closed on your way out?"

She pulled her dress over her body and picked up her purse. "I'm putting a flag next to your profile on Date-Match. And you know what else? I'm going to leave a review of our encounter, too. I'm going to make sure—"

"Do you normally talk as you get dressed?" I cut her off and took a seat on the bed. "I'm pretty sure it's something that doesn't require conversation."

Fuming, she slipped into her shoes and rushed out of the room—slamming the door behind her.

I waited until I heard the ping of the elevator and lay across the mattress. I tried my best to think of something or someone other than Aubrey, but she was all that came to mind.

What the fuck is happening?

I stared at the ceiling for another hour, unable to take my mind off of how her mouth felt against mine at the office earlier today. Even if it was only for a few seconds.

Needing to get to the bottom of this, I pulled my phone out of my pocket and called her.

"Hello?" She answered on the second ring. "Hello?"

"Why did you buy me that watch, Aubrey?"

"Why do you care?"

"I don't, but I read the inscription on the back."

Silence.

"I need to ask you something," I said.

"Only if I can ask you a few things first…"

"Go ahead."

"How can you possibly be so adamant about honesty when you haven't been completely honest with me?"

"I *have* been completely honest with you."

"I'm starting to believe that your name isn't really Andrew Hamilton…"

"So you're still stalking me and my past online? Do you not have any other hobbies?"

"Who is *EH*?" Her voice cracked. "Why are those two letters hanging on all your walls? Why are they engraved in all of your cufflinks?"

"Aubrey…"

"What's going on with you and Ava? I saw her walk out of your office last week, and she smirked at me."

"Is this a bad time to talk?"

"*Yes.*" She was breathing hard. "This is a very bad time. Why don't you just hang up and go to the Marriott so you can fuck someone else?"

"I *am* at the Marriott, and I was actually about to fuck someone else."

She was silent for several seconds. "I don't… I don't want to hear from you anymore, Andrew."

"What did you just say?"

"I said I don't want to hear from you anymore. Don't you ever fucking call me again." She hung up.

# Impasse (n.):
The inability of two parties to reach a negotiated settlement.

*A few days later...*

**Aubrey**

My heart was still aching—reeling, and although I'd told Andrew never to call me again, and that I didn't want to hear from him, I couldn't move on until I received an apology.

I *needed* it...

I felt sick to my stomach after giving him that watch, and I'd foolishly expected for him to call and say, "I love you, too," but he acted as if it meant nothing.

Without knocking, I opened the door to his office and shut it behind me.

He raised his eyebrow as I stepped over to his desk, but he didn't hang up his phone.

"Yes, that will be fine," he spoke into the receiver.

"I need to talk to you." I blurted out. *"Now."*

He motioned for me to take a seat, but he continued talking. "Yes. That will work as well."

I sat and crossed my arms, trying not to stare at him too hard. He was utter perfection today—looking more fuck-able than usual with a fresh hair-cut and a brand new grey suit. His eyes regarded me intensely as usual, and I noticed he was actually wearing the watch I gave him. He'd even paired it with matching cufflinks.

Maybe I'm overreacting after all...

"Right..." He leaned back in his chair and typed a few things onto his keyboard. "I'll see you at eight o'clock tonight, Sandra.

Room 225."

My stomach dropped.

"Something I can help you with, Miss Everhart?" He hung up the phone. "Is there any reason why you barged into my office without knocking?"

"You've fucked someone else already?"

"Is that a serious question?"

"Did you fuck someone else already? Did you?"

"Would it matter?"

"Yes, it would fucking matter..." My blood boiled as I stood up. "*Did you sleep with someone else?*"

"Not yet." He narrowed his eyes at me and stood up too, walking over to me. "However, I really don't see how that's any of your concern."

I looked at his wrist. "Why are you wearing that watch if you don't feel the same way I do?"

"It's the only watch that matches my new cufflinks."

"Are you seriously this blind?" There were tears welling in my eyes. "Are you—"

"I told you a long time ago that I don't do feelings—that if we ever did fuck, that would be the end of us." He tucked a strand of hair behind my ear. "However, I do realize that by crossing the line with you, personally and professionally, that a percentage of the blame is mine."

"A *percentage?*"

"Would you like me to bring in the firm's accountant? I'm sure he can work out the exact figure."

"Andrew..." I was on the verge of losing it.

"Since we did break the boundaries, and we were in fact friends before, I'm willing to revert to that arrangement."

I shook my head as he tilted my chin up and looked into my eyes.

"We can still talk on the phone at night," he said. "You can tell me about your ballet, your parents, your life...And, to be sensitive to your feelings, I'll tell you about my life but I'll leave out my one night stands until you're completely over whatever the hell you think we had."

"I told you that I loved you..." The words rushed out of my mouth.

"I told you that you shouldn't have."

"You can't really be this callous and cold of a person, Andrew…"

"What do you want me to say, Aubrey?" His tone changed. "Your pussy was so magical that it opened my eyes and made me want to change all my ways for you? That I can't live or breathe without knowing that you're by my side? Is that what you're expecting me to say?"

"No." I tried not to cry. "A simple apology for—"

"Kicking your inquisitive ass out of my apartment?" He was glaring at me. "For trying to prevent you from feeling like you do right now? *Fine.* I'm sorry I didn't do it sooner."

I resisted the urge to spit in his face and stepped back. I officially despised him. "You are so not the man I thought you were."

"Good, because I'm sure that man is quite pathetic." He briefly shut his eyes and sighed. "Look, Aubrey…"

"It's *Miss Everhart.*" I hissed as I walked toward the door. "Miss. Fucking. Everhart. But not to worry, you'll never have to worry about using it because you won't be seeing me again."

I slammed the door so hard it rattled the windows on the other side of the hall. I ignored the suspicious look from Jessica as I stormed to the parking lot, and sped all the way to the bank.

I withdrew every dollar out of my savings account, and called the bus depot downtown—asking what the fare was for a one-way ticket to New York City.

"That would be seventy nine eighty six," the operator said. "It's ten dollars cheaper if you buy a roundtrip ticket."

"I won't be needing a round trip ticket." I steered my car into my apartment's lot. "Can you tell me when the next bus leaves?"

"Tonight. Would you like me to book that for you now?"

"Absolutely." I recited my credit card info from memory, and listened as she told me about how I needed to take a walk on the Brooklyn Bridge whenever I had the chance.

The second I hung up, I arranged for a cab and sent a quick text to my roommate:

> Something has come up and I have to move out ASAP…I'll be wiring my half of the remaining rent to our landlord, and I'll find a way to have my belongings shipped to me. I'm leaving my keys under that rose

plant in the laundry room
—Aubrey.

Grabbing two large suitcases from my closet, I stuffed them with whatever I could find, and placed Mr. Petrova's recommendation letter into my purse.

As I was writing myself a reminder (*"That asshole still has my panties…Need to shop for more."*), my mother called.

"Yes?" I answered.

"Excuse me, Aubrey?" she said.

I rolled my eyes. "Hello?"

"Much better." There was a smile in her voice. "What time should I expect you at The Grove tonight?"

"Never. I'm not coming."

"Save me your tantrums, Aubrey. There's a lot of money riding on this first dinner. Would you like me and your father to pick you up?"

"I said I'm not coming. Did you not hear me?"

"Aubrey…" She lowered her voice. "I've been trying to hold back for the past few weeks, but you know what? I am sick and tired of you being so damn thoughtless and selfish about your father's aspirations. Neither of us personally give a damn about your thoughts on the election, but since you're a member of this family, I demand that you—"

"Go to hell." I hung up and continued packing, even faster now.

**Subject: Cab.**

Miss Aubrey Everhart,

Your cab has arrived at the address you specified. It will wait for exactly five minutes.

—Durham Cab Co.

I rushed into the bathroom and filled a plastic bag with toiletries, and then I placed them into my suitcase and headed outside.

"Bus station, right?" The cab driver, a woman, smiled as I approached.

"Yes, please."

She took my bags and placed them into the trunk as I slid into the backseat. I felt my heart hurting with every second that passed, and as much as I tried to block out the thoughts about Andrew, images of his face infiltrated my brain anyway.

I was picturing the last full night we spent together, the night before he kicked me out of his condo, and no matter how hard I tried to make sense of what happened the very next night, I couldn't. All I could do was cry.

*My phone vibrated against my knee and I flipped it over, hoping to see Mr. Petrova's name, but it was Andrew.*

*"Hello?" I answered.*

*"What are you doing?"*

*"I have ballet practice on Wednesdays…Shouldn't you know that by now?"*

*"If you were actually in ballet practice you wouldn't be picking up your phone."*

*Silence.*

*"Aubrey?" He sounded concerned. "Are you crying?"*

*"No." I lied, turning up the volume on my car radio.*

*"What's wrong?"*

*"Nothing. I just said—"*

*"Stop fucking lying to me, Aubrey," he said. "What's wrong with you?"*

*"I got sent home from practice today."*

*"Okay. And?"*

*"There is no 'And' about this…" Tears welled in my eyes. "I've never been sent home before. He made me feel like shit today. He even told the understudy to be prepared to take my place right in front of me, and then he told me not to come back until next week…"*

*"I've told you the reason why he does that. Why don't you believe me?"*

*"Because I really was bad today," I admitted. "My feet are swollen and I didn't bandage them properly, so I was off by an eighth of a count for most of the day…"*

*He sighed. "I'm sure you were still ten times better than everyone else. Don't you think?"*

*"No..."*

*"Trust me. I'm pretty sure he's just—"*

*"Can I come over tonight?" I cut him off, hoping for a yes, but all I heard was silence. I knew I'd pushed my luck the first couple nights we spent together, but I didn't want it to be a rare thing. I wanted more.*

*"Are you going to give me an answer, Andrew?"*

*"Yes," he said. "You can come over. Where are you?"*

*"Outside your door."*

*He opened it seconds later and looked me up and down, raising his eyebrow. "I would've picked you up."*

*"I almost asked you to..."*

*He grabbed my hand and pulled me inside, keeping his eyes locked on mine. As the door shut, he pulled me into his arms and shook his head at me.*

*"What are you doing, Aubrey?"*

*"What do you mean?"*

*"Why do you keep insisting on breaking every rule I have?"*

*"Why do you keep letting me?"*

*Without saying another word, his lips were on mine and his hands were sliding around my waist—deftly unbuttoning my skirt, quickly pushing it down to the floor.*

*His hands grazed my backside, searching for my panties, but there were none.*

*"Remind me to return your collection." He laughed softly and led me over to the couch.*

*He dropped my hand and then he sat on the floor, looking up at me. Unzipping his pants, he pulled out a condom and slowly rolled it over his cock.*

*I started to bend low so I could sit next to him, but he grabbed my thighs.*

*"Stop," he said. "I don't want you to sit on the floor."*

*"Okay." I looked over my shoulder. "Do you want me to sit on the coffee table?"*

*"No..." He trailed his fingers up my legs. "On my face."*

*"What?"*

*"Sit your pussy on my face."*

*I stood still, speechless—unable to process what he'd just asked me to do.*

*Smirking, he pulled me close and tapped my left leg. "Lift that onto the pillow behind me." He commanded me with his eyes and I slowly lifted my foot and pressed it into the cushion.*

*"Good girl." He rubbed his hands along the inside of my thighs, blowing kisses against my skin. "Grab onto my hair..."*

*My hands found their way onto his head as he slipped two fingers inside of me, as he slowly moved them in and out.*

*He darted his tongue against my clit and groaned. "Are you actually going to follow my directions today?"*

*"Yes..."*

*"I need you to be as still as possible." One of his hands cupped my ass, palming it as he continued to stretch my pussy with his fingers. "Can you do that?"*

*I nodded, letting a low moan escape my mouth.*

*"Is that a yes?" He didn't give me chance to answer. He drew my swollen clit into his mouth, instantly making my knees buckle beneath me.*

*Shutting my eyes, I screamed as he gripped my hips and slightly rocked me against his mouth—licking every part of me with his tongue, lapping up every drop.*

*"Andrew..." I could barely hear my own voice. "Andrew..."*

*My right leg lost its hold on the floor and I nearly fell forward, but he grabbed me and held me still—not moving his mouth away.*

*I pulled his hair hard, begging him to slow down, to let me attempt to control the pace, but it was no use.*

*He continued to fuck me with his mouth, ignoring my every scream.*

*As my hips jerked and quivers began to race through my body, he wrapped his arms around my legs and slowly pulled me down, lowering me onto his cock.*

*"Ahhhh...." I breathed as he buried himself inch by inch. "I...I..."*

*"You, what?" He kissed my forehead once he was entirely inside of me. "Do you not want to ride me this way? Would you prefer if I bent you over?"*

*I shook my head, and he covered one of my nipples with his mouth, swirling his tongue around it until it hardened.*

*Without him telling me to, I wrapped my arms around his neck and moved myself up and down his cock.*

*"Harder..." He bit my neck. "I want you to fuck me as hard as I fuck you..."*

*I grinded my hips into him again and again, as forceful as I could, but he grabbed me and began thrusting his own hips up from the floor.*

*"Andrew, I'm going to cum..." I cried out as he completely took over. "I'm going to—"*

*He slapped my ass as my body finally gave in, as his gave in, too.*

*Breathless, I leaned against his chest, but he didn't let me rest long. He eased me out of his lap and stood up—walking off to toss away the condom.*

*Heading back over to me, he scooped me into his arms and carried me into his bedroom, gently lowering me onto his sheets.*

*I rolled over to the side of the bed I preferred—the side by the window, and waited for him to lay next to me, but he didn't. He took a seat near the edge of the bed and lifted my feet into his lap.*

*I was too tired to ask him what he was doing, and the next thing I felt was a warm, soothing liquid dripping onto my skin. Then I felt his hands slowly spreading it around the places where the swelling hurt the most.*

*I moaned as his fingers massaged my soles, said his name as his fingers caressed every tender spot.*

*"Shhh," he whispered, rendering me speechless as he continued to soothe me.*

*Every few minutes, he looked back at me and asked, "Would you like me to stop?"*

*I shook my head and kept my eyes shut, relishing every moment of this.*

*After what felt like hours of bliss, after he'd given me the best foot massage I'd ever had, he climbed in bed next to me and pulled me against his chest.*

*"Goodnight, Aubrey," he whispered. "I hope you feel better."*

*Elated, I threaded my fingers through his hair. "You're not going to insist on taking me home tonight?"*

*"Not unless you keep talking." He growled. "Go to sleep..."*

*"Thank you for the foot massage...That was really—"*

*"Stop talking, Aubrey." He rolled me on top of him. "Go to sleep."*

*"I was just saying thank you. I can't say thank you?"*

*"No." He pressed his lips against mine and kissed me until I couldn't breathe, saying, "Don't make me fuck you to sleep," in between breaths.*

*I attempted to roll over, but his grip was too strong.*

*Smiling, I positioned my head against his heartbeat and whispered, "Can you hear me? Are you sleeping?"*

*No answer. Just deep, sleeping breaths.*

*I hesitated a few seconds. "I love you..."*

# Foreseeable Risk (n.):
A danger which a reasonable person should anticipate
as the result from his/her actions.

## Andrew

"Jessica!" I glanced at the slightly normal looking cup of coffee on my desk.

"Yes, Mr. Hamilton?"

"Could you ask Miss Everhart to come in here, please?" I needed to see her face.

She'd been avoiding me all week, and if all I had to say was "sorry"—whether I actually meant it or not, it was worth it. I missed seeing her seductive mouth in the mornings, remembering how it felt when she pressed it against mine.

"I would do that," Jessica said, "but seeing as though she put in her resignation letter last week, I'm pretty sure that's impossible."

"She *quit*?"

Without telling me?

Jessica raised her eyebrow. "She did. I gave you the letter she left, too. It was quite interesting."

"I never got a letter."

She walked over to my desk and sifted through the clutter.

"Here it is," she said. "She left you two letters…Anything else?"

"No…"

She tilted her head to the side and tapped her lip, looking as if she wanted to say something, but she smiled and left the room.

Locking the door, I tore the first letter open and read it.

*Dear GBH,*

*Thank you very much for hiring me as your undergraduate intern. I've had quite the experience working for you and am honored by all I've learned. However, due to personal reasons, I am resigning as of today.*
*I apologize for such short notice, and I wish your firm continued success in your future endeavors.*

*—Aubrey Everhart.*

I sighed and opened the other letter that was addressed directly to me.

*Dear Mr. Hamilton,*

*FUCK. YOU.*

*—Aubrey*

# Overrule (v.):
To reject an attorney's objection to a question of a witness of admission of evidence.

## *Aubrey*

New York City was an entirely different universe. It was nothing like I expected, yet everything I wanted all at once.

The sidewalks were persistently packed with people rushing to get somewhere, the streets were seas of taxis, and the cacophony of sounds—the shouting from the street vendors, the rumbling of the subway below, and the endless chatter between the executives and casual-ites all blended into an almost pleasing melody.

Not that I had much time to listen to it, anyway.

The second I arrived in New York last week, I'd checked into a cheap hotel and rushed to register for the NYCB audition.

Every day for the past week, I jumped out of bed at four in the morning and headed to Lincoln Center to learn the required audition piece—the hardest choreography I'd encountered in my life.

It was faster, choppier, and the instructors refused to show it more than twice a day. There was no conversation outside of tempo counts, no questions were allowed either. On top of that, the company's pianist only elected to play the accompanying music at full speed, never slowing down to make the learning process easier.

There were hundreds of girls vying for a place in the company, and from what I gathered from conversations here or there, most of them were already professionals.

I didn't let that deter me, though.

When the grueling practices came to an end, I took that chance to find a new place in the city to dance on my own: A rooftop in view of Times Square, an abandoned historical store on the Upper East Side, or in front of bookstore windows in the West End.

Despite my immediate love for this city, it wasn't enough to distract me from my heartbreak. Nor was it enough to distract me from the fact that today, official audition day, I was late.

Sweating, I jumped off the subway and ran down Sixty Sixth Street—paying no mind to my burning lungs.

Keep going...Keep going...

A man to my left stepped out of a cab and I immediately jumped in.

"Lincoln Center, please!" I shouted.

"It's right up the street." The driver looked at me through the rearview mirror, confused.

"Please? I'm already late."

He shrugged and pulled off as I tried to steady my breathing.

Not wanting to waste any time, I pulled my black tutu out of my bag and pulled it over my tights. I took out my makeup and applied it the best I could, and as we approached the curb, I tossed a ten dollar bill at the driver and jumped out of the car.

Rushing into the building, I headed straight for the theater, relieved that one of the directors was still standing outside the doors.

"Yes?" She looked me up and down as I approached. "May I help you with something?"

"I'm here for the auditions."

"For the *nine o'clock* auditions?" She looked at her watch. "It's nine fifteen."

"I'm sorry...I called an hour ago and said—"

"Your first cab broke down? That was you?"

I nodded.

She studied me for a few more seconds—pursing her lips. Then she opened the door. "You can change into your whites in the dressing room. Hurry up."

The door shut behind me before I could ask what she meant by "[my] whites," but as my eyes scanned the stage, I realized that every dancer was dressed in a white leotard and matching tutu.

Shit...

My cheeks heated as I looked over my outfit. I didn't have my whites in my bag. They were at home.

Nearing the stage, I set my bag in a chair and tried to ignore that dread that was building inside my chest. I just needed to focus on giving it my all during this routine. That was it.

I found an open spot onstage and stretched my arms—noticing the smirks and whispers that were being thrown in my direction.

Undaunted, I smiled at anyone who made eye contact and continued my routine.

"May I have your attention, please?" A man's voice came over the speaker. "Can everyone stop stretching and make your way to the edge of the stage, please?"

I set my leg down and followed the crowd, finding a spot on the end.

The man addressing us was a tall grey haired man with wiry glasses, and he was the definition of the word "legend": His name was Arnold G. Ashcroft, and I'd followed him and his choreography for years. He was once the most sought after specialist in the world, but when he dropped in the rankings, it was only to his Russian rival: Paul Petrova.

"We're happy to see such a huge turnout for this session of auditions," he said. "As you know, due to a series of unfortunate events, we are overhauling our entire staff. That said, we are keeping our current production schedule as is, which means we will be filling in the roles of principle dancers, soloists, and corps members within the next fourteen days."

"Rehearsals will be long and hard—four to ten, midnight if need be, and there will be no room for excuses or..." He looked me up and down, frowning at my attire. "*Mistakes.*"

"This is the first round of six. You will be told of your status once the music stops, and if you are sent home, please don't hesitate to try again next year. I see a lot of failures from last summer, so I'm hoping you've learned something between then and now..."

"For this round, we'll do a portion of the Balanchine routine in groups of eight. You may stretch for a few minutes and then we will begin."

He waved at the man who was taking his seat at the piano, and then he turned around and gave a thumbs up to three people who were sitting in the judge's seats. Smiling, he ascended the stage's steps, and greeted a few familiar faces.

I made my way over and tapped his shoulder.

"Yes?" He turned around.

"Um…" I withered under his intense glare.

"Good morning, Mr. Ashcroft. My name is Aubrey Everhart and I'm—"

"*Late.*" He cut me off. "You're also the only performer who isn't wearing the mandatory white."

"Yes, well…" I stammered. "That's why I want to speak with you."

"Oh?"

"I want to know if you would allow me to go home and change."

"And why would I allow that, Miss Everhart?"

"So I can audition with the group this afternoon and be judged fairly. I just think that I've already—"

"Stop." He pressed a pen against my lips. "Ladies, may I please have your attention?"

An immediate silence fell over the theater.

"I want you all to meet *Aubrey Everhart.*" He smiled. "She's just informed me that due to the fact that she was late and decided to wear improper attire to her audition today, that there's a chance she'll be judged unfairly."

The ballerina across from me folded her arms.

"Now," he said. "Since the world of ballet is fair and has always been about catering to the needs of the *unprepared*, is there anyone who would have a problem if I allowed Miss Everhart to go home, change, and return for the auditions at six?"

Every dancer on stage raised her hand into the air.

"I thought so." His tone was cold. "If you think a wrongly colored tutu is going to affect how well you perform, you should leave right now."

I swallowed, wishing I could disappear.

"You can dance in the first group." He shook his head at me and walked away.

Disregarding the soft snickering from the other girls, I returned to my former spot on stage and stretched once more. I tried to block out everything that had gone wrong this morning and pretended that I was in Durham again—dancing for one of the best directors in the world.

"Miss Everhart?" A woman said my name, snapping me out of my thoughts.

"Yes?"

"Are you going to take your place at center stage with everyone else, or do you need more time to find it?"

I smiled at the judge's table and stepped into the line.

The woman signaled to the pianist and he played the B-flat scale before starting the piece. As his fingers forced the notes, my arms went high above my head and I slowly spun around on my toes— wincing as my right pointe slipper cracked.

I ignored the pain and continued the routine. Terribly.

Each time I attempted a jump, I landed off balance and slipped an eighth of a count behind everyone else. My turns were awkward—frantically paced, and my pointe work was so choppy that I bumped into the girl next to me.

Embarrassed, I murmured sorry and spun around, but I lost my balance and fell onto the stage. Headfirst.

I ignored the loud outburst of laughter from the dancers in the audience and stood up, attempting to fall back into the routine.

"Stop!" Mr. Ashcroft bellowed from the side of the stage, making the notes come to an end.

He walked in front of our line and stepped directly in front of me.

"I just looked through your file, Miss Everhart." He looked unimpressed. "You recently studied under Mr. Petrova?"

I nodded.

"Use your words, please."

"Yes…" I cleared my throat. "Yes, I did."

"And he wrote an actual recommendation letter on your behalf?"

"Yes sir."

He looked at me in utter disbelief. Shock. "You expect me to believe that when you dance so stiffly? When you're a count behind each and every step?"

"Yes…" My voice was a whisper.

"Well…At least you can always say that you studied under one of the greatest choreographers of all time. You can leave my theater now."

My heart sank. "*What?*"

"I don't think you're a good fit for our company. We'll email you this evening with a link to purchase discounted tickets for the season's shows."

A tear rolled down my face, and as if he could see that he'd just broken my heart, he patted my shoulder.

"I can tell that you've had training," he said. "Very good training. And I can see that you have potential, but we're not interested in *potential* here. For the rest of you, congratulations! You've earned yourselves a spot in the next round of auditions. Now, please clear the stage so the next group of dancers may perform."

A loud applause arose from the hopefuls in the audience, and I felt as if I was watching my life fall apart in front of me. Hurt, I followed the dancers to the side steps—unsure of what to do next.

Grabbing my bag, I avoided the pathetic glances of the hopefuls and shook my head.

"That just goes to show you," Mr. Ashcroft said to the other panelists, laughing, "even Petrova picks duds sometimes."

I turned around.

Enraged, I marched up the stage's steps and took a seat on the white line. I untied my right slipper and prepared another one—bending it forward and backward until it felt right.

"You can change your shoes in the restroom, Miss Everhart." Mr. Ashcroft chided. "The stage is for actual performers. Or did Petrova not teach you that?"

"I need another chance," I said. "Just because I didn't nail the Balanchine piece that doesn't make me a bad dancer."

"Of course it doesn't, honey." He mocked me. "It makes you a *failed dancer*, who is currently using my stage and sucking up precious audition time for those who might actually make the cut in my company."

I walked over to the pianist. "Tchaikovsky, *Swan Lake*. Act two, scene fourteen. Do you know that piece?"

"Umm..." He looked confused.

"Do you know it or not?"

"Yes, but—" He pointed to another judge who was now standing and crossing her arms.

"Could you please play it?" I pleaded with my eyes. "It's only three minutes long."

He let out a sigh and straightened his back, strumming the keys of the piano. With no count off, he played the first few notes of the concerto and the softs sounds echoed off the theater's walls.

"Miss Everhart, you're wasting everyone's time..." Mr.

Ashcroft's face turned red as I slipped into fifth position.

I could hear him sighing and tsk-ing, could hear the other hopefuls murmuring, but as I twirled around the stage and transitioned from an arabesque to a grand jete, their talking stopped.

The notes lingered longer—darker, as the song progressed and I made sure each motion of my hands was smooth and graceful. As I leapt across the stage and completed a series of perfect pirouettes, I could see Mr. Ashcroft rubbing his chin.

Before I knew it, I was in a trance and I was dancing in the middle of Times Square, underneath flashing lights and a star-filled sky.

I continued dancing long after the last note, humming the additional refrain that most pianists ignored, and I ended by leaning forward on my left leg—holding my right one in the air behind me.

The panelists stared back at me. Their faces expressionless.

"Are you done, Miss Everhart?" Mr. Ashcroft asked.

"Yes..."

"Good. Now, get the hell off my stage."

I stood upright and bit my lip to prevent myself from breaking down in front of them.

"Thank you very much for the opportunity..." I grabbed my bag and rushed off stage—running down the hallway and outside the building.

I stopped in front of a trashcan and bent over, waiting for the inevitable vomit.

Deep down I knew that I was a good dancer—that I'd just danced my heart out, and I honestly felt like I deserved a second chance.

The thought of failing had never crossed my mind when I signed up for this audition, and the option of returning to Durham was too painful to bear.

Heaving, I tearfully weighed my options: 1) Go home and rejoin Mr. Petrova's dance program. 2) Go back inside and tell the panel they're all fucking idiots, or—

"Miss Everhart?" Someone tapped my shoulder.

I spun around, finding myself face to face with a stoic Mr. Ashcroft.

"Yes?" I wiped my face on my sleeve and forced a smile.

"What you just did on stage was rude, unprofessional, and

*horrible.* It was the worst thing I have ever seen a prospective dancer do and I didn't appreciate it all...That said, be here *on time* for the second round next week."

My jaw dropped and I didn't get a chance to scream or say thank you.

He was already gone.

I pulled out my phone, anxious to tell someone that I'd made it to the next round, but I had no one to call.

All I had were angry texts from my parents, tons of their missed calls, and I knew better than to reach out to them right now. They didn't really give a damn.

I searched for Mr. Petrova's number—hoping I'd saved it, but an email from Andrew appeared on my screen.

**Subject: Your Resignation.**

I was tempted to open it, but my heart wouldn't let me do it. He was the main reason why I fled here, and I didn't need him intruding on my new life.

I deleted his message and decided that I wasn't going to think about him anymore. All that mattered now was ballet.

# Months later…

# Rebuttal (n.):
Evidence introduced to counter, disprove or
contradict the opposition's evidence or a presumption,
or responsive legal argument.


## Andrew

The fall season came and went, taking the changing leaves and amber sunsets with it. New interns filled the positions at GBH, new cases and clients packed the calendars, and as winter enveloped the city, one thing remained clear: Durham was only one step above the shit ladder when compared to New York City.

At least when it came to the winter, anyway.

This was the coldest winter the city had experienced, and since it was a Southern town, they were ill-prepared. The courtroom I was currently sitting in featured blankets lined against the windows instead of proper insulation, and there were space heaters jutting from every outlet.

There were few salt trucks available to control the icy streets, even fewer people who actually knew how to drive in such weather, and for whatever reason, there were no more suitable women available.

"Andrew?" Mr. Bach tapped my shoulder. "The prosecution is done with the witness…Are you going to redirect? That last line might have influenced the jury."

"Permission to redirect, Your Honor." I stood up from the table.

The judge nodded and I stared at the woman on the stand. She'd been lying through her teeth since this trial began and I'd had enough.

"Miss Everhart—" I cleared my throat. "I mean, *Miss Everly*, do you believe that leaving your husband in his time of need was what was best for your company?"

"Yes," she said. "I told you that during our first meeting."

"No." I shook my head. "You told me that you loved him and that your sole reasoning for leaving him was because you thought he didn't love you back. Is that not true?"

"It is, but—"

"So, because he didn't say that he loved you on *your terms*, because he told you he was actually incapable of loving you that way, you decided to leave him. Didn't you?"

"No...I left him because he was spending the company's money on unnecessary things and cheating on me."

"Did you ever think about *his feelings*?" I asked. "Did you think to simply ask if your leaving would affect him—whether you were on good terms or not?"

"He was..." She was breaking down. "He was cheating on me..."

"Was he? Or did you just want more than what he was willing to give you emotionally, Miss Everly?"

"Please stop..."

"Is it possible that you could be making all of this up?"

"No, never. I would never—"

"Is it possible that you're a *fucking liar*?"

"Order! Order!" The judge banged her gavel and the jury gasped.

"Counsel, my chambers. NOW!"

I stared at the fake tears falling down Miss Everly's face. This case was a wrap.

I walked into the judge's chambers and shut the door. "Yes, Your Honor?"

"Are you out of your goddamn mind?"

"Excuse me?"

"You just called your own witness a fucking liar."

I looked through the window, seeing that the bailiff was handing her a box of Kleenex.

"Are you on a new prescription?" she asked. "Drinking? Smoking something other than Cubans?"

"Because I'm having one bad day in court?"

"Because you've had *several* bad days in court."

"I don't recall calling any of my other witnesses fucking liars…"

"You called for an objection during the reading of a verdict."

"Maybe I didn't like the sound of it."

"Maybe, but you never mess up in my court." She paused. "*Ever*…Please go get yourself checked out, Mr. Hamilton. I'd really hate to be the judge presiding over your very first loss."

She motioned for me to follow her out of her chambers. She took a seat in her chair and announced that the current trial was being postponed due to a rare rule brought up by the defense, and that we would reconvene two weeks from now.

Relieved, I closed my briefcase and ignored a red-faced Miss Everly.

"Mr. Bach," she said, glaring at me, "I would really like for us to win this case, so could you please—"

"It's already taken care of," he said, cutting her off. "No worries." He gave her a reassuring smile and asked Mr. Greenwood to walk her out to her car. Then he turned and looked at me.

"Andrew, Andrew, Andrew…" He sighed. "I think you need some time off. I'll take over this case, alright? And Mr. Greenwood and I will be in contact with any of your clients who have cases within the next few weeks."

"You're overreacting," I said. "It's one fucking case."

"One fucking case that you're on the verge of losing."

"I *never* lose."

"I know." He patted me on the shoulder. "Go home, Andrew. You've actually never taken a vacation anyway. Maybe it's what you need right now."

"No." I grabbed my briefcase. "I'll see you at the Reber consultation tomorrow morning."

He called after me, but I ignored him. I sped back to GBH, prepared to immerse myself in more work. I was avoiding my condo as much as possible lately; I could hardly stand to be there.

Unopened condoms lined my wet bar—a reminder of how long it'd been since I had pussy, empty liquor bottles lined all of my window sills, and my Cuban cigar selection was long gone.

"Are you okay, Mr. Hamilton?" the main secretary asked as I walked through the firm's doors.

I ignored her. Too many people were asking me that question lately and I was tired of hearing it.

I shut myself inside my office and pulled my phone's chord out of the wall. I didn't need any distractions.

For the rest of the morning, I read over my files in utter silence—not even answering emails from my own clients.

"Jessica!" I called her once the clock struck noon. "*Jessica!*"

"Yes, Mr. Hamilton?" She walked in right away.

"Is there any reason why you suddenly decided to stop organizing my case files by date?" I slid a folder across the desk. "Any reason why you've decided to stop doing your goddamn job?"

"You think I actually have time to organize all your case files by date? Do you know how long that takes?" She raised her eyebrow. "That was *Miss Everhart's* idea. I told her it was a waste of time, but I guess not. If I have some free hours in between the Doherty case next week I'll try to do that."

"Thank you." I ignored the fact that my heart skipped a beat when she said Miss Everhart. "You can get out of my office now."

I pulled the papers from the file and began reorganizing them. As I clipped all of the witness testimonies together, Jessica cleared her throat.

"You miss her, don't you?" she asked.

"Excuse me?" My head shot up.

"Aubrey," she said, smiling. "You miss her, don't you?"

I said nothing. I just watched as she sauntered over to me, slowly raising the sides of her skirt to show that she wasn't wearing anything underneath.

Smiling, she picked up my coffee cup and took a long, dramatic sip.

"*Jessica...*" I groaned.

"You don't have to admit to it." She plopped her bare ass atop my desk. "But it's clear that you haven't been yourself for quite a while..."

"Are your ass cheeks touching my desk right now?"

"You don't even insult me the normal way that you used to," she said. "I actually miss that."

I pulled out a box of Clorox wipes.

"She doesn't stay in her old apartment anymore, you know. I think she moved."

"What makes you think I care about where an ex-employee lives?"

"Because the address you gave me for that envelope and red

box delivery belonged to her."

"That was for an old friend."

"Yeah, well..." She slid off my desk. "Your old friend must share an address with Aubrey Everhart because I pulled up her records from HR and she definitely stayed there."

Silence.

"I thought so." She smirked. "So, since you and I are so close—"

"We are *not* close."

"It's my duty as a friend to let you know that you're really letting yourself go..." She actually looked saddened. "You're not shaving, you're coming to work every morning reeking of alcohol, and you're barely yelling at the interns...I haven't had a wet dream about you in a very long time."

I rolled my eyes and stood up, wiping the part of my desk where her ass had been.

"But, since I know your secret about Aubrey now, you can know one of mine," she said, lowering her voice. "Sometimes, in the mornings, when she would bring you your coffee and shut the door, I would stand outside and listen..." Her eyes lit up. "And I would just pretend that it was me..."

"Pretend *what* was you?"

"Aubrey," she said. "Clearly she was good enough for you to break the 'I don't fuck my employees' rule." She stepped toward the door. "I knew the second she started here that you liked her."

"You have no idea what you're talking about."

"Of course I don't." She looked over her shoulder. "But I do know that the second she quit, you've been a shell of yourself. You have yet to realize that you've been wearing the same blue suit for two weeks straight."

I took a long swig of scotch from the bottle, numbly staring at the images that were playing on my television screen. A little blond girl playing in the rain—stomping her red boots in every puddle she could find.

"It's time to go, Emma..."

I winced at hearing the sound of my old voice, but I continued watching the scene.

"Five more minutes!" She begged with a smile.

"You don't even know what that means. You've just heard me say it..."

"Five more minutes!" She jumped into another puddle, laughing. "Five more minutes, Daddy!"

"It's going to rain all week. Don't you want to go home and—"

"*No!*" She stomped her feet in a puddle again, splashing me. And then she smiled innocently into the camera before running away—begging me to chase her.

I couldn't bear to watch anymore. I turned off the TV and knocked the DVD player to the floor.

Fuck...

Walking down the hallway, I straightened the "E" and "H" frames that hung on the wall—trying my best not to look too hard.

I didn't need to make myself another drink tonight. I needed someone to talk to.

I grabbed my phone from the night-stand, scrolling down my contacts for the one person who'd once kept the nightmares at bay. Aubrey.

It rang four times and went to voicemail.

"Hi. You've reached Aubrey Everhart," it said. "I'm unable to take your call right now, but if you leave your name and number I'll get back to you as soon as I can."

The second the beep sounded I hung up. Then I called again, just to listen to that small snippet of her voice. I told myself that I wasn't being pathetic by calling her five times—knowing damn well that she wasn't there, but when I called the sixth time, she picked up.

"Hello?" she answered. "*Andrew?*"

"Hello, Aubrey..."

"What do you want?" Her voice was cold.

"How are you?"

"What do you want, Andrew?" she asked, even colder. "I'm busy."

"Then why did you pick up?"

"It was a mistake." She ended the call.

I drew in a sharp breath, shocked that she hung up on me. I started to type up an email, chastising her for being so rude, but I noticed that she hadn't responded to my last three in months:

**Subject: Your Resignation.**

Even though the last two words of your resignation letter were ridiculous and unprofessional, I'd like to take you up on your offer to fuck you.

Name the time.

—Andrew.

**Subject: My Suit.**

Since you have yet to pick up your final check, should I assume that's your way of letting me keep it to replace the suit you ruined?

—Andrew.

**Subject: BALLET.**

I stopped by your dance hall earlier. You weren't there.

Did you quit that, too?

—Andrew.

I decided that I needed to replace her. Fast.

I grabbed my laptop from my nightstand and logged into LawyerChat, looking for another Alyssa-type.

I spent all night roaming the chat rooms, answering questions left and right—gauging the personalities of the askers, but none of them grabbed me. Still, one woman who was listed as a high profile lawyer with ten years of experience seemed promising, so I clicked on her chat box.

"If you have ten years of experience, what could you possibly need help with on this site?" I typed.

"You're never too old to learn new things...Why are you on here?"

"I'm looking for a replacement."

"You're trolling for an employee?"

"No, just someone I can talk to and make cum occasionally."

She blocked me.

I tried talking to a few other women—keeping my true words to myself, but ultimately they just wanted to use me for information. They weren't open to talking about anything else, and since LawyerChat had expanded its site recently, there seemed to be an influx of law students using it as a complaint board about their professors.

I shut the laptop and took another swig from my bottle—immediately realizing that there was only *one* "Alyssa-type": Aubrey...

Maybe I made a mistake...

Out the corner of my eye I spotted an envelope under the slit of my door. It hadn't been there when I first arrived home, and it hadn't been there a few hours ago when I ordered my dinner.

Confused, I walked over and picked it up.

It was an official court summons to testify in a New York hearing, but it wasn't addressed to my new name. It was addressed to Liam Henderson.

# Remedy (n.):
The means to achieve justice in any matter in which
legal rights are involved.


## *Aubrey*

*The Firebird.*
*Jewels.*
*Swan Lake.*

I wrote down the roles I wanted to audition for in my planner, smiling as I ran my hands across my acceptance letter for the umpteenth time. I had ten copies of it—two of them were framed, seven were for inspiration whenever I was feeling down, and one was for my parents. (I just hadn't had the time or energy to draft an "I fucking told you so" letter to mail with it.)

I looked at the clock on my wall and checked my phone, trying to suppress the butterflies that were fluttering around my stomach.

The guy I was now dating, Brian—a fellow dancer in the company, was supposed to call me with something important he wanted to talk about.

Ever since I met him, he'd been trying his hardest to woo me— taking me on dates in between rehearsals, joining me as I danced on rooftops and icy park benches. He was kind, sweet, funny, and the perfect example of what it meant to be a gentleman.

He was like the nice guy in the Old Hollywood movies, the type that held your hand for no reason at all, the type that walked you to your door and waited until you were completely inside before stepping away. He was the type that kissed you—softly and tenderly, whispering that he liked your lips, but never taking things any further.

In other words, he was nothing like Andrew.

Nothing like.

Even though his kisses never left me panting and wet, and his touches never set my nerves on fire, he never made me feel like shit.

My phone vibrated and I looked at the screen. Brian.

"Did you receive the roses I sent you today?"

I grinned, looking over at the red and white blooms on my fireplace.

"Yes." I texted back. "Thank you very much. I love them."

"I placed something else in the vase for you, too...You should use it to relax tonight. I'll be calling you after I get out of rehearsal."

"Looking forward to it." I added a smiley face at the end of my text and walked over to the vase, lifting the flowers up by their stems. There was a huge packet of pink bath beads and rose petals with a handwritten note across the front:

*The next time you take a bath...Think about me...*
*—Brian*

My heart fluttered and I couldn't help but want to immediately take him up on the idea. I slipped out of my clothes and headed into the bathroom, tossing the beads under rushing water.

As I let down my hair, I turned the volume on my ringer to the highest setting, and before I could set it down, I noticed a new email. Andrew.

My heart nearly jumped out of my chest, as it always did when one of his sporadic emails or calls graced my screen.

Everything in me told me not to open it, to continue ignoring him, and to let him feel just how alone and underappreciated I felt months ago, but I couldn't help it.

**Subject: Thoreau & Alyssa.**

You once said that you missed when we were Thoreau and Alyssa because I supposedly treated you better. I don't think I treated you any differently. I just really wanted to fuck you. But when we did meet in person, I unfortunately wanted to fuck you even more.

184

I personally prefer us as "Andrew & Aubrey" because on a night like tonight, when there's nothing I would rather do than fuck you against my balcony until you cum, at least I can actually picture what your pussy feels like and no longer have to imagine.

Pick up the phone...

—Andrew

I shook my head and set the phone down, mentally erasing that message and stepping into the tub.

I lay back and let the hot water rise to my chest, exhaling as it warmed my skin.

It was becoming easier to avoid thinking about Andrew now that I was talking to Brian, but it was harder trying to force myself to forget. I still thought about him late at night when I was in my bed, often wishing he was inside of me.

Nonetheless, I wasn't running back to him and his asshole-ish ways, and I would never allow him to come back to me.

Never.

I scrubbed myself clean with a soft loofah, trying my best to ignore the intense throbbing between my legs that always came when thinking about Andrew. I filled a ladle with water and poured it over my head—unable to push away the thought of Andrew washing my hair in the tub, of him telling me to stand underneath the streams and hold the wall as he grabbed my waist and fucked me from behind.

My fingers found their way to my clit as I remembered him bending me over the vanity in his bathroom, saying "I need you to fucking take it...All of it..." as he palmed my breasts and kissed his way down my spine.

I rubbed my clit in circles—shutting my eyes as I pictured his lips on mine, moaning as it swelled with every caress.

"Ahhhh...." I felt my nipples hardening as the water cooled, and I was close—so close, to coming, but my phone rang.

Andrew?

I immediately stood up and wrapped myself in a robe, rushing to answer it—telling myself that I could pick up his call "just this once."

"Hello?" I held the phone up to my ear without looking at the screen.

"*Aubrey?*" It was Brian.

"Hi…" I sighed, trying to mask my discontent. "How are you?"

"Is this a bad time? You sound kind of upset."

"I'm not upset. I was just getting out of the bath."

"Oh, well good," he said. "Did you use the relaxation kit I bought you?"

"I did."

"Did you also think about me?"

"Yes…" I lied, feeling slightly guilty. "How was rehearsal?"

I walked to my dresser and slipped into a T-shirt, listening to him recount the many ways that Mr. Ashcroft was the devil reincarnate.

"He's worse than Mr. Petrova." I pulled my hair into a ponytail.

"Worse than Paul Petrova?" He laughed. "I don't believe you. I've seen that man's documentary, seen him make grown men cry."

"Well, maybe years ago. Don't get me wrong, he's still rude and overbearing, but he has a layer of softness that Mr. Ashcroft lacks."

"I'll take your word for it…" He cleared his throat. "How tired are you right now?"

"Not too tired, shockingly."

"Well…I wanted to talk to you tonight because I needed to know if you wanted to try something new in our relationship."

"Sure." I climbed into bed. "What is it?"

"Phone sex…" His voice became deeper. "Have you ever done that before?"

I held back a laugh and quickly took off my shirt, tossing it to the floor. "Yes."

"Would you want to do it with me? Like, right now?"

"Yes." I grabbed my vibrator from a box and slipped under the covers, happy that I wouldn't need to think about Andrew to have an orgasm anymore. "Yes, I would like that very much."

"Good," he said. "Well…"

Silence.

"Well, *what?* Are you there, Brian?"

"Sorry, I was taking off my shorts." He hesitated. "So, what are you wearing?"

"Nothing…I'm naked."

"You're naked, Aubrey?" He sounded as if he didn't believe me. "Are you sure you've had phone sex before? This is the part where you're supposed to tell me that you have on lingerie. Work with me, please."

"Okay...I'm wearing a black thong and a black—"

"No, not black. I don't like black. Try blue, navy blue."

"Okay, it's a navy blue thong and a blue bra."

"Yeah, that's more like it. Now, take off the panties with one hand."

I lay there motionless, not sure as to whether I should turn on my vibrator or not.

"Now, imagine me..." He groaned. "Imagine me impaling you with my cock—so deep inside of you, so deep..."

I sighed.

"Can you picture it?" His voice became hoarse. "I need you to picture it...and touch your vagina."

"*What?*"

"Your vagina. Touch it."

I stood up and put on a pair of pajama pants.

"Are you touching it, babe?"

"Ohhh yeah..." I pulled a sweater over my head. "I'm touching my *vagina*..."

"Are you thinking about me licking your folds? Running my tongue along your ass crack?"

"Brian, you're actually..." I shook my head. "You're breaking up..."

"I'm going to stroke you down real good with my tongue, babe. Then I'm going to ram my cock into you again and again—never stopping even if you say no...You can't say no..."

I grabbed a sheet of paper and crumpled it next to the phone. "I can't hear you anymore, Brian...Reception in my bedroom is getting really bad...." I hung up in the middle of his panting and scrolled through my old emails—breaking down and reading the old messages from Andrew, the only man who could ever make me cum with words...

Whether I hated him or not, I needed a release and I knew this was the only way...

188

# Stay (n.):
A court-ordered short-term delay in judicial proceedings.

## *Andrew*

"Mr. Hamilton?" The flight attendant tapped my shoulder. "All of the other passengers have departed the plane sir. Thank you for flying first class, and I hope you enjoy New York."

"I'll try." I stood up and grabbed my briefcase from the overhead bin.

I'd tried to get out of coming here for weeks, but it was to no avail. The second I booked my ticket, I canceled all of my consultations and meetings, asked for an extension on my current case, and packed one suitcase. Just one.

I didn't need to be in this city longer than a day, and I refused to even testify. I was going to submit a written testimony to the judge and immediately return to Durham.

As I walked through the airport, I noticed that a few things had changed, but not as much as I'd hoped. People still walked at a breakneck pace, the air still reeked of failure, and the top newspaper was still *The New York Times*.

I placed a few dollars into the paper machine, twisting the key so it could spit out my copy, and then I flipped to the middle section where the justice pieces were kept.

There it was. Section C. The story that covered the entire page:

# Another Hearing in the Ongoing Hart Trial: Henderson to Testify This Week

I skimmed the article, slightly impressed that the journalist was writing facts this time and not smearing my name for the hell of it.

I also noticed there were still no pictures of me.

Figures…

"Over here, Mr. Hamilton!" A brunette waved as I stepped off the escalator. "Over here!"

I walked over and she held out her hand.

"I'm Rebecca Waters, lead attorney."

"I know who you are." I offered her a firm shake. "How fast can we get to the judge's chambers?"

"The judge's chambers?" She raised her eyebrow. "I'm supposed to check you into the hotel so we can discuss your testimony…You're supposed to stay here for a couple weeks."

"My return flight leaves in fifteen hours."

She looked shocked. "You only want to submit a written testimony? After all this time?"

"I find it quite impressive that you know how to listen and comprehend at the same time." I looked at my watch. "Where is the town car?"

She groaned and led me down the bustling terminal, through the gates, and into the executive car lot. She was babbling about how "important" this case was, how it would finally close a chapter on my life, but I wasn't listening.

My mind was literally counting the seconds I had left in this place.

"Good morning, sir." The driver grabbed my bag as we approached the car. "I hope you enjoy your stay in New York City."

I nodded and slipped into the back seat, rolling my eyes when Rebecca sat next to me.

"Could you at least stay for one night and think about this, Liam?"

"What did you just call me?"

"I'm sorry," she said. "Andrew…I mean, Mr. Hamilton. Could you at least think about it?"

"I just did."

"Fine." She pulled out her phone, and I looked out the window as the car coasted through the city.

I winced as we passed a billboard where my old firm once held an advertisement, shut my eyes when we passed Emma's favorite toy store.

"Mr. Hamilton…" Rebecca tapped my shoulder. "As a lawyer, I'm sure you know how much more compelling an oral testimony can be over a written one. I am begging you to reconsider this."

"And I'm begging you to get over it." I looked her directly in the eyes. "He and Ava ruined my life and I don't have shit to gain by sitting in a courtroom full of strangers and explaining how. You want an emotional testimony? Hire a fucking drama student to read my words to the jury."

"Things have changed. It's not like it was six years ago."

"That's why *The New York Times* still won't print my picture?"

"They won't print your picture because they think you're an asshole." She snapped. "You also won a huge and expensive case against them years ago or have you suddenly forgotten that? Take it as a compliment that they're even mentioning you in a positive light." She tossed yesterday's paper into my lap. "They even ran that piece. Looks pretty damn good to me."

I picked up the paper and brought it close to my face, and before I could read the article, two words caught my eye: Aubrey Everhart.

Her name was at the bottom of the page, mixed in with several others, in a beautiful black ad:

> The New York Ballet Company to Celebrate New
> Cast Members with Saturday Night Gala.

Tomorrow…

"I just…" Rebecca was still talking. "I just think you should at least stay for a night, clear your head, and really think about this."

"I'll stay until tomorrow."

"Really?" Her eyes lit up.

"Yes." I stared at Aubrey's name again. "*Really.*"

# Harass (v.):
Systematic and/or continual unwanted and annoying
pestering, which often includes threats and demands.


### Andrew

The prosecutor shook my hand over coffee and tea the next night,
batting her light brown eyes.

"Thank you so much for agreeing to stay for a few weeks,
Andrew," she said. "This is going to be a real help in this case."

"I'm sure..." I stood up and walked over to the window,
looking at the snow covered streets below.

"Your old partner has definitely hired the best lawyers money
can buy, and has paid fines and suffered penalties for years, but I
think we can finally send him to prison with the new evidence that
we have. That, and your testimony, of course."

I said nothing.

"I'm not sure how you would feel about this, but..." Her voice
trailed off, and seconds later she was by my side. "Would you like
to catch up on all we've missed since you've been gone?"

"Excuse me?"

She rubbed my shoulder. "You left New York and you never
looked back. You didn't call anyone or keep in touch...We were
such good friends and you—"

"Okay." I cut her off and grabbed her hand, moving it away.
"First of all, *no*, I do not want to catch up on shit. I don't give a
damn about what I've missed." I looked her up and down. "But
from the look of things, it hasn't been much. Second of all, yes, we
*were* friends. Past tense. You didn't call or keep in touch with me
when everyone in this city was dragging my name through the mud,
did you?"

Her cheeks reddened.

"You didn't even call to ask me if the rumors were fucking true." I pointed to the door. "So, please don't think that just because I've agreed to help put an asshole where he belongs, that you and I are, or will ever be friends."

"I'm so sorry…"

"It's six years too late for that." I turned around. "I'll be in court when I'm needed. You can leave now."

I waited until I heard the sound of the door close and called the town-car driver. "What time do I need to leave for the gala if I want to be there once it starts?"

"Now, sir."

I hung up and slipped into my coat, taking the penthouse's private elevator to the lobby. Rushing through the hotel's exit doors, I spotted the car across the street and headed over.

"We should be there in about thirty minutes, Mr. Hamilton." He looked at me through the rearview mirror. "Are you meeting a date at this event tonight?"

"No," I said. "Why are you asking?"

"Because if you were, I was going to suggest that we stop at the floral stand that's three blocks down."

"We can stop." I looked out the window as he pulled off.

I'd thought about telling Aubrey that I was in town, or "good luck" for her performance tonight, but I didn't see a point. Besides, last night, in a moment of weakness, I sent her a rather vague email and her rare response didn't encourage further conversation.

**Subject: Happiness.**

Are you happy with your current life away from GBH? Are you pursuing your ballet dreams finally?

—Andrew

**Subject: Re: Happiness.**

Please stop emailing me and delete my number.

Thank you.

—Aubrey

"Mr. Hamilton?" The driver held the door open. "We've arrived…Do you plan on getting out of the car?"

"Thank you." I grabbed the bouquet of roses and lilies off the seat and gave him a tip, telling him that I needed him to stay close, that I may be bringing someone else back with me.

The line to enter the venue was wrapped around the block, so I skipped everyone and walked straight through the front door.

"Excuse me, sir?" An usher immediately stepped in front of me. "There's a line outside for a reason."

"I don't like to wait."

"None of us do sir," he said, crossing his arms, "but that's gala policy unless you already have a ticket. Do you have a ticket?"

"I don't like those either."

He unclipped a radio from his belt buckle. "Sir, please don't make me call security. You have to purchase a ticket just like everyone else, and you have to stand in line just like everyone else. Now, I'm going to kindly ask you to—"

He stopped mid-sentence once I handed him a clip of hundred dollar bills. "Did you say your ticket was in the front row, sir?"

"Yes. That's exactly what my ticket says."

He smiled and led me down the hall, into a colossal room that featured floor to ceiling windows, glimmering chandeliers, and freshly polished marble floors. Hundreds of tables were dressed in white table cloths—stamped with lavish gold and silver centerpieces, and the letters "NYCB" were etched onto every dinner menu and program.

There was no formal stage in this room, only a slightly elevated platform that stood in the center—in perfect view for all the dinner tables.

"Will this seat be okay for you, sir?" The usher waved his hand over a seat that was directly in front of the platform.

"Yes, thank you."

"Dinner will be served in about an hour, the sponsors of the NYCB will be honored shortly after, and then the short tributes and the dance portion of the gala will begin."

I thanked him again as I took my seat. If I had known the exact order of the program beforehand, I would've shown up much later.

Picking up the brochure in front of me, I flipped through the pages—stopping when I saw Aubrey's face.

Her picture was taken mid-laugh, as she tossed her hair over her shoulder and looked directly into the camera. According to the picture, her hair was much shorter now—it barely touched her shoulders, and her eyes looked more hopeful and happy than I'd ever seen them.

I stared at the picture long and hard, noting all her new changes.

The lights in the room flickered, and a soft applause arose as a woman dressed in all-white stepped onto the platform.

"We will begin now," she said. "Thank you ladies and gentlemen for attending the Annual New York City Ballet Company Gala. It is with great honor and pride that we present tonight's artists—principle dancers, soloists, and corps members. As you know, due to quite a few unfortunate circumstances, we had to replace nearly ninety percent of our group over the past few months, but as always, the show must go on. And, I truly believe that this is the best class we've had in a very long time."

The audience clapped.

"Our company will be performing several productions this year, but the ones that will be presented this winter are *The Firebird*, *Jewels*, and our company favorite, *Swan Lake*."

More applause.

"Tonight, our corps will introduce themselves to you personally and perform small tributes as a thank you for your continued support of the arts. And as always, when it comes to the art of dance, please do not applaud until after the last note has played. Thank you." She walked away and the lights transformed from a stark white to an airy blue, then they dissolved into heavy hues of purple and pink.

One by one, the dancers came out—reciting a short monologue and dancing to a short piece of piano music. While most of the performers were entertaining, a few of them made me wonder if they'd simply awoken this morning and decided try ballet for the first time.

In between the sets, I could hear a few murmurs from the crowd: "Are they sure this is their best cohort?" "Maybe they should've canceled the season after that accident..." "Hopefully, they'll be having nonstop rehearsals until the season actually begins..."

A man next to me was whispering about how he missed "the good old days of the company" when Aubrey stepped onto the floor.

She was wearing a thin black top and a pink tutu, and her lips were coated in a deep dark red.

"Good evening, New York City," she said. "My name is Aubrey Everhart, and…"

She was saying something else, something that made the audience clap loudly, but I could only focus on how good she looked. I'd never admit it to anyone, but I'd kept that photo frame of us on my nightstand ever since she left—looking at her pretty face at night whenever I had a bad day.

Tonight she wasn't "pretty," though. She was a fucking vision.

Her mouth stopped moving amidst another round of applause from the audience, and the soft sounds of a piano and harp slowly filled the room.

Aubrey shut her eyes and started her routine, dancing as if she was the only person here.

There was an immediate change in the gala's atmosphere. Everyone watching her was fully engaged—captivated, by her every move.

Out of nowhere, a male dancer joined her, picking her up and holding her high above his head—spinning her around as the music became harsher. After he set her down, the two of them completed steps together—smiling at each other and exchanging glances that made it clear that they knew each other a little too well.

The second the music stopped, the male dancer pulled her into his arms and kissed her lips.

What the fuck…

The crowd stood to its feet and clapped for the first time all night, but I remained seated, completely taken aback by what the fuck I just saw.

"Maybe I won't have to cancel my season tickets after all, eh?" The man next to me winked. "Bravissimo!"

I narrowed my eyes at Aubrey and her partner, seething as he wrapped an arm around her waist and strummed his fingers against her skin. He whispered into her ear and she blushed, making my blood pressure soar to an all-time high.

"Well, what a response!" The director took the floor. "Thank you, Miss Everhart and Mr. Williams. I want you all to know that those two will be headlining next month's Silver Moon Gala as well…" She continued talking, saying more about the program, but her words were soundless to me.

I was confused by what I just saw—not sure if Aubrey's mouth had actually been on someone else.

More dancers took the floor, more applause, more speeches, and my thoughts remained the same. It wasn't until the patrons took the floor, that I realized that the showcase part of this evening was over.

"Are you interested in donating to the NYCB?" A ballerina, still dressed in her white performance outfit, stepped in front of me. "Would you like to make a contribution?"

"My *contribution* was the ticket I bought for tonight." I stood up, leaving the flower bouquet behind, and walked off in search of Aubrey.

It didn't take long to find her.

Dressed in a rather revealing silver dress, she was in a corner laughing with her male dancer friend, batting her eyes as he handed her a drink.

"Excuse me, sir?" Someone tapped me on the shoulder.

"Yes?" I kept my eyes on Aubrey.

"Um, if you stay for the after-portion of the event, you have to donate…It's part of the rules. It was written in bold so—"

"Here." I handed her whatever bills were left in my wallet.

She disappeared.

Aubrey's friend kissed her forehead and stepped away, giving me the perfect opportunity to approach, but she was swarmed by a group of other ballerinas.

Friends, it seemed.

I waited for their conversation to end, until she told them she'd join them later, and then I made my move.

As she turned around, I placed my hand on her shoulder--feeling a jolt shoot through my veins. "Good evening, Aubrey…"

She dropped her glass to the floor and slowly turned around.

"*Andrew?*" She stepped back. "What are you doing here?"

"Does it matter?"

She didn't answer.

Neither of us said anything further, and that familiar tension that had always existed between us began to thicken with every second that passed.

She looked even more beautiful up close, and I was tempted to push her against the wall and reconnect, but I held back.

"Can I speak with you?" I asked.

She looked me up and down.

"Aubrey…" I looked into her eyes. "Can I speak with you?"

"No."

"Excuse me?" I raised my eyebrow.

"I said *no*." She crossed her arms. "As in, *no* you may not speak with me, and you can go back to wherever the hell you came from."

She walked away and headed to the dance floor.

I sighed and went after her, clasping her hand and spinning her around. "It'll only take five minutes."

"That's five more than I'm willing to give you."

"It's important."

"Are you *dying*?" Her face turned red. "Is it a life or death matter?"

"Does it really have to be?" My hand caressed her cheek, temporarily silencing her. "You look fucking beautiful tonight…"

"Thank you. My boyfriend thinks so, too."

"Your *boyfriend*?"

"Yes. You know, that person who doesn't treat you like shit just because he likes you and you like him back? Interesting concept, isn't it?"

I didn't get a chance to respond to that.

The orchestra struck a sudden loud chord that reverberated through the room, and a voice came over the speakers.

"Ladies and gentlemen," it said. "The Benjamin Wright Orchestra will now play their rendition of one of Tchaikovsky's most revered pieces. The tempo of this song has a similar pacing for what some of you may know as the waltz. Please join us on the floor for this classic homage…"

I grabbed her hand and entwined it with mine, securing my free hand around her waist.

"What are you doing?" She hissed and tried to pull away. "I'm not dancing with you."

I tightened my grip around her. "*Yes you are.*"

"Please don't make me scream, Andrew…"

"What makes you think I wouldn't love to hear that?"

She tried to move away from me, but I held her still.

"Five minutes," I said.

"*Three*," she countered.

"Fine." I loosened my grip and swayed her to the music. "Are you aware that your boyfriend is a *male ballerina?*"

"The correct term," she said, rolling her eyes, "is a danseur."

"He's a fucking ballerina…" I dipped her to the floor. "Is this what you've been doing for the past few months?"

"Living out my dream free from a certain asshole?"

"I expect more from you if you're going to date someone else."

"I don't give a damn what you expect." She hissed. "He's everything you'll *never* be…"

"Because he kisses you in public?"

"It's more than that…But that's on the never-ending list of things he has on you."

"Does he make you cum?"

"He doesn't make me *cry.*"

Silence.

I felt her pulling away from me, but I held her still. "Are you fucking him?"

"Why do you care?"

"I don't. I just want to know."

"We haven't had a conversation in months and you think you're entitled to know who I'm sleeping with?"

"I wouldn't necessarily use the term *entitled.*"

"No." She pressed her chest against mine. "No, I am not fucking him, but you know what? I will be soon."

"You have no reason to if I'm here."

She burst into laughter and stepped back. "You think I would sleep with you? Seriously?"

"Aubrey—"

"Do you really think I'm that stupid?" She cut me off. "I don't want anything to do with you, Andrew. You're nothing but a muse for an orgasm, a good visual for a hand-fuck, and I may miss you, but—"

"You miss me?"

"I miss the *idea* of you—of what you could've been."

"We can't be friends?"

"We can't be anything." Her lips were close to mine.

"Why am I finding that hard to believe?"

"You shouldn't." She glared at me. "Because in order for me to ever entertain you outside of this dance, I would have to take you back."

"Then take me back."

"*Please!*" She scoffed, looking angrier than I'd ever seen her before. "You would have to beg me to take you back, Andrew. Fucking *beg* me…"

"Hey Aubs." Her ballerina boyfriend interrupted us. "Is everything okay?"

"Yes." She stepped away from me and kissed his cheek. "Everything is more than okay."

"Who's your friend?"

"*No one*," she said. "Just some guy who made a donation."

"Thank you for your donation." He shook my hand like a woman and turned to Aubrey. "Are you ready to go home?"

"More than ready." She took his hand and walked away from me without glancing back.

I stood on the balcony of my hotel room, completely confused about what had happened a few hours ago. I was expecting Aubrey to leave with me, to come back to my hotel so we could fuck and catch up.

Unable to stop thinking about it, I sent her an email:

**Subject: Your Address.**

We need to finish our conversation. Tell me where you live so I can come over and talk.

—Andrew.


**Subject: Re: Your Address.**

I highly doubt you only want to talk. You just want to fuck.

Nonetheless, I'm pretty sure Brian wouldn't appreciate you coming over tonight.

—Aubrey.

**Subject: Re: Re: Your Address.**

He's more than welcome to watch. He might actually learn something.

—Andrew.

No answer.

She didn't respond for a long time, and when she finally did, all she sent me was a text:

"Leave me alone, Andrew. Please."

I couldn't. I emailed her again.

**Subject: Sponsor.**

I bought golden level season tickets. One of the benefits is getting a tour from the cast-mate of my choice. It will definitely be you.

—Andrew.


**Subject: Re: Sponsor.**

Thank you for that pointless information. If you do choose me, we won't be alone, and I'll make sure that our tour ends in the exact time allotted.

Now, please leave me alone. I'm out with someone who admires my brain more than my pussy.

You had your chance, you fucked up, and I'm not sure why you're in New York right now but I really don't care.

I seriously don't want to hear from you...Please go away.

—Aubrey

I sighed and scrolled down my contacts. I knew she was simply being difficult, and I wasn't going to let her get the last word. I pressed call on an old number and held it up to my ear.

"Who is this?" the old voice said over the line.

"I need an address."

"Who is this?"

"I need an address. Now."

"Liam?" There was a smile in his voice. "Is that you?"

"It's *Andrew*." I rolled my eyes. "Are you going to help me or not?"

"Well, since you asked so nicely..." There was a familiar humming sound in the background. "You know, I haven't heard from you since the last time I saw..." He stopped himself and cleared his throat. "What's the name?"

"Aubrey Everhart."

"Do you know what borough?"

"No," I said. "But the address can't be more than a few months old. She just moved here."

He was silent for a little while, tapping and touching buttons.

"Found it," he said. "7654 Fifth Avenue."

Five blocks away...

I thought about whether I should wait until morning to stop by, but I was already putting on my coat.

"It was nice hearing from you again, Liam..." the old man's voice brought me back to the present. "Good to know you're well and...getting over what happened."

"I'll never get over it." I hung up and headed outside, signaling for the town car driver to open the back door.

"Where to, Mr. Hamilton?" he asked.

"7654 Fifth Avenue."

"Right away."

It took less than twenty minutes to get there, and when we arrived I stared at the brownstone for a while. It looked like something I would've purchased years ago when I lived here, something far out of budget for a ballerina, so I figured her parents were paying the rent.

Stepping out of the car, I adjusted my coat and walked to her door—knocking five times.

"Coming!" She yelled.

The door swung open, but she wasn't standing behind it. It was her boyfriend.

"Um..." He looked confused. "Did you leave the pizza in your car or something?"

"I'm not a fucking pizza guy. Where is Aubrey?"

203

"It depends. Didn't we just see you at the gala?" He crossed his arms as Aubrey stepped into the doorway. "Who are you?"

"He's no one, *again*," she said, standing on her toes to kiss his lips.

He looked at me with his eyebrow raised as he returned her kiss.

"My cock has been in every inch of her mouth." I gritted my teeth.

Aubrey gasped, her cheeks turning bright red. "I am so sorry, Brian... Can you give us a moment please?"

He looked between the both of us, anger creeping onto his face, but he walked away.

"What do you fucking want, Andrew?" She fumed. "*What do you want?*"

"To talk."

"About *what?*"

"You and me, about us being friends again..."

"That will never fucking happen. Is that it?"

"Aubrey—"

"What brings you to New York, huh? Did you need to come back and fuck some familiar women on Date-Match? Did Durham somehow run out of pussy?"

"It's actually starting to feel that way."

She started to close the door, but I held it still with my hand.

"I miss you, Aubrey..." I looked directly into her eyes. "I really do, and I'm...I'm sorry for kicking you out that night."

"You should be." Her voice was a whisper. "And if you really miss me, you'll leave me alone."

"Why would I do that?"

"Because you're bipolar. Because the second I ask one too many questions, or suggest something outside of your comfort zone, you'll treat me like trash again and I'd rather cut my losses now." She wiped a tear from her eyes. "I was your only friend—your only fucking friend, and you treated me worse than any of the women you met online. If anything, *I'm* sorry that I ever let you do that. Please leave."

"Aubrey, listen..."

"Is there super glue on my floor?" She pushed me down a step. "Is that why you're still standing there?"

"Please, just—"

"Lie about one thing, lie about it all, right?" She pushed me again. "You're still the biggest liar between the two of us. Lying by omission is still lying."

"Can you please calm down and let me talk about this with you inside?"

"I thought you hated rhetorical questions." She slammed the door in my face.

# A Priori Assumption (n.):
An assumption that is true without further proof or
need to prove it.

*Aubrey*

I woke up the next morning on edge, in utter shock.

I couldn't believe Andrew was in New York, couldn't believe he'd admitted missing me on my front steps last night.

Seeing him again brought out every emotion in me, and even though I'd told Brian that Andrew and I were done, I'd spent the rest of our date last night thinking about him.

Him and his perfect suit. Him and his perfect lips that nearly pressed against mine as we argued. And, shamefully, him and his perfect cock that I felt hardening in his pants as he dipped me on the dance floor.

Ugh!

I got out of bed and sent Brian a text. "Today is my one on one day with Ashcroft...Wish me luck!"

His response came immediately. "Good luck, babe! Get some coffee, you're going to need it..."

Slipping into the shower, I scolded myself. "Brian is a sweetheart and he's good for you...He may suck at phone sex, and you may have no desire to sleep with him right now, but he treats you better than you've ever been treated before..."

When I was wrinkled and prune-like, I stepped out and checked the time.

4:30 a.m.

I had twenty minutes to make it to the closest subway station and avoid the ire of Ashcroft. Throwing on some old sweatpants, I grabbed my ballet bag and snatched my coat from the bannister in the hallway. I double checked my wallet to make sure I had my metro pass, and when I opened the door, I found myself face to face with a stranger and a cup of steaming hot coffee.

"Good luck at practice today," he said, handing it over. "This was made especially for you."

"Since when do coffee shops deliver?"

He shrugged. "They don't."

I stared at the cup as he walked away, noticing that my name was etched atop the whipped cream in thin caramel, and that "Good luck," was written in cursive on the label.

It was a signature, sweet Brian move, and I immediately felt guilty for not giving him my full attention last night. As I walked to the subway, sipping what was arguably the best coffee I'd ever had, I vowed to give him my full attention from here on out.

I deleted all of Andrew's old texts and emails, even the ones I'd fake deleted by placing them in the archive. I blocked his number, preventing his calls from ever getting through, and although I couldn't block his emails, I changed the settings of my inbox so they would go straight to my spam folder.

When I finally arrived at practice that morning, I danced better than I'd ever danced before…

*Later that night…*

"How do you find the time to take the subway just to meet me at practice and walk me home?" I looked up at Brian as we crossed the street. "Where do you find the energy?"

"I make time for all the things I really like." He kissed my forehead.

"Do you want to catch a movie this weekend? My treat? I owe you one…"

"What makes you say that?"

"I still feel bad about gala night and what that guy from my past said to you," I said. "I'm really sorry."

"No worries. I'm sure he's—" He stopped talking as we approached my house, pointing at the man who was leaning against the door.

Andrew.

I took a deep breath as Andrew walked down the steps.

"Good evening, Aubrey," he said, smirking. "And your name is *danseur*, correct?"

"It's *Brian*."

"Close enough."

Brian crossed his arms. "I could've sworn I overheard her say that she didn't want you anymore. Why can't you take the hint?"

"Because she says things she doesn't mean all the time." He looked at me, instantly setting my nerves on fire. "And I know she's just angry with me."

"Dude!" Brian let out an exasperated sigh. "I'm her boyfriend so clearly she's moved on...She has a *boyfriend*."

"I honestly don't feel threatened," he said, still looking at me. "Did you get my coffee this morning?"

*What?!* "That was from you?" My eyes widened. "I thought..."

"What coffee, Aubs?" Brian looked concerned. "What is he talking about?"

"Andrew..." I shook my head. "Thank you for the coffee, but that doesn't make up for anything..."

"I never said it did."

A cold wind brushed by and I felt myself being drawn to him, literally drawn to him, and I took a few steps forward. But then I took a few steps back.

"I'm with Brian now..." I grabbed Brian's hand and led him up to my door, refusing to look back at a seemingly hurt Andrew.

I shut the door and peeped through my blinds, noticing that he was still standing there. Confused.

"Look, Aubs..." The sound of Brian's voice got my attention. "I don't think the two of us are going to work."

"*What?* No, no, no. Of course, we will. This is just a minor issue."

"I think your heart and mind are elsewhere...I think they always have been, actually."

"Seriously?" I crossed my arms. "Because some psycho from my past shows up for one night and suddenly wants me again? That's what makes you think that?"

"That, and the fact that some psycho sent me a text earlier today that said, "Her pussy belongs to me." I'm just now remembering that..."

I sighed and he walked over, kissing my forehead.

"If it's a minor issue, and he doesn't mean anything to you anymore, we can try again in a month."

"A month?"

He nodded. "That way I'll know for sure, and our phone sex will be twice as amazing since we won't have had it in so long...Then, maybe we can upgrade to actual sex."

I said nothing, and he walked out of my place.

I peeped through the blinds again, watching him disappear into the night, and then I noticed that Andrew was still standing outside.

Livid, I stomped down the steps and headed straight toward him. "Do you have any idea how much I hate you right now?"

"Hate isn't something that can be adequately measured."

"You just ruined the one great relationship I had in this city. You just made him dump me."

"Good," he said. "I did you a favor."

"Is this how you're planning on getting me to talk to you again?"

"Part of it."

"It's not going to work." I pressed my finger against his chest, emphasizing every syllable. "I told you that you would have to fucking beg me, and since I know that's not how you operate—"

"You don't know how I fucking operate."

"Are you going to walk me to the subway station every morning?"

"I have a fucking car."

"Walk me back from rehearsals?"

"Same answer."

"Actually treat me with some goddamn respect?"

He cupped my face in his hands. "If you give me a chance to..."

I stepped back, still angry. "I'm not holding my breath."

# Omission (n.):
Inadvertently leaving out a word, phrase or other
language from a contract, deed, judgment or other
document.

### *Aubrey*

**Subject: Brian-gate.**

I'm not sure how many more times I'll have to apologize for
making your "boyfriend" dump you, but I am, in fact, sorry.
Then again, maybe I should have waited until after you fucked
him so you could be more appreciative.

—Andrew

"Ugh!" I tossed my phone across the room, nearly knocking over
the beautiful vase of lilies he sent me yesterday.

Ever since last week's "Brian-gate," I had to face him every day
in some capacity. In the mornings, he personally brought me my
favorite coffee, walked me to the block where my subway stop was,
and apologized profusely. In his own way, of course.

I never said a word back, though. I just sipped from my cup
and listened.

Taking a seat on my couch, I grabbed an ice wrap and placed it
on my shoulders. I was counting down the days to opening night,
wondering how much more pain my body could take.

My feet were now unrecognizable; I no longer soothed their
cuts and blisters. The muscles in my arms ached relentlessly, and
when I told Mr. Ashcroft that I needed a few extra minutes to
stretch my right leg yesterday, he said, "Then I need to replace you

with a dancer who doesn't."

I cringed at the memory and heard a knock at my door.

"Coming!" I walked over and opened it, tempted to slam it shut once I saw Andrew.

"Yes?" I asked.

"Practice starts in an hour. You're going to be late."

"I'm not due there until the afternoon session. Thank you for the reminder."

"Can I come in until then?"

"No."

"Why not?"

"Do I really need a reason?"

"I just want to talk to you for a few minutes, Aubrey."

"We can do that over the phone."

"You blocked my fucking number." He narrowed his eyes at me. "I've tried that already today. Twice."

"Have you tried email?"

"Aubrey, please…" He actually looked sincere.

"Fine." I held the door open. "But you have to leave in five minutes so I can take a nap."

He stepped inside and looked around, running his hands over the artwork in the halls.

Looking slightly impressed, he rubbed his chin. "Are your parents paying for this?"

"No, I haven't spoken to them since I left." I admitted. "A retired dancer from the company rents out all her condos to the newest cohorts."

"Is it expensive?"

"Not at all." I sat on the couch. "It's the only way I can afford to live in this part of town. Otherwise, I'd be sleeping in a cardboard box."

He stared at me for a while, not saying a word.

"What is it?" I asked.

"Nothing. It's just been awhile since you spoke a full sentence that wasn't filled with malice."

"Don't get used to it." I winced and placed another ice wrap on my shoulder. "I'm just trying to make your five minutes with me somewhat memorable."

"They will be."

Silence.

He walked over and sat next to me on the couch. "You got an A on your final assignment at GBH."

"Did you give it to me out of sympathy?"

"I gave it to you because your work was the best." He looked into my eyes. "Although, I could have done without the "FYI: Mr. Hamilton used to fuck me in his office" note that was at the end."

I held back a laugh.

"Jessica misses you by the way."

"Really?"

"She claims I was much more desirable when you were around," he said. "And apparently she used to listen to us have sex."

"What?"

"There's no point in even trying to fire her anymore…I think she grew on me."

"Do all the interns still hate you?"

"No." He smiled. "For some strange reason, they started to like me shortly after you left."

"Are you insinuating that your asshole behavior was my fault?"

"No." He pulled me into his lap and took the ice wrap away. "I'm insinuating that I no longer pretend to care about any interns when my favorite one is missing."

I blushed and he started to massage my shoulders—slowly kneading his hands against my skin.

I shut my eyes and exhaled, slightly tilting my head back instead of telling him to stop.

"Do you plan on ever accepting my apology?" he asked, pressing a kiss against my neck.

"No."

"Is there any way that I could *make you*?" His fingers gently rubbed my collarbone, alleviating the pain.

"You could tell me the real reason you're in New York…" I felt him unsnapping my bra. "I know you didn't come all the way here just to see me."

He kissed my shoulder. "You *don't* know that."

"I'm serious, Andrew."

"As am I." He pressed his palms into my back, temporarily rendering me speechless. "You're a huge part of the reason why I'm still here, actually."

"And the other part?"

He tilted my head back so I was looking directly into his eyes. "The other part doesn't really matter." He looked as if he wanted to kiss me, but he held back.

Instead, he slipped his hands underneath my legs and flipped me over so I was lying in his lap. "What time is your rehearsal again?"

"Four..." I barely managed. His touches felt too good.

"Can I drive you?" He softly kneaded the back of my shoulders. "I can do this to you for longer if you don't take the subway..."

I nodded and shut my eyes, falling asleep at the mercy of his hands.

Hours later, Andrew pulled over to the curb at Lincoln Center.

I unbuckled my seatbelt and looked at him. "Are you going to be standing outside the ballet hall when I get done today?"

"Probably."

"With hot chocolate?"

"Would you prefer something different?"

I smiled. "No..."

He leaned over and tucked a strand of hair behind my ear. "I thought I was doing the right thing by kicking you out that night, by pushing you away...It was definitely a mistake."

"I'm not coming back to you just because you said that."

"I didn't ask you to." He trailed his finger against my lips. "I would, however, like you to consider forgiving me."

"I'll think about it. Just because you—"

His lips were on mine—kissing me, begging me, saying all the things he couldn't say with words. And this time I was listening, missing everything we once had before he pushed me away.

Not letting me go, he ran his fingers through my hair and caressed my neck.

"Go think about *that*," he whispered, slowly pulling away from me.

"Um..." I struggled to catch my breath as he stepped out to open my door.

"I'll see you tonight." He kissed my lips before leaving me standing in the middle of the street, completely breathless again.

Shit...

I headed toward the dance hall, confident that I would dance like I was on air today. I opened the doors and felt someone grabbing my shoulder from behind.

"Aubrey?" The voice asked. "Aubrey, is that you?"

I turned around, shocked. "*Mom*? What are you doing here?"

"I wanted to see you…"

I noticed the pin on her suit, "Vote Smart. Vote Everhart," and knew that wasn't true. She was in town for something that had to do with my father's campaign; I was only a pit stop.

"Well, now you've seen me…" I turned away and slipped inside the building.

"Wait, Aubrey." She followed me. "Do you really think that moving across the country was the best way to get me and your father's attention?"

"I didn't leave North Carolina to get your attention."

"Well, you certainly have it."

"And look, it only took twenty two years…"

She sighed. "We've decided to talk to the department chair about letting you pick up where you left off during the summer semester. We can do that since you're so upset about being a part of the campaign."

"I'm not upset. I honestly don't care."

"Of course you do." She sounded offended. "But if it makes you feel any better, we placed a picture of you and one of your ballets in our campaign brochure."

"Did you do that so you could look like you actually care about college arts?"

"No, we donated fifty thousand dollars to Duke's dance program to look like we actually care about college arts. The brochure picture was *personal*, although it would've been even better if you wrote that essay we begged you to write. We could've put that next to the picture. "

I felt a pang in my chest. "When does your flight leave, mother?"

"Excuse me?"

"When does your flight leave?" I repeated, my voice cracking. "I'm pretty sure it's in three hours or less so you won't have to spend a full day here, so you can go back and tell Dad that you tried to convince me to come home after you fulfilled your campaign work. I'm sure that's still all that matters to you."

She was silent.

"I left Durham because I'll be living here for at least three years—which is the length of my contract with the company, where I'll be pursuing my real dream. And I must say, it's just a bonus that I won't be anywhere near you."

She gasped.

"Have a safe flight. Tell Dad I said hello."

"You're just going to leave me standing here?"

"You've done it to me my entire life." I left the building. I was too angry, too hurt, to completely focus.

I sent Ashcroft an email—letting him know I was using a sick day, and headed for the street.

"Aubrey!" My mother called from behind, but I kept walking. "Aubrey, wait!"

She finally caught up to me and grabbed my arm. "I can miss my flight…"

"And why would you want to do that?"

"So I can spend time with my daughter before she forgets that I exist…"

I held back tears.

"I can stay here for a few days and we can catch up in between your dance schedule," she said. "I'll make your dad fly up too if that's okay with you?"

"That would be perfectly fine…" I nodded, but then it hit me. "No campaign talk, though."

"Done deal."

"No talking about me going back to law school, either."

"I can live with that, too." She nodded.

"And no talking shit about ballet."

She hesitated, but she nodded again. "Okay, fine." She hugged me. "Can you hail us a cab so I can book a room at the Four Seasons?"

"Why? You can just stay at my place."

"Oh, please." She slid a pair of shades over her eyes. "I looked up what professional ballerinas make. I know what type of apartment you can afford in this city, and daughter or not, I refuse."

I didn't want to laugh, but I couldn't help it. I knew making up would be a long process, but I was willing to give it a try.

She walked over to a newspaper stand, and I held out my hand for a cab.

"Oh, *The New York Times* always picks the best cases to cover."
She flipped through the paper. "There's one hell of a trial going on
this week."

"Criminal or corporate?" I asked as a taxi flew right past me.

"Both," she said. "And I actually know this guy. Well, I know *of*
him anyway...Absolutely incredible lawyer..."

"We're never going to get a cab at this rate." I shook my head at
being snubbed again.

"I doubt he'll ever get recognition for that government case..."

"What are you talking about?"

"Liam Henderson." She held the paper in front of me, pointing
to a picture-less article. "Remember? He's on me and your dad's
list of lawyers who'll never be given the credit they deserve because
they went against the government. This guy was your favorite, I do
believe."

"Oh, yeah." I remembered. "So, why is he in the paper now?
Did he mess up because he didn't receive his due fame? Is he in
trouble?"

"No, looks like he's just testifying in a case. Article claims he's
been living down in the South and even partnered at some firm,
but that can't be true. Any firm down there would be bragging if
they had him, and I haven't heard anything."

"I'm sure they would." I finally waved down a cab. "We can go
now."

"It's quite weird though." She tapped her lip. "In all of his
career, I've never seen a picture of him—maybe one or two, but
they were stock pictures from his college days. I'm sure he looks
different now."

"Mom," I said, opening the car door. "The cab charges by the
minute."

"Now the article claims he's been living in North Carolina
under an assumed name for the past six years. But of course,
they're not revealing *that* name. They need to get better researchers,
don't you think? How could a lawyer of that status manage to
change his name, switch states, and still practice the law?" She
handed me the paper as she stepped into the cab. "He'd have to
erase his entire identity and start all over. Who would do that?"

I gasped and flipped to the article as I sat in the backseat. I read
it word for word, over and over, and everything around me became

a blur. I could practically feel my jaw dropping as I flashed back to my first interview at GBH:

*Miss Everhart, are there any lawyers that you wish to model your own career after?" Mr. Bach smiled at me.*

*"Yes, actually," I said. "I've always admired the career of Liam Henderson."*

*"Liam Henderson?" Andrew looked up at me with his eyebrow raised. "Who is that?"*

## Suppression of Evidence (n.):
The improper hiding of evidence by a prosecutor who is constitutionally required to reveal to the defense all evidence

*Andrew*

# Former Partners to Finally Appear in Court Opposite Each Other: Hart Case Continues This Week.

That's what the headline in the judicial section of *The New York Times* read this morning. To those who knew nothing about the case, I was sure that it was simply another story to pass the time, another superficial scandal to devour with their morning breakfast.

But for me, it was the end of a six year chapter that had gone on for far too many pages. It was part of the reason why I left, part of the reason why after I testified in a few days, I would leave this city for the very last time.

I looked outside the window at the Waldorf Astoria's restaurant, wondering how it could possibly be raining so heavily in the dead of winter.

"Mr. Hamilton?" A woman in a suit stepped next to my table.

"Yes?"

"I'm Vera Milton, the general manager," she said. "You've had several calls from a Miss Ava Sanchez… She keeps telling us that it's important and that she needs to speak with you. She's on the line for you now…"

I sighed. "Could you patch her call to my room in two minutes please?"

"Certainly sir."

I left the newspaper on the table and headed straight for the penthouse suite. As soon as I unlocked the door, the phone in the parlor room rang.

"Hello?" I answered.

"It's me…" Ava said softly.

"I'm aware. How did you find out where I was staying?"

"Really?" She scoffed. "I need you to do me a favor…"

"Goodbye, Ava."

"No, wait." She sounded frantic. "I really am sorry for everything I did to you, Liam."

"What did I tell you about calling me that?"

"I remember when you visited me when I was being held in jail—before all the hearings started…Remember?" She paused. "I know how hard seeing me must have been back then, how lonely you had to be to come and visit *me* of all people…You even told me you were contemplating changing your name to Andrew and leaving New York…And then I begged you to save me. Remember that?"

"I'm really not in the mood for story time right now."

"You were such a softie back then…So compassionate, so caring—"

"Get to the fucking point, Ava."

"At the trial this week, I know that Kevin—"

"I.e. my former best friend that you fucked?"

"Yes." She sighed. "Him…"

"What about him?"

"He's not the monster you think he is."

"Are you calling about a favor that's never going to happen, or are you calling to be his fucking character witness? I'm confused."

"He's still sorry for what he did…He was—"

"Which one is it, Ava?" I snapped. "I'm not a fan of this vague shit."

"Do you really want to hurt him?" Her voice softened. "I think you've already punished us enough. I'm already behind bars, so there's really no need for him to suffer at this point. "

"The two of you will never suffer enough." I hung up and sent a text to an old contact I had at corrections, telling him that Ava had contraband in her cell.

The last thing I wanted to think about was my old partner and former best friend. The only time he needed to be thought of was during the upcoming hearing, and never again after that.

I scrolled through my text messages, noticing that Aubrey had sent me a simple "Okay" when I asked how today's audition went.

With the exception of the day I massaged her shoulders, she was still being short with me.

I opened my inbox to send her a longer message, but I saw that she'd sent me one first.

**Subject: Yes.**

I just received your newest set of flowers and your note about going on a date tonight...I have a few stipulations, though.

—Aubrey

**Subject: Re: Yes.**

Name them.

—Andrew

She sent a new message.

**Subject: Date.**

I'm allowed to ask you whatever I want and you have to answer truthfully.

—Aubrey

**Subject: Re: Date.**

I always answer truthfully. Is the word "stipulations" not plural?

—Andrew

**Subject: Re: Re: Date.**

You have to be a complete gentleman. I don't want to be fucked
in another bathroom...

What time are you picking me up?

—Aubrey

**Subject: Re: Re: Re: Date.**

I actually wasn't planning on fucking you tonight, but since
you've clearly entertained that possibility, I'll be sure to send a list
of potential locations prior to the date.

Eight o' clock.

—Andrew

I knocked on her door at 7:58, dressed in a black designer suit I'd
purchased hours ago.

There was no answer, and before I could knock again, the door
swung open and she stepped out wearing a short black dress that
left little to the imagination.

"Are you aware that it's still winter?" I trailed my finger along
her exposed shoulders. "You're going to need a coat."

She looked behind me. "You took the subway here?"

"Yes."

"We're taking the subway on our *date*?"

"The car will come later." I smiled as confusion spread across
her face.

She grabbed her coat from inside and shut the door, looking up
at me. "Do you even know how to use the subway?"

"Of course I do," I said, clasping her hand. "I wasn't always
well-off when I lived here..."

A light snow fell as we made our way to the subway tunnel, and
she leaned against me—pressing her body closer to mine. Holiday
lights were strung about the tallest buildings—sparkling against the

night, and a faint sense of excitement swirled through the air.

There weren't that many people out tonight, and as we boarded a nearly empty train, Aubrey laughed at that fact.

"This is the first time I've ever seen a subway like this," she said. "I usually have to fight for my own tiny space."

"Hmmm." I prevented her from taking a seat, instead making her share a pole with me. "How did your audition really go today? Surely you have more to say about it than okay."

"I was crying when I sent that text. I was overwhelmed."

I raised my eyebrow.

"I landed Odette/Odile in *Swan Lake*—on a *professional* level." She looked as if she was about to burst into tears. "I still can't believe it...All of my dreams are actually coming true."

"Maybe you're meant to play that role..." I wiped a stray tear from her eyes.

"Maybe." She leaned closer. "I'm just happy that they're giving us the next few days off...I think I'll be able to relax and keep up with the news a bit more. You know, actually have some semblance of a life outside of the dance hall."

"You could spend more time with me if you want to take a break. The news in this city is overrated and mostly false."

"Is that so?"

"Yes," I said, looking into her eyes. "I wouldn't believe half of the shit in any of these papers."

She smiled. "Have you heard anything about the huge trial that's happening this week?"

"I'm pretty sure there's more than one."

"No..." She shook her head. "Not like this one..."

I hesitated. "What makes this one so special?"

"It's more intriguing than special...It's about two lawyers who once shared a firm—both of them were big shots, you know? One of them even won against the government in his very first case."

"It was probably a lucky break."

"I don't think so." She looked into my eyes. "I've read the transcripts. He knew exactly what he was doing, and the verdict actually affected public policy."

I said nothing.

"But the thing is, he never got credit for his work—outside of word of mouth from people who knew the details, you know?" She paused. "But anyway, from what I've read and pieced together, it seems like he was falsely accused of a laundry list of federal charges a few years later."

"*Aubrey…*"

"It looks like everyone ran with the story—all of the papers, all of the news outlets, and the truth wasn't filtered until months later, after his name was already tarnished."

I stared at her, begging her to stop, but she continued.

"The charges are still pending against his old partner to this day, that's just how many there were. But *him*—this upstanding lawyer with one hell of a track record, he just vanished. Into thin air."

"If he was that upstanding, then I'm pretty sure that's impossible."

"Is it?"

"*It is*," I said.

"I thought that, too…" She searched my eyes for answers. "But I think the guy I'm talking about is capable of anything."

"What are the names in this case you're speaking of?"

"The accused is Kevin Hart, and the key witness is Liam Henderson."

"I'll google it tonight." I sighed, not wanting to continue this conversation.

A voice came over the speakers, announcing our stop, and I took her hand again.

"I know you made me agree to stipulations," I said, looking at her as we stepped off, "but can you agree to one of mine?"

"Depends on what it is."

"Ask me the deep conversation questions after dinner."

"Is that where we're going right now?"

"No." I led her up the steps. "I wouldn't dare. I don't want you accusing me of treating you like all my other dates."

"Does that mean you won't fuck me at the end?"

"It means I won't leave you at the end."

She blushed, and I kissed her forehead as we walked through the streets of flashing lights and sparkling billboards.

She didn't say much of anything else as we moved from block to block, only blushing each time I looked at her.

"Here," I said, stopping her as we approached our first destination.

"Broadway?" She looked up at the grand marquis.

"You mentioned you haven't had the chance to come here yet,"

I said. "I used to come here all the time when I lived here…"

"All the time?"

"At least once a week." I held the door open for her. "Twice when this particular play was performed." I ran my fingers across the words, *Death of a Salesman*, before handing our tickets to the usher.

She smiled as he led us to the private balcony, as he offered us complimentary wine since we were so early.

"I would've never taken you for the drama type," she said, taking a sip from her glass. "You've never mentioned that to me before."

"I actually almost went to theater school instead of law school."

"What made you change your mind?"

"A law degree attracts a higher percentage of pussy."

"What?!" She rolled her eyes, laughing. "I'm being serious."

"I received a bigger scholarship for law school." I resisted the urge to pull her into my lap. "Best decision I ever made."

She opened her mouth to respond, but the lights began to dim and she leaned closer to me, whispering, "I would've liked to see you as an actor…I think you would've been really good at it."

I felt her placing her hand on my thigh. "I don't think I would've wanted to see you play anything serious though. I think I would prefer—"

"Are you going to talk through this entire play, Aubrey?" I cut her off, ignoring the tell-tale look on her face—the one of severe longing, needing.

"Am I not allowed to make comments?" She sounded offended. "Am I not allowed to do that until *after dinner* either? If that's the case, why even take me out? Why would you even—"

"I've seen this play a million times…" I pressed my finger against her lips as the lead actor stepped onto the stage. "And although I want you to experience it too, if you would rather me entertain you in a *different* way, just tell me."

"What?"

"Would this balcony make it onto your list of approved places?" I asked. "If I fucked you here, would that still count as me being a gentleman?"

Her eyes widened and she quickly moved her hand away from my lap. "I was just teasing you, Andrew…"

"I'm aware." I kissed her neck. "And I've told you on numerous occasions that I don't appreciate that, whether you're mad at me or not..."

She sucked in a breath as I slid my thumb underneath her panties.

"I'll stop asking questions," she said. "I'll watch the play..."

As she turned her face toward the stage, I moved out of my seat and kneeled in front of her.

"Andrew?" She whispered harshly as I spread her thighs apart. "What are you doing?"

"Making sure you enjoy the show."

I didn't give her a chance to respond. I quickly ripped off her panties, and buried my head in between her legs, running my tongue against her bare pussy—enjoying a taste I'd missed for months. I sucked her clit between my lips, shutting my eyes as it swelled in my mouth.

"Andrew...." She moaned as she squeezed her legs around my neck, grabbing onto my hair and begging me to slow down.

I couldn't. She tasted too fucking good.

I forced my tongue deeper inside of her, claiming every part, marking what was mine.

Her hips began to rise off the seat, and I pushed them down—punishing her with stronger strokes, slipping my fingers inside of her and commanding her to stay still.

"I can't..." She thrust her hips up again. "I can't..."

A loud applause arose from the theater below us, echoing off the walls as the first scene ended.

I sucked her clit harder, darting my tongue against it repeatedly until she couldn't help but scream my name across the theater.

Shaking, she grabbed my shoulders, gripping me harder than ever as she came into my mouth.

I held her thighs as she continued to shake, as tremor after tremor ran through her body.

As she came back down, I caressed her legs and kissed the inside of her thighs.

Grabbing her ripped panties off the floor, I wiped her clean. Then I stuffed them into my pocket before taking my seat again.

"Is something wrong sir?" An usher stepped into our balcony. "I heard a disturbance."

"A *disturbance?*" I looked at Aubrey then back at him. "No, I don't think there was one here."

"Are you sure?" he asked concerned. "What about you, Miss? Are you okay?"

"Yes sir." Aubrey nodded, attempting to look as normal as possible. "I'm more than fine."

He walked away, and within seconds, she seemingly transformed into the Aubrey I remembered from months ago, the one that was incapable of not asking questions.

Not that I minded, though.

By the first intermission she'd asked all that was possible about the play and leaned against me, whispering, "This is perfect, Andrew...Thank you." And then she didn't speak again until the show ended two hours later.

"The lead was amazing," she said as the curtains closed. "I really felt all of his emotions in that last scene..."

"Me too." I helped her into her coat. "Do you have a curfew? Any time that I need to get you back home?"

"I'm twenty two years old."

"I'm well aware." I rolled my eyes. "I found that out the hard way, thank you. I meant, do you have a few more hours to spend with me or do you have to get up early?"

"Not until the afternoon..."

"Good." I led her out of the theater and signaled to the town-car driver across the street. "I want to take you somewhere else. Can I?"

"I would love that..."

I helped her into the town car and after I slid inside, she moved into my lap—pressing her lips against mine, whispering thanks once again.

Holding her close, I gave her a brief tour of my past as we drove through the city—grateful that the driver avoided driving by my former firm.

I showed her my favorite restaurants, my favorite places to relax, and a few places I would like to take her to before I left.

"We've arrived at the Waldorf Astoria, Mr. Hamilton." The driver looked at us through the rearview mirror. "Will this be the final stop for the night?"

"Yes," I said, noticing Aubrey narrowing her eyes at me.

"I thought you said—"

"Relax..." I kissed her forehead. "This is where I've been living since I flew here."

"Oh…"

I took her hand and walked her through the lobby and onto the elevator that led to the roof.

Opening the doors, I noticed everything was set up exactly as I asked: A lone white clothed table sat in front of a dancing fire, soft lights hung in waves across the trellis, and through the falling snow, the words "I'm sorry" twinkled against the building directly across from us.

"This is so beautiful, Andrew…" she said, looking around. "When did you change your mind about dinner?"

"I didn't." I pulled out her chair and uncovered the platter of chocolate and vanilla covered strawberries. "It's dessert."

"Did you think of all this yourself?"

"I did." I sat next to her and put my arms around her shoulders.

"You know," she said, "typically on a date the two people sit across from each other."

"Did you miss the memo about me making sure that I wouldn't treat you like any other date?"

"Not at all." Her mouth was on mine within seconds and my hands found their way into her hair.

Pulling her forward, I bit her lips and looked into her eyes.

She was silently telling me to take things further, rubbing her hand against my cock.

"Stop touching me, Aubrey," I whispered, warning her. "I'm not going to be able to be a gentleman anymore if you don't stop…" I stood up and walked to the door, giving myself some space. "I'm trying to prove to you that I can get through a date without fucking you…"

She followed me, smiling. "I'm pretty sure you already failed at that…" She threaded her fingers through my hair and hastily unbuttoned my shirt.

I wedged my knee between her legs and slid a hand across her thighs, sighing as I felt how wet she was.

"Aubrey…" I groaned as she reached into my pocket and pulled out a condom. "I can wait…"

"I can't." She freed my cock from my pants and rolled the condom onto me without letting my lips go.

I secured my arms around her waist and lifting her up, carrying her over to the rooftop's railing. "You have no idea how much I've missed your pussy." I kissed her lips. "And your mouth."

"Is that all you miss?" Her hands went around my neck.

"If it was, then we wouldn't be here right now." I slowly slid inside of her, filling her inch by inch, staring into her eyes as I remembered just how good she fucking felt.

Without saying another word, I slid my hands down to her sides and moved her up and down—groaning as her pussy gripped me tighter and tighter with every stroke.

Her lips found their way to mine, and neither of us let go—grinding into each other as a second light snow fell over us.

Her nails dug into my back as she came close to coming, her teeth trapped my bottom lip to prevent herself from screaming out.

"Don't let go yet, Aubrey…" My cock was throbbing inside of her. "Wait…"

She shook her head, fighting it, but she held on for a few more seconds—looking into my eyes.

"I missed you so much," I whispered. "So fucking much…"

Falling forward into my chest, she came with me—biting my skin as her legs went limp around my waist.

Both of us were breathing heavily, staring at each other as we once did months ago, and we remained entwined.

I kissed her lips, repeating how much I missed her, and she smiled—softly telling me to pull out of her.

"Would you like to stay the night?" I asked, picking up my jacket and holding it out for her. "You can tell me more about that case you're so intrigued with lately."

"The Henderson & Hart one?" she asked. "You really haven't heard anything about it?"

"No, but if you spend the night we can google it together."

"I don't think so." Her voice was suddenly flat. "I need to go." She adjusted her dress and walked over to the table, picking up her purse. '

"Is something wrong?"

She didn't answer. She pulled out her phone to check the time and sighed.

"Aubrey, what are you doing?"

"Forcing myself to see that you're still the same and you'll never change." She looked hurt. "Your idea of the truth is, and will always be, duplicitous. That's all."

"Excuse me?"

"Thank you for a wonderful night…I'll always remember this

and cherish it, just so you know."

"I'm really starting to wonder if you are, indeed, *bipolar*..."

"Why didn't you tell me that your name was Liam Henderson tonight?" She shook her head, and I inhaled a sharp breath.

"I gave you every opportunity to," she said, looking hurt. "I practically begged you to tell me, but you opened up about everything except for that."

I hesitated. "I was going to tell you everything later tonight, in bed."

"Sure you were." She scoffed. "Is there any reason why you didn't even tell me this when I said you were once my favorite lawyer in my interview?"

"Once?"

She nodded. "Yes. *Once*. The essays I used to read by Liam all stressed complete and utter honesty. I guess that all changed once he became *Andrew*."

"Aubrey, don't..." I stepped forward and she took a step back. "I was honestly going to ask you to come to the final hearing."

"Can I use your town car to get home or do I need to call a cab?"

"Stop this. Now."

"Cab it is." She shrugged. "I wish you the best of luck with your testimony. And I hope you treat the next girl you find nicely from the beginning so she won't have to love and leave you alone in the end."

"Give me a chance to talk, Aubrey..."

"We have nothing more to discuss." She opened the door. "*Please* do not follow me, Andrew. You can't trust me and I can't trust you, so I don't want anything to do with this anymore and I need you to finally respect that."

I opened my mouth to respond, but she spoke first.

"Goodbye Andrew, *Liam*," she said, "whatever the hell your name is."

"Aubrey..."

The door slammed shut and I knew it was pointless to go after her in that moment.

She was gone.

# Swear (v.):
To declare under oath that one will tell the truth.


## Andrew

"Do you swear to tell the truth, the whole truth, and nothing but the truth so help you God?" The judge said to me a few mornings later.

I said nothing, the sudden departure of Aubrey still fresh on my mind.

"Mr. Hamilton, I asked you a question." The judge chided.

"I apologize," I said. "I do swear to tell the truth, the whole truth, and nothing but the truth so help me God."

"We may proceed."

The defense lawyer stood up and cleared his throat. "Mr. Hamilton, your legal name was formerly Liam Henderson, correct?"

"Correct."

"Could you please tell the court how you know my client, Kevin Hart?"

"We were once partners at Henderson & Hart."

"Partners *and* best friends, correct?"

I looked over at an expressionless Kevin. He was dressed in a grey suit, still incapable of wearing a matching tie.

"Yes," I said to the lawyer. "Once upon a time."

"Is it true that you got into an altercation with him at a bar six and a half years ago?"

"Define altercation."

He picked up a sheet of paper. "Did you walk into a bar and punch him? Leaving him with a broken jaw and a fractured ribcage?"

"He was fucking my wife."

The jurors gasped and the judge banged his gavel.

"*Mr. Hamilton...*" The judge spoke sternly. "That type of language is not allowed in my courtroom. Please answer the question."

"Yes," I said. "Yes, I did injure Mr. Hart...*Severely.*"

"Similarly to how you injured your own wife?"

"*Objection!*" The prosecutor stood up. "Relevance, Your Honor?"

"Sustained."

"Fine." The defense lawyer held up his hands in surrender. "Is it true that you blame Mr. Hart for the downfall of your former firm?"

"Clearly the Department of Justice does since he's the one on trial today."

"*Mr. Hamilton...*"

"Yes." I clenched my jaw. "Yes, I blame him for the demise of our former firm."

"Is it true that you also blame him for the unfortunate death of your daughter?"

"*Your Honor!*" The prosecutor shot me a look of sympathy. "Relevance?"

"Overruled...Answer the question, Mr. Hamilton."

I looked away from Kevin and balled my fists. "Yes."

"Your daughter died amidst the weeks leading up to the complete collapse of your firm, and within those weeks you managed to severely beat your partner, batter your wife—"

"I didn't batter my fucking wife. She made that shit up. Have you done any fucking research?"

The judge banged his gavel, but I continued talking.

"I'm not sure what low level community college was dumb enough to issue you a law degree, but the case between me and my wife was thrown out years ago because she lied about numerous things to a grand jury. And seeing as though she was sent to prison and I was cleared of all charges, you can accept that as a fucking fact. So, before you ask me another bullshit question and try to damage my character, remember that *your* client's livelihood is at stake during this trial. Not mine."

The judge let out a deep sigh, but he didn't say anything further. He just motioned for the defense to continue.

"During your partnership, is it true that your wife was in charge of all the firm's monetary dealings?"

"Ex-wife. And yes."

"And you never thought to double check where she was allocating most of the funds?"

"I had a degree in law, not accounting."

"So, you never thought it was slightly suspicious that your new firm was bringing in seven figures monthly?"

"No." I sighed, thinking back to those days, those clients. Everyone we dealt with had far more than I would earn in my lifetime and I thought nothing about the monthly profits Ava reported; I trusted her.

"Is it fair to say that the demise of your firm could be due to your wife's handling of funding?"

I gritted my teeth. "Yes."

"Interesting." He picked up a sheet of paper and asked the judge if he could approach me. "Could you read this to the court please?"

"I'd rather not," I said.

"You'd rather not?" He laughed. "Mr. Hamilton, as a lawyer yourself, surely you know that you will be held in contempt for refusing to read requested evidence."

"Read it, Mr. Hamilton." The judge demanded.

"You're a fucking liar, Ava." I read my old words. "You've fucked so many people behind my back that I've lost count. As far as I'm concerned, you deserve to rot behind bars. Maybe then your overworked pussy will get a much needed break."

A juror covered her mouth in shock, but I continued reading.

"Thank you for telling me that my cock was never up to par, that after all those years of marriage you were never satisfied…Since you and Kevin have not only managed to take away my firm, but have also ruined the one thing that made my life worth living, accept this letter as a goodbye." I looked up at the defense.

"Could you also read what you wrote after the PS?"

I rolled my eyes. "Since you'll only be around women for the next fifteen years, I suggest you give pussy a try. The taste is quite impeccable."

"Objection, your honor." The prosecutor stood up. "I don't see how this document is relevant to the case. The defense also failed to produce that letter during discovery. I move to strike."

"Sustained. Consider it stricken." The judge looked at his watch and then stood up. "Let's adjourn for lunch. Testimony will continue this afternoon."

As the jury and the courtroom attendees filed out, I sat still. I had nowhere to go.

"I didn't know he was going to bring up your daughter. I'm so sorry..." The prosecutor offered me a small smile. "I'll redirect once he gets done...Your partner is definitely going down, he's just trying to discredit your character a bit, to make him look a little more sympathetic to the jury."

"You are aware that I'm a lawyer as well, right?" I stepped off the stand. "I know exactly what he's trying to do."

I stepped out of the court and outside into a heavy snowfall, looking up at the sky. I considered leaving the courthouse and risking contempt, but a part of me wanted to help seal the deal on Kevin's fate.

It'd been a long time coming—all the lies, the betrayal, the pain, and he deserved whatever he was going to get.

Someone tapped my shoulder from behind.

"You got a minute?" A familiar voice asked. Kevin.

"I don't."

"I figured..." He sighed. "Whatever happens at the end of this trial—"

"Did you not hear what I said?" I spun around to face him, taken aback by how haggard he looked up close. Time hadn't been good to him at all.

"I'm sorry for everything me and Ava put you through," he said with a genuine look in his eyes. "The money and clients were coming in so fast and we were all so young..."

"Young?"

"Yeah." He nodded. "Young and dumb, you know? It was—"

"Dumb as fuck." I clenched my jaw. "But it was more than stupidity, Kevin. It was greed. And when the newspapers started to put the pieces together, when the clients started demanding answers, you both turned on me. You blamed me...You filed for custody of Emma, knowing damn well you didn't really want her. You just wanted to hurt me since you were her biological father."

"Liam..."

"And you did." I could honestly admit that once and for all.

"You really fucking did…"

"If I could take it back—"

"You can't." I cut him off. "But you can tell me one thing…"

"What is it?"

"The night you ruined my life…Well, not the first night, the night that came months later, were you drinking?"

"What does it matter now?"

"Were you fucking drinking that night?" I glared at him and he sighed, looking down at the ground.

"Yes…"

"Thank you for finally being honest." I scoffed. "I'll sleep even easier at night knowing that you'll be joining Ava behind bars after this week."

"Ava's back in prison?" He looked hurt, disappointed.

"Nine more years." I smiled, but it quickly faded. "Six more than what Emma got."

I didn't give him a chance to respond. My heart was clenching at the thought of losing Emma again, at imagining all the pain she must've felt on her last day, so I shut my eyes—trying to block another dark memory from passing by.

# Reasonable Doubt (n.):
Not being sure of a criminal defendant's guilt to a
moral certainty.

*Six years ago…*

### Liam Henderson

Living in New York never felt ordinary. Every day there was
something new to discover, something I'd never seen before.

Even though I was still running on the fumes of winning one of
the biggest, yet non-reported cases in the state, I was still trying to
find myself—personally and professionally. I was realizing that
national popularity would always elude me, but as long as I was
under-rated and not over-rated, I was perfectly fine with that.

I dropped a book of essays on my coffee table once I heard a
loud knock at the door. It was a familiar loud and annoying one
that my best friend Kevin always used.

"You know, you can't keep coming over in the middle of the—
" I stopped talking when I realized it wasn't Kevin. It was a woman
and a man, dressed in grey suits.

"Are you Liam Andrew Henderson?" The woman asked.

"Who's asking?"

"Are you Liam Andrew Henderson?" The man spoke sternly.

"Depends on who wants to know."

They both blinked.

"Yes," I said. "I'm Liam Henderson."

"You've been served." The woman thrust a thick blue envelope
into my hand, the tenth time this had happened to me this week.

"Is this some type of joke? Is the *New York Times* trying to get a rise out of me again?"

They exchanged glances, confused.

"I was just doing my job," I said. "If they want to continue their pettiness by refusing to print my picture for the rest of their paper's life, that's fine. I'm okay with that, really. But serving me papers as a prank every day for a week and a half—"

"The SEC doesn't do pranks," the woman said, before they both walked away.

I shut my door and immediately called Kevin.

"This better be an emergency," he answered. "Do you know what time it is?"

"Has our firm pissed anyone off lately?"

"Of course we have. Why?"

"I just got served papers by the SEC, again."

"Have you actually opened any of the other ones?" he asked.

"Two of them," I walked over to my coffee table and pulled out a drawer. "Something about a client named Ferguson who claims we haven't been putting his money in escrow? He's suing us for five million and supposedly contacting our other clients. Do we even have a client named Ferguson?"

"We have three clients named Ferguson."

"Have we pissed any of them off?"

"Not to my knowledge." He sounded concerned. "I'm pretty sure they would've contacted us first before filing the charges, don't you think? Are you sure it's not *The New York Times* playing a mean joke on you? This is like the tenth letter you've received."

"That's the first thing I asked tonight. They said it's not them."

We were both silent for several seconds.

"It's them." We laughed in unison.

"Sorry for calling at this hour." I stuffed the envelope into the drawer with all the others. "I'll talk to you later." I hung up.

"Daddy?" Emma walked into the living room, wiping her eyes as she walked over to me. "Can I go play?"

"It's three in the morning, Emma." I shook my head. "What do you think?"

"I want to go play..." She smiled, giving me that look that made me incapable of saying no.

I smiled back and kissed her forehead, thinking of where we could possibly go out at this hour. Central Park was out of the question, as was any park, really. There was a twenty four hour donut shop nearby that we could walk to or—

I stopped mid thought. Kevin was having a special playroom built for her at the office, a room that was twice the size of his own. He'd said it would prevent me from using "I have to go check on Emma" as an excuse when we worked on demanding cases.

"I know somewhere we can go." I picked her up and carried her to her room, helping her into her favorite shoes—a pair of red rain boots she wore every day, even when it wasn't raining. "Okay, go sit on the couch so I can get dressed and then we'll go okay?"

She rushed out of her room without saying another word. I really needed to find a way to curb her wake-up-at-three-in-the-morning routine ASAP, but a part of me liked it. It was our special time together.

I put on a sweatshirt and sent my wife a quick email.

**Subject: Emma.**

Taking Emma out to play. Are you still at the coffee shop?

Love you,

Liam

**Subject Re: Emma.**

What are you going to say when she asks you for a pony?

(Yes, I'm still here…Tax season is going to be the death of me. Want me to bring you a cup back? Want to try a latte?)

I love you more,

Ava

**Subject: Re: Re: Emma**

Nothing. I'll just buy the pony.

(No, thank you. You know I really hate coffee.)

Impossible. I love you more than you'll ever know,

Liam

"I'm ready! I'm ready!" Emma rushed into my room, knocking over a stack of folders. "I'm ready!"

Laughing, I put my phone in my pocket and attempted to stuff the papers back in order—stopping once I saw my signature. Forged.

Confused, I sifted through the other papers-noticing the same thing.

What is this?

"Let's go, Daddy!" Emma tugged on my pants.

I tucked the folder underneath my arm and clasped her hand. "Your nap today is going to have to last for at least five hours. Do you know that?"

"I don't like naps."

"Of course you don't…" I walked her out of our apartment and to my car. As usual, Ava had slipped a note underneath the windshield wipers.

*Dear Husband,*

*I love you—so very much, and it pains me to see you, someone with as much money and status as you have, driving a car like this. I know you're modest, and the most expensive suit you own probably costs eighty dollars, but come on! You have to live, Liam!*

*I'm taking you car shopping next week and I'm not taking no for an answer,*

*Ava.*

*P.S.—Thank you for the roses you sent me yesterday. I got you something special and placed it on your desk at the office.*

I smiled and secured Emma into her car seat, giving in when she requested to listen to her favorite song on repeat while riding to the firm.

The sleek design of the building still took people's breath away when they saw it for the first time. It was the one thing I spared no expense on when constructing; I made sure the translucent gold panels were state of the art, that the law scale statues were properly erected on marble ledges, and that the stone letters above the entrance—"Henderson & Hart" were polished every week.

And, as a giant "fuck you" to the government for burying my first case, the case that should've made me a household name and landed me on billboards all over this country, I had the office built right in front of their Social Security Office.

Pulling into the reserved parking spot, I looked in my rearview mirror—seeing that Emma was fast asleep.

Figures...

I stepped out and carried her inside anyway. I was sure she'd wake up soon.

"Good morning, Mr. Henderson." An intern greeted me as I walked inside.

"Good morning, Laura," I responded. "Am I in a different time zone today? Why is everyone awake and working right now?"

She blushed. "It's tax season."

"I keep hearing that..." I stepped onto the elevator. "I'll see you later."

Emma stirred in my arms, murmuring, but only soft snores followed.

When the elevator doors glided open, I walked through the massive "H&H" glass doors headed to Emma's half-finished playroom. I gently lowered her onto the massive pink bed and tucked her under the covers, whispering "I love you," before I dimmed the lights.

I took a seat in the corner and pulled out the folder that was under my arm, reading over what seemed like written receipts and accounts of money exchanges. Things I didn't recall doing.

I pulled out my phone to text Ava, to see if this was just another elaborate joke—something she was prone to pulling, but I heard her voice.

"Fuck!" She yelled.

I jumped up and headed to where the shouting had come from, pausing once I heard a familiar voice.

"Your pussy feels so fucking good..."

"Ahhhh...." Ava was moaning. "Just fuck me...Fuck me harder..."

I completely froze, unable to take another step. I didn't want to believe another man—Kevin, from the sound of things, was fucking my wife or that she was cheating on me.

I couldn't believe it. I trusted her way too much.

But, as she screamed a few more times—the same screams she yelled when having sex with me, I knew it was true.

"Is this how you always conduct business, *Mrs. Henderson?*" Kevin asked, laughter in his voice.

"Are you seriously going to call me that after we just fucked?" She groaned. "Can we actually get back to work now? That's the third interruption tonight and I'd actually like to get something done."

"Fine, fine…"

Papers shuffled, windows opened, but I remained frozen—still in disbelief. It wasn't until I peered through the slit of the door that my brain actually began to process what was happening.

"What are we going to do about this Ferguson shit?" Kevin asked.

"Ferguson shit? That's what we're calling it?"

"Oh, right. Here's a better name for it: Five to ten years for me. Fifteen years for you."

"I was thinking twenty."

"*Twenty?*" He slammed the table. "Are you out of your fucking mind? Twenty years? Are you suggesting that we just turn ourselves in?"

"No…" she said. "Just Liam."

"What?" He sounded appalled. "Are you joking right now?"

"Do you hear me laughing?"

Silence.

"Ava, look…" He sighed. "Liam is like a brother to me—"

"Says the man who's currently fucking his wife…Some brother you are."

"This is a mistake."

"A mistake would be one time," she said, lighting a cigarette. "Once a day for the past few years isn't necessarily the same thing. Sorry."

My heart sank.

"It was a mistake, Ava." He looked conflicted. "Tonight was going to be the last time anyway. I can't keep doing this to him."

"I don't want to stop." She walked over to the window and sighed. "I can't…"

"What?"

"He doesn't give me what I need anymore…"

"You'll have to find a way that he can. Now actually might be a good time to start, seeing as though he might have to be your lawyer."

She turned around in tears. "Is this really the last time?"

"The first time should've been the last time." He walked over and massaged her shoulders. "You were only using me…You tend to forget that."

"I wasn't—" She choked back a sob. "I wasn't using you…"

"Yes you were." He kissed her lips. "And that's okay. I sympathized."

"Did you think I was a horrible person?

"No."

"You promise?"

He nodded, cupping her face in his hands. "He couldn't give you a baby and you wanted one…Naturally…That's completely understandable."

I held back a gasp.

"He doesn't fuck me like you do..." she whispered.

"Stop it, Ava." He kissed her cheek. "Stop it."

I didn't want to hear anymore.

I couldn't take it.

As the two of them kissed and held each other—completely immersing themselves in their own world, I forced myself to walk away.

I hit the lights in my office and noticed a bright blue box on my desk. It read, "To: the love of my life. From: Your first and only love."

My heart ached again as I tore the wrapping and looked inside: A new set of cufflinks, a set that probably cost more than all of my suits combined. My initials were engraved in them, and she'd enclosed a quote from my favorite authors:

*"Do not be too moral. You may cheat yourself out of life much so. Aim above morality."*

*-Henry David Thoreau*

I sighed. She'd left out the last part of the quote, the "Be not simply good; be good for something."

I pulled out my phone and sent her an email:

**Subject: Coffee.**

I think I will try some coffee…Are you still at the coffee shop?

—Liam

**Subject: Re: Coffee.**

Yes. I think I'll be here all night.

What kind would you like?

—Ava.

**Subject: Re: Re: Coffee.**

Whatever you think is best for a first timer…

Have you talked to Kevin today?

—Ava

**Subject: Re: Re: Re: Coffee.**

Not at all. He's been weirder than usual lately. (We really need to find him a girlfriend…) Have you?

—Ava.

I didn't answer.

I left my office and walked over to Emma's playroom, looking at her as she slept peacefully. I wanted to make her wake up, make her look at me, so I could study her features and pick them apart, so I could see for myself that she was indeed Kevin's, but I couldn't.

She was *mine*, biological father or not.

I carried her out of the firm and rushed home. As soon as I set her down, I flipped over the coffee table and opened the envelope I'd filed away hours earlier.

It was a standard summons, a demand to appear in court, but the charges listed didn't end on one page. They didn't even end on two.

It was a ten page manifesto, a laundry list of bullshit that I would never attempt: bribery, racketeering, tax fraud, mail fraud, wire fraud—every fucking fraud.

What the hell is this?

I pored over the documents for hours, my mind racing a mile a minute. Still, I couldn't completely process everything—my mind was still thinking about Kevin and Ava.

How she'd lied to me.

How he'd lied to me, too.

And now, this.

The door opened at five in the morning, and Ava set a hot cup of coffee in front of me.

"We need to talk," she said.

I said nothing. Just closed all the folders and looked at her.

"I just got served by the SEC…" She paced the floor. "Served, like *legit papers*…They came to the firm and—"

"I thought you were at the coffee shop."

"I was." She swallowed. "I stopped by the firm after getting your coffee so I could pick up a few things."

"Was anyone there with you?"

"Of course not." She scoffed. "Look at what time it is. Anyway…"

I couldn't hear anything else she was saying. I could see her lips moving, make out some of the sounds that were coming out of her mouth, but the lies she'd just told me were blocking out everything.

"Why are you cheating on me?" I blurted out, suddenly annoyed by the tears falling down her face.

She sucked in a breath and looked me up and down. "Liam, the SEC has just unreasonably served me papers. Are you seriously accusing me of infidelity right now?"

"I'm not *accusing* you. An accusation would imply that there's a chance you could be innocent. Why. Are. You. Cheating. On. Me?

She toyed with the gemstones on her necklace. Then she started to hum the refrain of a classic Sinatra song, "New York, New York."

"Don't make me ask you again, Ava," I said. "I know you've fucked Kevin."

Her eyes finally met mine. "Fine...Yes, I fucked him. Now, what?" Tears formed in her eyes. "I didn't mean for it to happen. I never thought I would cross the line with him of all people..."

"You told me Emma was a surprise..." I said. "That you didn't want to have kids until we were in our mid-thirties."

Her face paled. "You were at the office tonight weren't you?"

"I was..."

Silence.

"So," I said, mentally putting together the puzzle pieces. "Either you're lying to him about me not being able to give you a baby—because last time I checked, right before Emma was *miraculously* conceived, you were still making me wear condoms and we weren't even trying to have a fucking baby. Or, you're lying to me, and you just wanted to fuck my best friend for an ulterior motive you're saving for later. Which is it?"

"I still love you, Liam, It's just—"

"*Which is it?*"

She said nothing, she just stood there with more tears falling down her eyes.

I held up one of the folders I'd been reading through. "I was looking through these tonight...At first, I thought they were standard mail-outs that you'd signed for me while I was gone or too busy, standard office supply orders, things like that..."

"Where'd you find those?"

"But it turns out," I said, ignoring her question, "That these are all fucking favors from judges and clerks that I don't recall asking for. Ever."

"Liam..."

"Is there anyone in this city that you haven't fucked to get something in return?"

She looked as if she actually had to think about it.

"I send you flowers every day—every. fucking. day." I stepped forward. "I tell you that I love you and that you complete me, every day and this is what I get in return?"

"I understand how you feel, Liam, but—"

"No, you don't fucking understand." I clenched my fists. "I've never even entertained the thought of being *friends* with another woman. I make sure everyone knows I'm completely unavailable, that no one else stands a damn chance."

"I cheated for your benefit, Liam. I did it for you."

What the fuck?

I'd heard a lot of bullshit in my life, but that line officially took the cake.

"How do you think you won the Luttrell case?" She wiped away her tears and narrowed her eyes at me. "You think you did it with your award winning rhetoric and charm?"

"Do you have a mental disorder that you failed to tell me about?"

"I fucked the judge three days before the verdict. You were going to lose. And if you lost that case, there's no way some of our current clients would've picked our firm to handle their account."

"*Our* firm?"

"You think you built it alone?" She laughed. "Liam Henderson, warm-hearted, loyal, and too nice for his own fucking good? Please. I had to intercept every contract you sent out and redraft half of the terms. If I'd left it up to you, your firm would be nothing more than a pipe dream. You should be thanking me because you have no idea how much work I've done to put you where you are."

"You've never argued a single case."

"No, but I've fucked a lot of powerful people to make sure you never lost one."

"I've never lost because I'm a damn good lawyer."

"And I'm a damn good lay." She shrugged. "Of course, my own husband has been so busy this year that he probably wouldn't even know."

"You're blaming me for throwing your pussy around?"

"I'm shocked you even know what the word *pussy* means." She hissed. "We lay in bed together every night and you never want to fuck me."

"You always say that you're tired. Or is that a lie, too?"

"I was only tired of fucking you." She brushed past me and shut the door to Emma's room. "What do you want to do now, huh? Divorce me?"

"Is that a serious question?"

"It is." She smirked and a knock came to the door.

We both stood rooted to the floor, and the knock came again.

"I'll get it." I warned. "You stay there."

I walked away and opened it, expecting to see Kevin so I could punch the shit out of him, but it was a different woman in a suit.

A young blonde.

"You've um…" Her cheeks reddened. "You've been…"

"*Served!*" Someone whispered loudly from around the corner. "Tell him he's been *served…*"

"You're an intern at *The New York Times*, aren't you?" I rolled my eyes.

She nodded, but then she added. "My boss says you can go fuck yourself, and that even though we'll never run your picture, we'll make sure everyone knows that your firm is about to be run into the ground starting tomorrow." She handed me the copy print for an article in tomorrow's paper. "He says it's your turn to feel some karma."

I slammed the door in her face.

"I think you need to seriously weigh your options before you act out on your emotions." Ava was right behind me, holding a sleeping Emma.

"Is this a threat?"

"It's a promise…"

I raised my eyebrow. "And what exactly are the proposed terms?"

"If you help me sort this thing out—if you get the SEC off the firm's back, both of us can avoid serving any time."

"I'm not serving any fucking time. I didn't do anything wrong. And if you think I won't be the first person in line to help the state put your ass away, you're sadly fucking mistaken."

"Awww." She pouted. "Look at you. Trying to sound all masculine and tough for a change, sounding like the man I wish you could've been."

"Fuck you, Ava."

"Not a chance." She narrowed her eyes at me. "Let me try phrasing this another way: I know that you're Mr. Lawyer of the Year and you'd never willingly lie because you have a conscience and all that. But if you don't help me, or if you refuse to tell investigators that you were partly responsible for what happened— that we *all* played a small part, I'm filing for sole custody of Emma."

"File away. No judge in his right mind would give you sole custody."

She laughed. "This is actually why people fuck to get what they want, *honey*. It comes in handy for times like this. Besides, you're not even her real father." She kissed Emma's forehead. "Did you overhear that part while you were watching us fuck or were you too busy taking notes?"

I didn't get a chance to answer.

"Do not fuck with me, Liam." She hissed. "You have no idea how far I'm willing to go to stay out of prison."

"Even though you deserve to be there?" I snatched Emma away from her, making her stir. "You sought out clients using my name and you misappropriated the money. For what?"

"Status. Something you'll never understand."

"Something you'll never need." I countered. "Everyone behind bars shares the same level of popularity."

She rolled her eyes. "I'm going to give you a few days to come to your senses."

"Or else what?"

"You don't want to know the answer to that." She walked out, slamming the door behind her—waking Emma.

She looked at me with her bright blue eyes, smiling. "Can I go play?"

I nodded, unable to even speak. Carrying her to the balcony, I didn't even bother grabbing an umbrella for myself. I set her down and helped her into a coat, trying not to think about what Ava could possibly have up her sleeve.

Emma tilted her head up to the sky and swallowed raindrops, and then she dashed away from me—running in circles.

A loud thunder roared in the distance, and as if she could tell what I was about to say, she looked at me with a wide grin. "Five more minutes!"

*The New York Times* didn't waste any time printing the story. Well, stories.

## Henderson & Hart, Revered Law Firm, Embroiled in Scandal.

## Hart Agrees to Cooperate Against Henderson, Following Brutal Bar Brawl.

## Henderson Arrested, Questioned, After Wife Claims Recent Domestic Abuse.

The only story they didn't mention, out of a hanging thread of respect, was my losing custody of Emma. Of me having to hand her over to Kevin.

I was innocent of every charge I faced, but due to the fact that I'd bashed Kevin's head in, and Ava had claimed I was just as violent with her, it left the judge no choice but to put her in custody with her supposed "loving and biological father per the mother's request."

I thought it would only be for a week or two, a month at most, but as the charges piled up and the cases were trudged through the courts at a snail's pace, the months wore on and on.

To make matters worse, Kevin and Ava purposely took Emma to places they knew I frequented: My favorite place at Central Park, my spot on the Brooklyn Bridge, my favorite restaurants.

In between my court appearances, I followed them to the park—resisting the urge to yell at them for letting her get too close to the streets, holding back the urge to take her back and flee the state.

Instead, I filed injunction after injunction—fighting multiple cases at once. I searched through every loophole of custody, documenting cases after case of non-biological fathers retaining rights.

Eventually the truth about Ava and Kevin's scheme began to surface, and on the same day that Ava confessed to lying about me beating her—when she admitted that she'd made that all up, I won custody of Emma.

It was three days before her fourth birthday, so I arranged for a few of her neighborhood friends to come by with their parents. The theme was the rainforest, of course, and the party favors were umbrellas and rain-boots.

Kevin, still foolishly proclaiming his innocence in regards to the fraud, had grown quite attached to her over the past few months. He asked if he could still see her on the weekends once he returned her to me, but I didn't even bother answering that question.

He'd seen her long enough.

Standing outside my brownstone, I called him two hours before her birthday party, making sure he was still dropping her off on time. Instead of talking to me like an adult, he made Emma repeat his every word to me.

"We'll be there soon," she said, a smile in her soft voice. "Can you please let us enjoy our last few hours alone? She's my daughter, too."

"See you soon, Emma."

"Goodbye, Daddy!" She hung up and I rearranged the party decorations for the umpteenth time, greeting the early guests and directing them into the living room.

Half an hour passed.

A whole hour.

Two.

I called Kevin, annoyed that he was pulling this bullshit of a stunt—as if it was even *half* as difficult as it had been for me, but there was no answer.

Upset, I dialed the police and they showed up to my door within minutes.

"Are you Liam Henderson?" They asked.

"Yes, I'm the one that called."

I pulled the court order out of my pocket and explained what was happening, how Kevin was technically committing kidnapping, but they interrupted me.

They weren't at my house to take a report.

They were there to give one.

As they calmly explained what had happened, how she was less than a block away when the car collided with a truck, my world stopped.

I asked which hospital she was being flown to, which route was the fastest to take, but the cops simply sighed and looked past me, as if they didn't want to say anything further.

They didn't have to.

Their looks said it all.

Emma's funeral was held on a grey and wet day, another harsh blow to my chest. I sat through speeches from the few people she'd crossed paths with, from her young friends who had yet to fully comprehend what her death really meant.

My next door neighbor, a four year old named Hannah, said, "I hope you come back next week, Emma. You can come to my birthday party."

I stared at the tiny casket as they lowered it into the ground, half of me wanting to jump in with it and risk being buried alive. At least then I wouldn't have to feel anything anymore.

As the crowd dissipated one by one—tapping my shoulder and saying, "I'm so sorry for your loss," as they left, I spotted Ava walking into the cemetery.

Flanked by two prison guards, she fell to her knees and bawled once she reached the uncovered grave.

"You made me late for my child's funeral." She cursed at the guards. "I fucking missed it...How cruel can you possibly be?"

"All furloughs have the same time constraints, ma'am," one of them said flatly. "We couldn't have left any earlier."

She shook her head and continued to cry, beating her hands against the ground. As if she needed to distance herself from the guilt, she stood up and walked towards the podium, reading the papers that were left behind.

She broke down again and I walked over.

"Liam..." She held out her arms. "She's really gone, isn't she?"

"*She is.*" I refused to console her. "And it's all your fault, Ava. Your fucking fault."

"Don't you think I know that?" She sniffled. "Don't you think I *feel* that?"

"It should be you down there in the ground right now. It should be you."

"Liam..."

"She didn't deserve to be taken away from me and you know it."

"I do know that...I was just—"

"Trying to prove a point? To do whatever it took to hurt me because you fucked yourself over and you wanted to bring me down with you?"

"We can get through this...We can still find a way to restore your name in this city, and you're the best lawyer I know so...I know you can turn everything around and maybe help me too. Maybe forgive me?"

"I'm going to do everything in my power to make sure you rot in prison, to make sure you never get out and that the parole board never gives you an ounce of sympathy."

"You don't mean that, Liam…"

"If I ever find a way to get away with murder, you and Kevin will be my first victims."

The guard across from us gave me a look.

"Don't be like this, Liam…"

"My name won't be Liam for too much longer just so you know. It'll be Andrew."

"Are you leaving? Are you about to leave me here?"

"That should be you in the ground right now…" I noticed the funeral director stacking the chairs, mindlessly breaking down what was just another ceremony to him. "That should be you…"

One of the guards began speaking with the funeral staff, inquiring as to whether they should leave the premises or not. Noticing her time here was limited, Ava grabbed onto me. "Liam, I mean…*Andrew*. You clearly still love me because you're trusting me with that…We can rebuild everything we had, we can start over, you and me…We can do this if you help me…"

I grabbed her hands and moved them away as one of the guards stepped closer.

"You know I don't belong in prison," she said, crying. "They're transferring me to a permanent location next week…Save me, Andrew…Save me…"

I said nothing.

"If I could take everything back, I swear…I swear I would. Don't you think I love Emma, too?"

"Loved," I said. "It's past tense now, don't you think?"

She sighed. "Please don't leave me…"

"I won't." I stepped back so the guards could escort her back to the van. "I'll write…"

"Really?" Her eyes looked hopeful as she walked away. "Okay, I look forward to your letters…I look forward to fixing us…"

The rain picked up its pace, transitioning from a drizzle to a downpour, but I remained standing—unable to walk away from Emma. I re-read her tiny tombstone, crying as her face crossed my mind.

*Emma Rose Henderson,*
*A Daddy's girl, through and through.*
*Gone too soon,*
*But never forgotten…*

I stared at those words for hours, letting the rain drench me to the bone. It wasn't until the director informed me that the gates were closing, that I walked away.

Lost and heartbroken, I spent the next few months in a dizzying haze. Despite the fact that Ava was the one behind bars, the paper continued spouting her lies as facts, slandering me, and I didn't even bother disputing it.

I didn't have the energy.

I submitted written testimonies through lawyers I'd hired—knowing that eventually things would sort themselves out. I didn't even care that Ava had hired her own high profile team to block me from getting a divorce.

I no longer gave a fuck about anything.

My firm collapsed before my very eyes—everything down to the sink-ware was sold off in parts, and in the legal community, the downfall became a warning, a tell-tale of what happened when status and greed consumed one of us.

I drank every morning, letting the alcohol numb my pain. And whenever I awoke from passing out, I drank again. It was only when I started drinking coffee that I could somewhat function well enough to get anything done.

Visiting the cemetery was too painful, almost as painful as stepping inside Emma's room. So, I hired a few people to pack it away in boxes, telling them to leave out the "E" and "H" frames; I could bear to look at those since she'd hand-picked them.

For months, I mourned the life she would never have—attempting to make sense of it all. I knew deep down that I couldn't stay here, but I couldn't leave as the same man that I was; I knew that I'd never get over Emma, but I needed a way to cope. A way to slowly re-integrate myself into the real world.

Stopping by a newspaper stand, my eyes caught an article about the newest hotshot lawyer in town—Michael Weston. Dressed in one of the expensive suits that Kevin once raved about, he was the talk of the city and from the words I was reading, he was cocky—

only slightly cockier than I had become recently.

"Oh, you got the last one…" A woman said as she stepped next to me.

"You want this paper?"

"Well…" She blushed. "Not really the paper. I just want the ad of Michael Weston so I can show my friends my ideal dream guy."

"Have you read some of the shit he's said in this interview?" I raised my eyebrow. "He's an asshole."

"That just makes him more loveable, don't you think."

"They asked him what he does when he gets less than favorable reviews." I couldn't believe how fucking gullible this woman looked. "Do you want to know what he said?"

"Sure." She crossed her arms. "What does he do when he gets bad reviews?"

"He looks at his bank account," I said. "And then he claims, and I quote, 'I don't recall learning that someone needs to be well-liked in order to be successful.' He really said that."

She practically melted into the sidewalk. "I bet he really knows how to fuck…"

I gave her the paper and walked away. Her bringing up sex was a reminder of how long it'd been since I slept with someone.

And then it hit me: Sex.

I needed some, badly.

I signed up for an online dating site, Date-Match, and slowly shed the layers of the man I used to be. I bought expensive suits— one for every day of the week. I slowly curbed my excessive drinking to make room for a new appetite, and instead of punching my walls to de-stress, I invested in Cuban cigars.

Still, the women I met online were average, and none of them seemed to be about sex. They just wanted to talk about bullshit— always leaving me restless and alone at the end of the night to drink away my sorrows; forcing me back to square one with my experiment.

Like the woman who was sitting on the edge of the bed right now, a goddamn mile-a-minute talker. She was a few years older than me, a teacher of some sort, and she couldn't shut up for shit.

She was talking about her life in college, about some boy named Billy she once loved—some boy who never loved her back. Before she could start elaborating about the campus bond-fire where the two of them met, I realized that I couldn't take this shit anymore.

"Billy and I would've been perfect together, I think," she said. "There was even this one time that—"

"Are we going to fuck or what?" I cut her off.

"*What?*" She clutched her chest. "What did you just say?"

"I said, are we going to fuck *or what?*" I emphasized every syllable. "I didn't reserve this hotel room so I could sit and listen to you talk all night."

Her jaw dropped.

"I thought that..." She stuttered. "I thought that you liked me."

"I like you enough to fuck you. That's about it."

Her eyes went wide and she stepped back. "All this time that we've been dating you've only been thinking about sleeping with me?"

I mentally added "rhetorical questions" to the list of shit I wasn't going to put up with anymore.

"I was under the impression that all those dates you took me on was because—"

"I took you on all those dates so we could scratch the surface of each other's personalities. So I could know that you're not some psycho-murderer, and so you could be assured that I'm not one either." I grimaced at all the time I'd clearly wasted. "The purpose was so the both of us could be comfortable enough to fuck, and then after that we could go our separate ways."

"It was only going to be *once?*"

"Do you have a hearing problem?"

She looked completely lost, and I wasn't in the mood to make this picture any clearer.

Before I could say another word, she looked into my eyes.

"So," she said, still in shock, "all the things on your profile were a lie?"

"No. Everything on my profile is one hundred percent accurate." I pulled out my phone. "I specifically wrote what I'm in for, and I've been more than lenient spending my time with you. You seem like a nice person, but after tonight—whether we fuck or not, I won't be speaking to you again. So, what's it going to be?"

She stood there, her jaw dropped once more, and I glanced at my profile.

Sure enough, I'd forgotten to adjust the default settings when I'd signed up for Date-Match, and my "What I'm Looking For" box was still set to bullshit: "Long conversations, a connection with someone I can truly relate to, and finding my one true love."

Ha…

I quickly erased all of the text and looked up, noticing that my date for tonight was still in the room.

"If you continue standing here," I said," I'm going to assume that you do want to fuck tonight. If not, the door's right behind you."

The sound of her huffing was the last sound I heard before the door slammed so hard it rattled the mirror on the wall.

Unfazed, I contemplated what I wanted to write in my profile's box. Over the past few months, I'd found disappointment after disappointment—wasting too much of my time and money on women who were not on the same wavelength as me.

And now it all made perfect sense. All those unnecessary dinners, late night conversations, and utter bullshit was about to end right now.

I didn't need another relationship—those days were gone forever, and I would never spend more than a week talking to the same woman on the phone.

As the sun set outside the hotel room's window, the perfect phrasing came to me, and I typed: One dinner. One night. No repeats.

Then I highlighted it and placed it in bold.

Staring at it, I realized how bare it looked, how someone might actually think I wasn't dead ass serious, so underneath, I made things completely clear:

Casual sex. Nothing more. Nothing less.

# Condone (v.):

To forgive, support, and/or overlook moral or legal failures of another without protest, with the result that it appears that such breaches of moral or legal duties are acceptable. An employer may overlook an employee overcharging customers or a police officer may look the other way when a party uses violent self-help to solve a problem.

## *Aubrey*

I sat in the back of the courtroom, listening to Andrew break down on the stand. Twice, when the defense purposely brought up Emma, he lost all composure.

Yet, as I saw the look in his eyes at the mere mention of her, of the "slip" of her name, I felt his pain.

I kept my head down the remainder of his testimony so our eyes wouldn't meet, so he wouldn't know I was here, and when the judge called for a short recess, I slipped outside.

Reporters were murmuring in the hallway, hoping he didn't read any of their old articles about him years ago, and suddenly they were shouting questions.

"Mr. Henderson! Mr. Henderson!" They hounded him the second he stepped outside of the courtroom. "Mr. Henderson!"

He stopped and looked at them. "My name is *Mr. Hamilton.*"

"How do you feel about potentially sending your former partner and best friend away to prison?"

"He's sending himself to prison," he answered.

"Do you have any intentions of reconnecting with him while he's behind bars?"

He ignored that question with a blank stare.

"Your name was cleared years ago and yet you still left New York," someone else asked. "Now that everything is in the open for good, any chance that you'll come back and re-open your firm?"

"I'm about to spend my last hour in this city on the way to the airport," he said, pulling shades over his eyes.

The throng of reporters followed him out of the courtroom, and he slipped inside the car without a second glance.

Sighing, I pulled out my phone and re-read the messages he'd sent me this morning, somewhat regretting that I didn't respond.

**Subject: NYC.**

I would like to see you one last time before I leave. Can I pick you up for breakfast?

PS—I really was going to tell you everything that night…

—Andrew


**Subject: Your Pussy.**

This message is actually not about your pussy. (Although, since I'm on the subject, it is number one on my list of favorite things.)

Come to breakfast with me. I'm outside your door.

—Andrew

As I was rereading that email, a new one popped onto my screen:

**Subject: Goodbye.**

—Andrew

I knew my lack of response was immature, that it was my fault that I didn't get to see him before he left, but I felt as if he could've made more of an effort. And I still felt that he was wrong for not being open with me when he should have.

Leaving the courthouse, I headed home and thought about all the half-truths and lies that had swirled our relationship. Alyssa.

His wife. My real name. His real name.

Everything we had was built on lies…

Letting tears roll down my face, I opened the door to my house, prepared to shower until I couldn't cry anymore, but Andrew was standing in my living room.

"Hello, Aubrey." He glared at me.

"Breaking and entering is a crime." I crossed my arms. "Shouldn't you know that?"

He said nothing, just continued glaring at me—looking me up and down.

"Don't you have a flight to catch?" My voice cracked. "Shouldn't you be spending your last hour in New York on the way to the airport?"

"I realized I still have something to say to you."

"Do you have another fake name you want to tell me about? Another secret identity that you want to—"

"Stop." He stepped closer and closer until I backed into a wall, and he looked directly into my eyes. "I need you to listen to me, Aubrey. Just fucking listen…"

I tried to move away from him, but he grabbed my hands and pinned them above my head. Then he used his hips to keep me still.

"You're going to stand here and listen to me for the next five minutes whether you like it or not." The words came out rushed, heated. "Since you suddenly care about knowing the truth, I'll tell you the fucking truth…"

I tried to say something, but he leaned down and bit my lips. Hard.

"I liked you when you were Alyssa and I was Thoreau—when we spent nights talking about your ridiculous homework and my law firm… I even liked you after you fucking lied to me and I saw you at your interview—I *liked* you…" He tightened his grip around my wrists. "And even though I knew I shouldn't have chased you down and showed up to your apartment that day, I did, and I fucked you…After that, I *really* liked you."

"Are you being serious right now?"

"Dead ass serious." He glared at me and bit my lips again, silently commanding me to keep quiet. "I didn't want to like you, Aubrey. I wasn't supposed to, and I didn't need to, but every day after that you were all I could think about. You and your smartass mouth, and how your lies maybe weren't so bad after all."

"What about *your lies*? Do you still think that you're above morality? That—"

"*Stop talking.*" He choked out. "Let me finish."

I swallowed and he stared at me a few seconds before continuing.

"Yes, I hid the fact that I was married from you, and although it was unintentional, it was still a lie."

"A *huge* lie."

"*Aubrey*…" He gripped me tighter. "I hadn't thought about Ava in a very long time…On the contrary, I've been thinking about you every day since you left."

"No, you haven't…"

"I have." He looked directly into my eyes. "I drove to your ballet class twice a week, trying to see you, trying to talk to you and apologize…I sent things to your apartment. I even showed up twice, but that was before I knew you'd moved."

"You're just saying all this so you can fuck me…" I shook my head and turned away, but he made me face him again.

"I'm saying all of this because I love you…"

I gasped and tears formed in my eyes.

"I fucking love you, Aubrey…" he repeated, wiping my face. "And I'll do whatever it takes to show you that." He brushed his lips against mine. "Do you still love me?"

"No, I don't… Not any—" I felt his lips against mine, silencing me.

I didn't want to kiss him back, I wanted to push him away and tell him to leave, but I parted my lips and let his tongue slip inside of my mouth.

Slowly, he freed my hands from his grip and locked his arms around my waist—keeping his lips attached to mine. He didn't give me a chance to talk, to breathe. He just kissed me senseless until I couldn't take it anymore.

"If you can honestly say that you don't love me," he whispered, slowly pulling away from me, "then I'll leave you alone."

"And if I can't?" I asked, breathless.

"If you can't, you're going to show me to your room so you and I can become reacquainted."

"Reacquainted?" I moaned as he cupped my ass. "Is that code for conversation?"

"It's code for fucking."

"Would it kill you to say make love just once?"

"Depends on if you actually love me or not."

Silence.

His fingers were now trailing the zipper on the back of my skirt, gently pulling on it as I looked into his eyes.

"I hate you," I said, making him raise his eyebrow. "If you said all of those things just to get my hopes up, I'll never forgive you."

"You still haven't..." He kissed me gently. "I meant every word I said." He pulled my zipper down. "And I really need to know whether or not you still love me because..." He stopped talking.

My skirt fell into a puddle on the floor and he tugged my thong away from my waist until it snapped.

"Aubrey, tell me...Tell me right now."

I gasped as he slipped a finger inside of me, as he groaned at how wet I was.

"Yes..."

"Yes?" He moved his finger in and out. "Yes, what?"

"Yes, I—" I paused as he kissed my lips. "Yes, I still love you."

"Where's your bedroom?"

I looked to my left and he immediately tugged me down the hall, shutting the door behind us. He didn't give me a chance to get undressed. His hands were all over me—unbuttoning my shirt, ripping my bra, and caressing my breasts.

I reached forward and unbuckled his pants, pushing his pants down. Then he tossed me onto the bed, climbing on top of me.

I spread my legs beneath him, lifting my hips up so he could fuck me, but he didn't. Instead he kissed my neck—whispering how much he missed me, how much he needed me.

"Andrew..." I felt his cock rubbing against my thigh.

He slowly moved his mouth to my chest—swirling his tongue across my nipples as he palmed my breasts. His kisses traveled further and further, all the way down to my thighs.

I shut my eyes as he pressed his tongue against my clit, as he teasingly darted it against me in slow, sensuous circles.

"Ahhhh..." I tried to clamp my legs shut, but he pinned them to the mattress and looked up at me.

"Aubrey..." His voice was low.

"Yes?"

He circled his thumb around my clit, making it swell in pleasure.

"Tell me that I own this."

I shut my eyes as he increased the pressure, rubbing his thumb around and around.

"Tell me that I own your pussy, Aubrey."

"Yes..." I writhed underneath his hand. "Yes..."

"Say it." He prevented me from rolling over. "I need you to say it."

Tingles traveled up and down my spine and I finally stared back at him. "Yes...You own it."

He smiled and pressed his head between my legs again, devouring me—making me scream at the top of my lungs, but he didn't let me cum.

Instead, he flipped me over. "Get down on all fours."

I caught my breath and slowly obliged, and the next thing I felt was him palming my ass, kissing his way down my spine.

"I still haven't claimed every inch of you..." he said, squeezing my cheeks harshly. "But I'll save that for when I think you're ready..."

I murmured as he slid into my pussy inch by inch, making me lean forward. He took the elastic out of my hair and pulled me back, whispering, "It's going to feel just like this...Maybe even better..."

"Ahhhh..."

"And when it happens, you're going to let me cum inside of you..." His other hand skimmed my sides and squeezed my breasts. "I want you to feel every last drop..."

"Andrew." I gripped the sheets.

"Yes?"

I didn't answer. I couldn't.

He was slapping my ass as he pounded into me, giving it to me rough as he whispered my name.

I met him thrust for thrust, unable to let go of the sheets, and when I felt myself nearing the edge—coming close to it as he tortured my clit with his fingers, he denied me once again.

He pulled out of me, making me whimper, and then he made me face him once again. Immediately burying himself inside of me, he stared into my eyes—slowly sliding his cock back and forth, suffocating my screams with his mouth.

I felt his cock throbbing inside of me, felt my muscles clenching as he cursed against my lips and as we locked eyes again, we both came at the same time.

I fell forward against his chest, panting. "Andrew, I..."

He cut me off with a kiss. "I love you, too..."

We lay there connected for what felt like forever—him threading his fingers through my hair, me rubbing my hands against his chest.

"Are you okay?" he asked.

"Yes..."

He rolled out of bed and stood up to toss away the condom. "Come here."

I couldn't move. I was still feeling weak from my last orgasm.

He shook his head and slipped his hands underneath my thighs, picking me up and carrying me out of the room, checking each door we passed. When we reached the bathroom, he set me down on the floor.

"I don't think I can stand up long enough for a shower..." I whispered.

He ignored me and turned on the water. "We're not going to take a shower." He picked me up and gently placed me into the tub.

Climbing in behind me, he grabbed an empty bottle and filled it with warm water. Then he gently poured it over my head.

He grabbed some shampoo from the ledge and squirted a few drops into my hair, lathering it to suds.

I heard him asking me questions, something about how I was feeling or if I wanted to talk to him about whatever I had on my mind, but as his fingers continued to massage my scalp, everything went black.

I woke up in bed alone.

There was no note from Andrew, and all of his clothes were gone.

I was starting to think having sex with him was all a dream, but I spotted his wallet sitting on top of my nightstand. I pulled the covers off of me and smiled once I saw that he'd dressed me in a silk slip.

I made my way out of the room and down the hallway where he was standing out on my balcony smoking a cigar.

"Since when do you smoke?" I stepped behind him.

"I don't often," he said. "Only when I need to think."

I nodded and looked out into the night sky, but I suddenly felt him pulling me against him.

"Aren't you going to ask what I'm thinking about?" He smirked. "Surely you have questions."

"I do, *Liam*."

"We can talk about it."

"Now?"

"If that's what you want…" He put out his cigar and walked me over to a chair, pulling me into his lap. "How long have you known about that?"

"A couple weeks…"

"Hmmm."

I shook my head. "Do Bach and Greenwood know who you really are?"

"They do."

"So, why do you have to hide it from everyone else?"

"Esteemed lawyer or not, no one wants to take on someone who has a history in the papers…It makes a high profile firm look bad." He kissed the back of my shoulder.

"What was Emma like?"

He sighed, looking at me. "She was perfect…"

I thought of a way to change the subject, but he continued talking.

"She hated when I went to work, and she would beg me to come sometimes, so I'd let her…" His voice was low. "And then I wouldn't get any work done because the park was right across the street and she always wanted to play…Always."

"Did she follow you around at home?" I asked.

"She was my shadow. She would come sleep on the couch if I was up working, and if she saw me leave the room to take a call, she would cross her arms and look offended if I didn't invite her to listen." He let out a short laugh, but he didn't say anything else.

"Can I ask you something?" I leaned against his chest.

"If I say no I don't think it'll stop you…"

"Where do we go from here?"

"What do you mean?"

"I mean…What happens now with us?"

He looked at me, confused. "*Us?*"

REASONABLE DOUBT

"Are we in a relationship? Are you going to stay with me, or are you going back to Date-Match?"

He stared at me for a long time. "I can't stay in New York, Aubrey. I think you can understand why..."

"You had no plans to stay past tonight did you?"

"No."

"And you leave in the morning?"

"Yes." He tried to kiss my hair, but I moved away. "So, was this some type of way to get your Aubrey fix before you went home? Say all the right things so you can feel better about yourself when you leave?"

"I wanted you to know that I loved you before I went home."

"And to get some pussy on the side, of course."

"Of course." He smirked, but I didn't return his smile.

"I told you not to get my hopes up, Andrew." I stepped back. "And you did it anyway."

"What do you want me to do, Aubrey? Move in with you? Fucking propose?"

"I want you to stay...And if you can't stay, I want you to leave...Now."

"Aubrey..."

"*Now*," I said. "We can still be friends, but I don't want to—"

"Stop." He pulled me close and pressed his mouth against mine. "We're more than friends...We always were. I just can't be with you right now."

I opened my mouth to protest, but he kissed me again and again, whispering as he cupped my breasts, "I would really prefer if we spent the rest of night in bed and not arguing..."

# Adjourn (v.):

To suspend proceedings: to suspend the business of a court,
legislature, or committee indefinitely.

*Weeks later...*

## Aubrey

I stood on my toes backstage—tilting my head toward the ceiling,
rehearsing the final move of the production one last time. I
should've been happy and smiling—overjoyed at the fact that I was
about to debut in the leading role in a New York Ballet Company
production, but I wasn't. Far from it.

I felt alone, and I knew no amount of applause or accolades
would take those feelings away.

I was still hanging onto my last few moments with Andrew: The
early morning sex in the shower, the sex against my door, the sex in
the town car on the way to the airport. (And there was also the
final romp in the airport's bathroom...)

He told me that he loved me each time—that he didn't want to
leave me, but he left anyway.

Our relationship was now relegated to talking on the phone
every night—recapping our days, getting off on each other's
fantasies in between, but it wasn't enough. And I knew it wasn't
going to be enough for me for too much longer.

I needed him here.

"Forty minutes everyone!" A stage hand slipped past me.
"Places in forty!"

I took a deep breath and walked to a mirror that hung near the
wing. Staring at myself, I looked over tonight's costume—a

glimmering white visage that looked like it'd been plucked from a dream: Sparkling crystals adorned every inch of the leotard, the tutu was freshly fluffed and sprayed with glitter, and my feathered headband was far more defined and layered than the one I'd worn in Durham.

"Aubrey?" A familiar voice said from behind.

"Mom?" I spun around. "What are you doing backstage?"

"We wanted to come and tell you good luck in person." She nodded at my father.

"Thank you…"

"We also want you to know that despite the fact that we still wish you'd pursued law school, we're very proud of you for pursuing your own dreams."

I smiled. "Thank you, again."

"And we are also very, *very* honored to have you as our daughter because you're such an inspiration to all the college students who will be heading to the polls in this year's election—students who have similar dreams and ambitions regarding careers in the arts."

"What?"

"Did you get all that?" She turned to the reporter behind us who was shutting off his device. "Make sure you use that last part as a sound bite for the next commercial."

"Seriously?"

"What?" She shrugged. "I meant every word of that, but it's also good to get it on tape, don't you think?"

I didn't bother with a rebuttal.

My father stepped over and hugged me, posing for an unnatural photo-op, but when the photographer walked away he smiled.

"I'm happy for you, Aubrey," he said. "I think this is where you belong."

"You're just saying that because you think me being here means I won't mess up the campaign at home."

"No, I *know* you being here means you won't mess up the campaign at home." He laughed. "But I'm still happy for you."

"How reassuring…"

"It's true," my mother chimed in. "We're excited for you."

"Ladies and gentlemen we are about to begin our show in exactly one hour!" Mr. Ashcroft bellowed. "If you are not a ballerina, a danseur, or a stagehand please find your way off my stage. Now!"

My parents embraced me—holding onto me for a long time. As they pulled back, they took turns kissing my cheek before they walked away.

I adjusted my headband one last time and checked my phone. Sure enough, there was an email. Andrew.

**Subject: Good luck.**

I'm sorry I couldn't make it to your first opening night, but I look forward to hearing about it tonight when you call me.

I'm sure you'll be quite memorable to everyone in the audience.

—Andrew.

PS—I miss you.

**Subject: Re: Good luck.**

I am not calling you tonight. You should've been here. I'll *think* about recapping it for you next week.

—Aubrey.

PS—You "missing me" would be a lot more convincing if the subject of the email you sent two hours ago wasn't "I miss your pussy."

**Subject: Re: Re: Good luck.**

I know I should've been there. Hence the aforementioned apology.

And you *will* call me.

—Andrew

PS—I miss you both.

**Subject: Re: Re: Re: Good luck.**

I really wanted you to be here…

—Aubrey

I turned off my phone so I wouldn't have to continue messaging him. I needed to focus.

All the rehearsals and dance lessons I'd taken over the past twenty-two years had brought me to this moment. In thirty-six minutes, my every move would be on display for one of the biggest audiences in the dance world.

It would draw critiques from the staunchest critics—the most advent admirers of ballet, and the papers would run early reviews that could make or break the remaining production run. But right now, in this moment, none of that mattered.

This was my dream, I was finally living it, and I could only make sure I was the best I could possibly be.

"Are you ready, Miss Everhart?" Mr. Ashcroft placed his hands on my shoulders. "Are you ready to show this city that you belong here?"

I nodded. "Very much so, sir."

"Good, because I'm ready for them to see that, too." He clapped his hands above his head, signaling the rest of the dancers to circle us.

"Ladies and gentlemen, it is officially opening night," he said. "You've worked hard for months, logged every necessary hour and then some, and I do believe that tonight's execution of *Swan Lake* will be the best execution this audience will ever see." He paused. "If it isn't, I'll make sure you pay for it at tomorrow morning's rehearsal."

There were groans. We knew he wasn't kidding.

"I'll be sitting in the balcony at center stage, and I will not give you one clap, no inkling of applause, if the show is anything less than perfect. Are we clear?"

"Yes sir." We collectively murmured, still intimidated by his power.

"Good. Take your places now." He walked away from us and snapped his fingers. "Make me proud."

I took my place at center stage and turned my back to the curtain—raising my hands above my head. I heard the orchestra giving their instruments one final tuning, heard the pianist replaying the refrain he missed at this morning's rehearsal, and then I heard silence.

Ear deafening silence.

The lights in the gallery flickered, slow at first then faster, and everything went black.

Five...Four...Three...Two...

The pianist played the first stanza of the composition and the curtains rose, cueing the spotlight to shine against my back.

The swan corps—twenty ballerinas dressed in complementing white tutus, formed a circle around me, and as they stood on their toes, tilting their heads back, I slowly turned around to face the audience—pausing, taking all of the nameless faces in, and then I became lost in my own world.

I was Odette, The Swan Queen, and I was falling in love with a prince at first sight, dancing with him underneath a glittering orb of lights, telling him he needed to pledge his love for me if he wanted to break my lake's spell.

The gasps from the audience could be heard over the music, but I kept my focus.

I seamlessly transitioned from the white, sweet swan who wanted nothing more than to fall in love, into the black, evil swan—Odile, who wanted nothing more than to prevent it from happening.

I illustrated love, heartbreak, and devastation over the course of two hours, never stopping to catch my breath, never missing a beat.

In the final frame, where the love of my life vows to die with me instead of honoring his mistaken promise to the black swan, I can't help but deviate from the choreography.

Instead of taking his hand and letting him lead me into the "water," I leapt into his arms— letting him hold me high for all the other swans to see. And then the two of us spun into oblivion— "dying" together.

The music began its decrescendo—half-somber, half-light, and the lights shut off—leaving nothing. Ending everything with blackness.

And silence.

All of a sudden, a raucous applause arose from the audience and a collection of cheers—"Bravo!" "Encore!" "Bravissimo!" echoed off the walls.

The stage lights brightened and I took a bow, looking out into a sea of well-entertained faces: Mr. Petrova was front and center, nodding as he clapped, mouthing, "Good job, good job." My mother was wiping a tear from her eye and looking up at my father, saying, "That's our daughter." Even Mr. Ashcroft, still stone faced, was standing and applauding, stopping once his eyes met mine.

"Bravo." He mouthed before turning away.

I kept a smile plastered on my face as I scanned the room, looking for the one person I wanted—the one person I *needed* to see, but he wasn't there.

"Thank you ladies and gentlemen for attending our opening night," one of the directors said as she took the stage. "Per our opening night tradition, we will now introduce the members of our corps to you..."

I tried to focus on the introductions, tried to focus on someone else other than Andrew, but as I was lifting my head up from another bow, I saw him.

He was there in the front row, in the last seat on the left. He was looking at me and smiling, mouthing, "Congratulations."

"And last but not least, our leading lady of the night and a new principle dancer here at NYCB—Aubrey Everhart!" The director said into the mic, and the audience cheered loudly.

"Miss Everhart?" She nudged me, whispering, "Miss Everhart, you need to take your final bow and leave the stage..."

I didn't move. I continued staring at Andrew.

"Miss Everhart?" She whispered, more harshly now. "Take a bow and get backstage...*Now*..."

I walked away from her and headed straight toward Andrew— taking my time down the stage's side steps. I stood in front of him, looking directly into his eyes—ignoring the confused murmurs of the crowd.

The director said a few more words, Mr. Ashcroft gave his regards, and the curtains closed without me.

As the audience gave one final applause and started to file out of the room, I finally found my voice.

"I thought you said you weren't coming..." I whispered. "Did you come here just to see my show or are you staying a little bit longer?"

"I'm staying a little bit longer."

"Does that mean permanently?"

"No." He wiped away my tears. "It means I'll stay here until you realize how terrible this city is—until you're ready to leave."

"I signed a contract for three years."

"Every contract is negotiable." He smiled and pulled me into his arms. "And if you don't apologize for ruining the closing credits tonight, they just might risk breaching it and fire you…"

"Where will you work?" I asked. "Are you going to practice law? *Can you* practice law?"

He kissed my lips. "I'll be teaching at NYU."

"What?" My heart immediately felt for the future students. "Why?"

"What do you mean, why?"

"You're a terrible teacher, Andrew…All of the interns at GBH hated you."

"I don't give a fuck."

"I'm serious…" I was actually worried. "I think you should reconsider. Teaching isn't for everyone, so—"

"First of all," he said, cutting me off and tightening his grip around me. "I *am* a good fucking teacher. It just depends on the subject matter…" He trailed his finger across my lips. "I can recall teaching you how to do something very well…"

I blushed.

"Second of all, last time I checked, all of the interns at GBH were quite unteachable and they were dumb as stones—all except one."

"The one that was a fucking liar?"

"Yes," he said. "That one."

"I heard she broke all your rules." I brought my hand up to his face. "I heard she ended your one dinner, one night, and no repeats streak… "

"I'm pretty sure that she didn't."

"Is that so?" I narrowed my eyes at him. "Is it still going on? Is that still your personal motto?"

"To a certain extent," he said, pressing his lips against mine. "Since I still like the sound of it, and will only be dating her from here on out, I'll just replace the word 'one' with '*more*'…"

# Epilogue

*Six Years later…*
*New York, New York*

## Andrew

I stood in front of a classroom at New York University—counting down the seconds, asking myself why I'd ever agreed to this.

"Are there any questions?" I looked at my watch.

Several hands flew into the air.

"I'm only answering three of them." I pointed to a young woman in the front row. "Yes, you. What is it?"

"Um…" She blushed. "Good morning, Professor Hamilton. My name is—"

"I don't care what your name is. What is your *question*?"

"Um, it's been about two weeks since the semester started and you have yet to give us a syllabus…"

I ignored her and pointed to a jock in the back row. "Yes?"

"You also haven't told us what books we need to buy…"

"Does anyone in this classroom know the definition of the word, *question*?" I picked the last student, a redhead sitting by the window. "Yes?"

"Is it true that we're required to take turns bringing you coffee every day?"

I looked at the coffee mug on my desk, at the sign-in sheet that listed which student had brought it today.

"It's not a requirement," I said, picking up the cup. "But if you miss your day to bring me my coffee, I'll make sure everyone in this class regrets it."

They groaned collectively and shook their heads. A few of them still had their hands raised, but I was officially done for the day.

"Read pages 153 - 260 from the printout by next class. I expect you to know the ins and outs of each case. Class dismissed." I walked out, saying nothing further.

Slipping into my car, I noticed a new email on my phone.

**Subject: Bathroom.**

Thank you for sending me that very inappropriate note with my flowers today. Everyone in my cohort now knows that you and I have yet to fuck in our brand new bathroom.

Why are you so ridiculous?

—Aubrey.

**Subject: Re: Bathroom.**

You're very welcome for the flowers. I'm hoping that you liked them.

And that wasn't a "note" that I sent you. It's a demand that's about to be addressed within the next few hours.

Why do you deny that you love it?

—Andrew.

I could picture her rolling her eyes at my last message, so I revved up my car and sped back toward our home.

Even though I'd spent the last six years here, I was still building my tolerance for the things I once hated, things that now bothered me less and less, but I still had a long way to go.

Some memories can never be replaced...

Aubrey was completely captivated and entranced by this city, though. Whenever she wasn't incessantly touring with the ballet company, she was insisting that we try every restaurant, theater, and tourist attraction possible—trying to make me fall in love with everything again.

I parked in front of our brownstone—a newly purchased brick

building in Brooklyn, and walked up the steps.

"Aubrey?" I said as I opened the door. "Are you in here?"

"Yes." She called from a distance. "And I'm not in the *bathroom.*"

"You will be eventually." I walked down the hallway, stopping when I saw her hanging another frame in her office.

The walls were covered in pictures of her standing at center stage, a different picture for every night she'd opened a show.

"Do I need to have another room built for you and your photos?" I asked. "You're running out of space."

"No, I think this is the last one."

"Are you still retiring at the end of the month?" I stepped behind her and kissed her neck. "Or have you changed your mind yet?"

"I'm not changing my mind." She turned around to face me. "I think it's time for me to focus on something new."

"Becoming the female version of Mr. Ashcroft when you teach?"

"I won't be that bad," she said. "But I do need a break like you said, I think…"

I nodded. I'd been extremely supportive throughout her professional career—traveling with her out of the country to see some of the shows, hiring a personal massage therapist who was at her beck and call, and documenting all of her achievements from the newspapers.

But I'd recently noted a change—a shift, in her attitude: Although she was happy when she went to rehearsals, even happier when telling me about new things the company was trying, she seemed to be more interested in a life outside of the company, so I suggested that she take a short break.

I was still trying to figure out how she'd interpreted my suggested "break" as a "retirement."

"I loved dancing in Russia." She smiled, pointing to the picture. "Do you remember that?"

"I do remember that…" I said, continuing my assault of her neck, slipping my hand under her shirt.

She murmured as I rubbed my thumb around her nipple, as I gently bit her skin. But then she stepped away. "I actually need you to go fax my revised contract to the company…I have to let them know officially by five o'clock."

"*After* the bathroom." I clasped her hand. "We have four hours."

She rolled her eyes, but she gave in, taking my lead into the bathroom.

I turned on the water and pulled her dress over her head. "If you're hell bent on retiring from performing and simply teaching, we'll have more time to spend together."

"More time for you to convince me to leave New York?"

"We really don't have a reason to stay," I said, threading my fingers through her hair. "If you're going to teach, you can commute."

"And if I don't teach? If I decide to continue dancing instead?"

"I'll buy season tickets." I cupped her face in my hands, raising my eyebrow. "I never asked you to retire, Aubrey...I just think you need a break. You haven't taken a week off in more than six years..."

"I *am* going to take a break..."

"Is it going to last longer than two days?"

"A lot longer..."

"Two weeks?"

"It'll be at least nine months..."

"What?" I backed up, shocked. We'd stopped using protection once we moved in together, but she'd still taken birth control. "What are you saying, Aubrey?"

"I'm saying you're going to be a father," she said, nearly whispering. "And I think that's a good enough reason for us to stay..."

I was silent for several seconds, pressing my palm against her flat stomach.

"Are you okay?" she asked. "Is this not something that you wanted? I wanted to tell you this morning, but you were in a rush, so—"

I cut her off with a deep kiss and pulled her close, rubbing my hands against her bare back. "I'm more than okay..." I looked into her eyes. "It *is* something I wanted..."

She murmured, "I love you," against my lips and I said it back.

Breathless, she leaned against the shower door. "Can you go fax my letter now? It would really be nice if, for once, I wasn't late doing something because you have no self-control and were too busy fucking me."

"I'll definitely fax your letter..." I drew her lip into my mouth and squeezed her ass. "*After* the bathroom."

She tried to dash away one last time, but I pinned her to the wall and kissed her until her body went limp.

Pulling away as she gasped for air, I lifted her leg around my waist—sliding my cock inside of her inch by inch.

Her arms went around my neck as she tilted her hips up, as I gripped her sides and pulled her into me.

"When we get back from dinner..." I whispered and skimmed a hand down her stomach and to her clit, swirling my thumb around it. "I'm going to fuck you until you can't take it anymore..."

She groaned and dragged her nails across my skin. "*Ahhh...*"

"Now that you're quitting, I'm going to be inside of you every day..."

"*Andrew...*"

I felt her body tensing and lifted her other leg around my waist—pressing her back further into the tile. "Every day..."

Her pussy clutched my cock tighter and throbbed against me, so I held her taut and watched as she reached her climax— as she completely let go.

Biting her bottom lip, I held her close to me as another orgasm made its way through her body. "Stop fighting it..."

"I'm....I'm not..."

"Aubrey..." I looked into her eyes as I came seconds after her, and the two of us remained entwined for several seconds as the shower's water poured over us.

"I hate you sometimes..." she whispered, motioning for me to let go of her legs.

"I love you, too." I gently set her down.

I grabbed a loofah, and slowly ran it over her body—pausing when I reached her stomach. "Did you go to the doctor yet?"

"No." She shook her head. "I just took a test...I'm going there tomorrow."

"*We're* going there tomorrow."

She looked as if she was going to say something else, but she simply moaned as I pressed the loofah against her thighs.

"Here," she said, grabbing a different loofah when I was finished. "Let me—"

"No." I gripped her wrist and pointed to the shower bench. "You can sit."

"What?"

"Go sit down."

"Seriously?" She crossed her arms and narrowed her eyes at me. "You're not going to let me return the favor because I'm *pregnant?* Is that what this is?"

"Yes." I washed my chest. "That's exactly what this is."

She sighed. "Andrew..."

"I can't lose another one." I looked into her eyes. "I don't want you doing anything at all."

Nodding slowly, she stepped back and sat on the bench, keeping her gaze locked on mine.

When I was finished, I turned off the water and wrapped her in a towel. Clasping her hand, I led her into our bedroom.

"Do I need to put a cover sheet over your letter?" I asked.

"No, but if you're in an accommodating mood, I would prefer if we skipped your faculty dinner tonight."

"That's not happening." I rolled my eyes and grabbed her sheet off the headboard. "You have plenty of time to get ready for it. I'll be back."

Ignoring her deep sighs, I left the room and headed into my home office. It, too, was covered in frames of her ballet shows. And, much to my annoyance, she'd placed a picture of us kissing right above my desk—a picture that always found its way there no matter how many times I placed my framed law degree there.

I turned on the fax machine and pulled out the tray, stopping once I actually read her letter:

*Dear Mr. Ashcroft, staff of NYCB, and current cohort,*

*I am writing this letter to officially resign as a principle dancer from the company. As we discussed previously, I would like to take on a more instructive role for at least two years, in which I will be pursuing some personal dreams of mine. I have full intent on returning to the stage once the time is right, but at this current moment, I need to do what is best for me and my future family.*

*—Aubrey Everhart*

## *Aubrey*

I adjusted my seatbelt and looked over at Andrew. "How long are you planning to stay at this event tonight?"

"Until it's over."

I rolled my eyes, thinking about the last dull faculty dinner we'd attended. Half of the awardees were sleep an hour into the ceremony.

"Are you nominated for an award or something?" I asked.

"What makes you think someone would *ever* nominate me for an award?"

"Seeing as though you somehow managed to win 'Professor of the Year' three times in a row, I'm pretty sure it's not impossible."

"No." He smiled. "The Professor of the Year banquet is next week."

"And tonight is?"

"Does it matter?" He placed his hand on my exposed thigh, rubbing it gently. "I want you to be here. When do you plan on telling your parents that you're pregnant?"

"Tomorrow…Are you going to tell anyone?"

He was silent for a few minutes. "Jessica."

"*Jessica?*" I laughed. "Seriously?"

"Seriously," he said. "She's a good friend."

I couldn't deny that. Even though she once had an unrelenting crush on him, she'd been nothing but supportive of us since we moved to New York. She called once a month to say hello, but to also ask him for dating advice. She even asked me sometimes.

Pulling the car into a parking garage, he looked over at me. "You stopped taking birth control months ago, didn't you?"

I nodded.

"Why?"

"Because you've talked about wanting to have a child more than you'll ever admit…"

"I told you I wanted you to have a career, to achieve everything you wanted first."

"I have," I said as he put the car in park.

He cupped my face in his hands and stared at me, looking deep into my eyes. He opened his mouth to say something, but there was a sudden knock on the window.

The valet.

He sighed and leaned back, letting a man in a white tuxedo take the keys as another man helped me out of the car.

"Enjoy your night," the two of them said in unison.

Andrew pulled me close and we strolled along a walkway that was adorned with bright lights. As we approached the glass entrance of the restaurant, a host nodded at us.

"Good evening, Mr. Hamilton," he said as he opened the doors. "Miss Everhart."

"Good evening," I said, wondering how he knew my name.

I felt Andrew kissing my hair as we stepped into a dimly lit room where patrons were sitting around white clothed tables.

He led me over to a spot by the windows and pulled out my chair.

I looked around the room, noticing that the usual signs for an over-the-top faculty meet and greet were nowhere to be found. None of the faces looked familiar, and there was no special mention of anything NYU related on the restaurant's menu.

As I turned to face Andrew again, to ask him what was going on, I noticed he'd placed a small black box at the center of the table.

"I was going to wait until after dinner..." He grabbed both of my hands and my heart stopped. "But..."

Everything around me blurred and I took several deep breaths. "But *what?*"

"I want you to have this now. I think I've been very patient regarding this matter, so—"

"Yes." I let his hands go. "I say *yes*...Can I open it?"

He smiled. "Sure."

I took one last deep breath before opening the box, before pulling out the—

"Earrings?" I asked, trying to keep a smile on my face as I looked over the sparkling diamond pointe slippers.

"Yes." He nodded, smiling. "You mentioned wanting some of those two weeks ago, so I figured with your news about the baby..."

I tuned the rest of his sentence out and stared at the jewelry.

"Do you not like them?" He tilted my chin up.

"Yes, but I...I thought..." There were tears welling in my eyes. "Yes...Yes, I like them very much, *Andrew.*"

He raised his eyebrow. "Why does it look like you're about to cry?"

"I'm not..." I stood up. "Can you please excuse me for a minute?"

I didn't wait for him to respond. I walked away and grabbed the elbow of a waiter, asking where the restroom was.

Rushing in that direction as quickly as I could, I checked all of the stalls before releasing a pent up, "Is he serious?!" cry. Then I let the rest of the tears fall down my face.

*I should've known better...*

I shook my head, knowing that I wasn't going to be able to finish tonight's dinner without showing my emotions. I immediately pulled out my phone and started to type a message for him, but he walked through the doors.

"This is the *women's* restroom," I said. "Get out. Now."

"So you can send me an email?" He smirked.

"Yes. So I can send you an email." I stepped back. "I'm almost finished with what I have to say, so if you could just—"

"Why are you crying, Aubrey?" He stepped toward me, making me step backward until I was pressed against the wall. "Was it something I said?"

"I'm about to have your baby, Andrew. We're going to be parents..."

"I'm aware." He glanced at my stomach and wiped tears from my eyes. "Although I'm pretty sure your hormones shouldn't be affected this quickly if you're only a few weeks pregnant."

"Are you ever going to propose?" I couldn't hold that question back anymore. "It's been *six years*..."

"I don't recall setting a time frame."

"You said after I was settled with my career and..." I sighed as he wiped away another stream of tears. "I just want to know if it's a yes or a no so I won't get my hopes up again...If you don't plan on ever marrying me because of your past, because you think I'll hurt you like Ava did, or you just have no desire in ever committing to me for the long-term, I just need you to tell me right now so I can—"

I stopped talking once I felt him slipping a ring onto my finger.

"You only had to wait twenty more minutes." He kissed my forehead, and I looked down at the ring—gasping once I held it in front of my face.

It was a massive princess cut design that featured small bits of blue sapphire around the platinum band. And along the setting that held the main jewel in place, a line of intertwined "As" glimmered beneath the light.

I looked at him in utter shock. "You were going to propose to me here?"

"No." He kissed my lips. "On the roof."

Silence.

"Were you going to get down on one knee?" Another tear fell past my cheeks.

He nodded.

"In front of other people?"

He nodded again.

"Can you still do that?"

"Why would I?"

"For memories sake."

"You already said *yes*."

"I know, but I can temporarily take the ring off so I can still hear whatever you were going to say." I twisted it around my finger, but he stopped me.

"If you take the ring off, I'm going to assume that your answer is *no*..." He glared at me. "But since I know you'll never let it go if I don't actually say the words, I'll say them for memories sake." He grabbed my hand and led me out of the restroom and up a set of steps.

Opening the doors ahead of us, he pulled me through the outdoor section of the restaurant, where patrons sat underneath a white heated canopy. He walked me over to the ledge and placed his jacket over my shoulders before picking me up and setting me atop a cold stone.

Then he looked over his shoulder, at the diners who were now eyeing us suspiciously as he got down on one knee.

"Do you want the edited or the non-edited version?" He looked into my eyes.

"Non-edited..."

"Okay." He took my right hand and held it in his. "Aubrey...The beginning of our relationship was a lie, a huge fucking lie, but for some odd reason, I couldn't be happier that that was the case."

He paused. "Over the past six years, we've dug our way to the truth, and as much as it hurt sometimes, I can honestly say that it was more than worth it."

I blushed as the people behind him fell silent, as they strained to hear what he was saying.

"I wanted to propose to you several years ago, but I didn't want to hold you back or distract you from focusing on your career, so I bought the ring and decided I would wait until you accomplished everything you wanted, until we could actually enjoy some time together."

A woman stood up and put her hand over her heart, mouthing, "Awww…"

"And even though you get under my skin like no other, and you continue to push me out of my comfort zone…There's no one I'd rather be with, and there's nothing I would rather do than fuck your pussy for the rest of my life."

There was a collective gasp, a chorus of "What did he just say?"

"So…" He circled his thumb around my ring. "Will you marry me?"

I nodded, feeling fresh tears fall down my face as he stood up and pulled me into his arms.

"Did you really have to say that last line?" I whispered as he claimed my mouth with his.

"Yes." He trailed his tongue along my lips. "I want you to be well aware that ring or not, I'm still the same Andrew."

"Or Liam…"

"No, *Andrew*." He kissed me again, more passionately this time. "Liam fell in love with the wrong woman…"Andrew" didn't…"

**\*\*The End\*\***

# Dear Incredible Reader,

(Before you read this...Did you read the extended epilogue at the end of RD3? YES...It's there...Go back and read that before this LOL)

When I began working on this series, I was terrified. I'd never written in the erotica genre before, and I was still learning about the romance genre as a whole. Gone were my days of reading Orwell, Didion, and Baldwin; they'd been replaced with the likes of awesome authors who specialized in steamy stories that sent shivers up and down my spine.

So, quite naturally, it took me a while to understand the difference between contemporary romance and erotica. And when I was putting the final touches on Reasonable Doubt 3, I realized that the ending was falling back into my former terrain.

The scenes that showed Aubrey & Andrew in the future were a tad bit too contemporary. Okay, they were sappy...LOL

But since there was no real "flow" to those scenes, and I felt like they might have led you into thinking that there would be an RD4 (I promised you a *trilogy*), I decided to simply end it with their HEA.

Now that their story is complete though, and since quite a few readers have asked about those scenes, the deleted glimpses of their future follow this letter.

**(Back at home after accepting Andrew's proposal)**

*Aubrey*

I slowly rolled on top of Andrew, feeling weak after yet another orgasm. "Hi…"

"Hi." He rubbed his hands against my bare back and kissed my lips.

"You owe me a dinner…" I whispered. "A cooked one, not delivered."

"You think I'm going to get up and do that right now?"

"I think you're going to do whatever I want for the next few months." I smiled, knowing it was true; I could tell. "Do you prefer a boy or a girl?"

"No preference." He shook his head. "It doesn't matter. What about you?"

"I'm partial to a girl…"

"And why is that?"

"I've just always wanted a little girl," I admitted. "To treat her better than my parents treated me, you know?"

"So, you'll cry if it's a boy?"

"I'll cry if he ends up being anything like you."

Laughing, he sat up and pulled me with him. He slipped into a pair of sweat pants and helped me into a slip. Then he took my hand and led me into the kitchen, setting me on one of the bar stools.

I leaned against the countertop as the two of us settled into what had become a routine since we started living together: Contrary to my comment about delivery, Andrew cooked for me whenever I asked. (Of course, there was an oral price that came with it afterwards, but it was one I was more than willing to pay.)

When my touring schedule became hectic and I only had five hours in between the next show and a rehearsal, dinner had always been waiting for me. And every opening night, he'd sent a boxed entrée along with a bouquet of flowers backstage just in case I wanted to eat right away.

"What if it is a girl?" He placed a small chicken salad in front of me. "Do you have any names in mind?"

"Aubrey, but we can spell it with an 'i' instead of an 'ey,' you know?"

He rolled his eyes. "That's not happening."

"I was joking." I plucked a strawberry from my plate. "I was thinking Autumn..."

"Autumn? Is there a reasoning behind that?"

"It's our favorite season," I said. "It's also when I fell in love with you, and when you fell in love with me."

"I fell in love with you in the winter."

"No. You *realized* that you loved me in the winter. You already loved me in the fall."

"I'm pretty sure I didn't." He poured me a cup of juice before sitting next to me. "I need to ask you something."

"Since when do you need permission?"

Cupping my chin, he turned my head so I was facing him. "Do you want a wedding?"

I nodded, running my finger along my ring for the umpteenth time.

"Before or after the baby?"

"Before..."

*A couple months later ...*

**Andrew**

I wasn't sure why Aubrey selected a vineyard in upstate New York for our wedding, but she insisted. We'd toured the venue no less than twenty times per her request, and on every occasion she'd swooned over the acres of lush plants, the small white cottages that stood in the distance, and the massive trees that shaded the area where we would be married.

One of the biggest benefits of being married here, though, was the unlimited fresh wine that was served at the outdoor bar.

"Andrew?" A male voice said from behind as I picked up a glass.

I turned around, finding myself face to face with Aubrey's father. "Governor Everhart."

"Ah, that title has such a nice ring to it, doesn't it?"

I didn't answer.

Sipping a glass of wine, he sighed. "I never thought this day was coming, never thought my Aubrey would get married." He took a longer sip. "To her former *boss*, no less."

I didn't answer that either.

"You're ten years older than Aubrey..." He finally said something that deserved a response.

"Yes, I am. Are you insinuating something?"

"Not at all," he said. "It's clear that you two are in love...You'd have to be to attend all of those overseas ballet shows without falling asleep."

"It's called being supportive."

"I know...Not that it matters now, but I would like to know for sure: Were you two having a relationship while she was your intern at GBH? Did you really just happen to meet again in New York after she quit?"

"Mr. Everhart..." I set my glass down, tired of playing into the story Aubrey had concocted years ago. "Since you asked me so nicely, I'm going to say this once and only once. Me and your daughter were actually—"

"There you are!" His wife came over and slipped her hand in his. "I was looking for you. Are you harassing the groom on the big day?"

"I wouldn't necessarily call it harassment," he said. "I was just asking him a few questions..."

"Oh?" She looked back and forth between us. "What type of questions?"

"He wanted to know if I was sleeping with your daughter when she was my intern."

She gasped, putting her hand on her chest. Then she looked up at him. "Seriously? I think you're really letting this governor thing go to your head. Of course someone like Andrew would never do something like that."

"Of course, I wouldn't." I smiled, nodding my head in agreement. "That's a very terrible rule to break, don't you think? Sleeping with an *intern*, especially an undergraduate intern, since that's what she was at the time, correct?"

He said nothing.

"See?" His wife kissed his cheek and then she turned around and hugged me. "Maybe after the baby you can convince her to reconsider law. Then the two of you can be just like us."

I held back my comment and returned her hug.

Before our lively conversation could go any further, the wedding director walked over with her clipboard.

"The bride-to-be is ready now," she said, smiling. "Time to head on over."

Mr. Everhart looked at me one last time and slowly extended his hand. "She thinks the world of you, and I've never seen her this happy before. Thank you…"

His wife hugged me one last time, and the two of them walked away.

I found it quite ironic that he'd seen Aubrey recently, because I hadn't seen her in three days. She'd scheduled her bachelorette party for this past weekend and claimed that she needed to get a few last things for the wedding on her own.

As I walked down the path of petals that led to the altar, I looked over the small crowd: Aubrey's parent, a few of my coworkers, Mr. Bach and Mr. Greenwood, and a group of dancers from Aubrey's cohort.

I didn't attempt to invite anyone from my family. I didn't see a point in asking them to come, or pretending that we had any type of relationship for the sake of a wedding.

"What took you so long?" Jessica tilted her head to the side as I took my spot next to her. "I told you that this is supposed to be the happiest day of your life."

"I told you that you could wear a dress." I looked over her tailored tuxedo.

"I wanted to commit to playing the role of the best man. You know, do my best to look like one of your guy friends."

"Your hair is in curls."

"Yes, but…" Her cheeks reddened. "My boyfriend loves when I wear my hair like this, especially when we're in bed because he likes to—"

"*Jessica*…" I couldn't help rolling my eyes, but then I laughed. "Thank you for being here."

"My pleasure." She hugged me. "I'm very happy for you and Aubrey. It's about time you finally married her."

I didn't get a chance to reply. The small orchestra to my right had begun to play, and the audience was standing to its feet.

Stepping out all alone—just like she wanted, Aubrey locked her eyes on me as she slowly made her way down the aisle.

There were whispers from everyone, flattering comments about how beautiful she looked, and I honestly couldn't take my eyes off of her.

Her hair was pulled to one side, in a bevy of curls that fell past her shoulder and lightly grazed the top of her chest. She was wearing a thin crystal headband that featured a few white feathers and matched her stunning dress: It was strapless and hugged her hips-perfectly—hiding her small baby bump. Adorned with subtle crystals that glimmered on every inch of the fabric, its long train stretched down the aisle.

As she stepped closer, I wiped her eyes with my fingertips.

"Stop crying," I whispered, taking her hand.

She nodded, but more tears made their way down her face.

As the small crowd took their seats, the pastor began to read scriptures.

"The couple has elected to keep this ceremony short and simple," the pastor said, holding back a laugh. "Their exact words to me were, Just marry us and get everyone to the reception. We're only paying you for one hour."

The audience laughed, and I slipped my arm around Aubrey's waist—pulling her close to me.

"I guess that's my cue." The pastor laughed louder. Then he cleared his throat, whispering that I needed to let her go, but I ignored him and kissed Aubrey.

"Mr. Hamilton?" He cleared his throat again.

Briefly letting Aubrey's lips go, I spoke. "We both told you not to give a speech. Just skip to the 'now pronounce' part." And then I claimed Aubrey's mouth once more, ignoring everything else around us, whispering in between breaths that she was forever mine.

*A few years later….*

### Aubrey

Our three year old daughter, Autumn, absolutely adores Andrew. She follows him around whenever he's at home, refuses to let anyone else tuck her in at night, and if she wakes up late, she runs into our bedroom in the morning just to make sure "He's here."

With the exception of her blond hair, she's inherited all of his features—his piercing blue eyes, his smile, and unfortunately, his personality.

She's also strangely addicted to Pop-tarts—*coffee flavored* Pop-tarts.

"Don't even think about it, Autumn." I cross my arms as she pushes her plastic ladder across the kitchen floor. "You had two for dessert, so you can't have another one until tomorrow morning."

She stops for a moment—looking as if she understands. But then she continues pushing the ladder across the floor.

"*Autumn…*" I step in front of her just as she presses it against a lower cabinet. "Tomorrow morning."

"Daddy said—"

"I don't care what *Daddy* said. I said no."

Seemingly hurt, she gasps and rushes out of the room.

I sigh and start to silently count.

*And in five…four…three…two…*

Andrew walks into the kitchen, carrying her at his side. Without glancing my way, he strolls right over to the countertop and opens a new package of Pop-tarts, handing one to her.

"Thank you!" She squeals as he sets her down, and as if she's trying to ease her betrayal, she breaks the tart and hands me a piece.

"I want to share with you, Mommy," she says, looking into my eyes. "Will you share with me?"

I resist the urge to roll my eyes as I take her peace offering. "Thank you, Autumn."

"You're welcome!" She gives a bigger piece to Andrew, and then she rushes off again.

"Andrew," I say, taking a deep breath. "We need to talk."

"About a fucking Pop-tart?"

"This is not about a Pop-tart. This is about your continued inability to say no to a three year old. If I say no, she immediately runs to you. And instead of being on my side about it, you simply say yes."

"Then maybe you should just start saying *yes.*"

I narrow my eyes at him and step closer. "She's going to be spoiled rotten if you keep this up…You don't have to say no all the time, but once or twice wouldn't kill you."

"It actually would." He pulls me into his arms and kisses me until I'm breathless. "I don't want to make her cry. Ever."

I suck in a few breaths as he rubs my back.

"She only asks for treats every now and then," he says. "She doesn't really ask for much else."

This is true. Outside of her growing doll collection, her attention has lately been geared toward the empty studio Andrew had built in our apartment last year.

She's starting to show slight interest in ballet: She watches me rehearse on the weekends, laughs whenever I show her my numerous tutus, and she even imitates me by holding her hands above her head from time to time.

"Daddy, can you tuck me in now?" Autumn returns to the kitchen and looks at Andrew—still chewing on that Pop-tart.

"Of course," he says, clasping my hand.

We follow her into her bright yellow bedroom, and as usual, wait for her to pick a book from her shelf.

She selects *Cinderella* today, and surprisingly hands the book to me. "I want Mommy to read it."

Smiling, I wait for Andrew to tuck her under the covers, and then the two of us sit on the edge of the bed—taking turns reading until she falls asleep.

"She didn't even make it to the midnight part this time." I kiss her forehead.

"Are you complaining?"

"No, I'm just surprised."

"You probably bored her to sleep with your monotonous tone." He pulls me up and turns off the lights. "She stays up to the very last page whenever I read."

"Would you like to sleep on the couch tonight?"

"Only if you'll be putting your pussy on my face."

"I won't be." I follow him into our room and get into bed. "You'll be lucky if I even let you kiss me tonight."

He slips in next to me and pulls me close—calling my bluff by kissing me again and again.

"When's the last time we had sex?" I whisper against his lips.

"This morning in the shower." He slides a hand between my legs, gently rubbing my clit. "You don't remember?"

"Yes…" I moan softly as he bites my bottom lip and rolls me

on top of him.

"Are you sure?" He kisses my neck. "I can fuck you again to make you remember."

"Ahhh…" I feel his cock hardening beneath me, feel him palming my ass as he continues kissing my skin. "Andrew…"

I draw my head back and kiss his lips, running my fingers through his hair. I feel him pulling at the back of my bra, unsnapping the first hook, but a familiar sound breaks our moment.

It's the patter of little feet against the hallway's hardwood floor.

Sighing, Andrew kisses my forehead and gently rolls me off of him.

"I'm scared…" Autumn says as she walks into our room. She walks over to Andrew's side of the bed and lifts her hands up. "Can I sleep in here?"

"Yes." He immediately picks her up and places her between us, tucking her in once again. His hand reaches out for mine and he caresses it, silently saying we'll finish in the morning.

"How much longer do you think she'll do this?" he whispers an hour later. "It's starting to happen twice a week."

"Is it bothering you?"

"Not particularly."

"Good." I sit up and lean over Autumn, briefly kissing him on the lips before returning to my pillow. "Because I'm pretty sure it'll keep happening until you learn to tell her no…"

# Acknowledgments

WHOA. JUST WHOA.

This is probably going to be one of the most unprofessional author notes ever, but if you know me, you shouldn't be surprised. LOL.

Thank you Tamisha Draper for being there for me throughout my entire career—for pushing me to do my best each and every time, and for reminding me what's most important. I could never do this without you, and even though I'm sure your husband shakes his head at the forty times my name crosses your phone's screen a day, I'm happy you ignore him and still pick up. You are the best friend a girl could ever ask for, and I couldn't be more grateful that you've stuck by my side through all the good, the bad, and the utterly insane. I love you.

Tiffany Downs, OMG I'm so happy to have you back again. You are the balance—the perfect balance, and your support, advice, and friendship mean the world to me. Thank you for telling me that my "style" is just "my style" and that it's okay to be different.

Alice Tribue, OMG. OMG. THANK YOU for being my anchor in the sea of self-publishing. I had no idea that authors could be friends. No. idea. But I'm so happy to have someone like you who understands my version of crazy, someone who's there for me through thick and thin, and someone who actually thinks I don't suck. LOL

Keshia Langston, you are the most humble and honest author I know and I can't tell you how refreshing it is to know someone who just "gets" me, you know? #FLY HARD (Or as you would say...#FLYbitch LOL)

Brooke Cumberland, I'm sure I won't be winning any "book signing assistant of the year" awards and that I'm like the worst texter ever (Okay...There has to be someone worse than me...has to be LOL), but I want you to know that your friendship is invaluable to me. You are kind, thoughtful, compassionate, and even though you're crazy (Yes. You are crazy LOL), I wouldn't trade you for the world.

Laura Dunaway, even from afar, even thousands of miles away, I feel your support and love and I can't thank you enough for being there with me through it all.

Bobbie Jo Malone Kirby, I'm struggling with the words to write right now because how can I possibly say that I love you more than you'll ever know? That you believe in me more than I believe in myself, and that you keep me sane through it all? I am so damn happy that you walked into my life last year—still can't believe how seamlessly everything fell together, and now that you're here, you're mine forever and I'm never letting you go.

Natasha Gentile, thank you for being the crazy, nonstop emailing, nonstop *shut up Whitney and finish this book* person that you are. You're awesome inside and out, and I just might see you in Montreal soon...

Natasha Tomic, I'm utterly speechless at the amount of love and support you've shown to me and this series, for the magical strings you managed to pull while you were in NOLA back in May (THANK YOU), and for the heart filled messages you sent me when things were in disarray. I can't seem to find the proper phrasing that says, "I heart you big, I think you're incredible, and I'll never ever forget all you've done for me," so I will leave it at this...and then re-upload this book with the proper phrasing LOL

Nicole Blanchard, thank you for the teasers that saved my book.

Literally. You have no idea how critical those were for RD1, and I'm so honored that you stepped in to be my PR/PA during this series when things were getting bigger than I could've ever imagined. THANK YOU.

Kimberly Brower, THANK YOU, THANK YOU, THANK YOU for reading this book over and over and helping me smooth out all of the flaws while I was losing my mind. You have no idea how much that means to me! You kept me sane during a very stressful time period, and I will never, ever forget that.

Thank you to all my friends, new and old, that I've made so far— Kimberly Kimball (You're going to kick ass this September, don't' worry), Stephanie Locke (I can't wait to meet you in St Louis, in person), Michelle Kannan (Did you catch your name in this? LOL), Lisa Pantano Kane (Thank you for reading everything, and I'm serious about that beta gig lol), & Lauren Blakely (You are my role model and you seriously inspire me more than you'll ever know…).

Thank you to every single blogger who promoted the hell out of this series and made it as successful as it became—to list a few, Milasy & Lisa at The Rockstars of Romance, Jenny & Gitte at TotallyBooked, Christine at Shh Mom's Reading, Nadine Colling at Hook Me Up Book Blog, Michelle Cole at The Blushing Reader Blog, Lori Economos at Sinfully Sexy, Tara and Tracie at Halos and Horns, Alison East at Three Chicks and Their Books, Hetty Rasmussen at BestSellers and BestStellars, Christine Cheff at Unhinged Book Blog, Miranda and Amie at Red Cheeks Reads, Cara Arthur at A Book Whore's Obsession, and COUNTLESS more! (Okay, now seriously…I *am* a scatter brain, so if I left you out, it wasn't intentional (I promise!), and since I self-published this, I can definitely add your name/blog and re-upload this book. LOL But seriously, though just tell me…)

Thank you to Evelyn Guy for the final proofing as always.

Thank you A MILLION TIMES OVER to Erik Gevers for stepping in to do the formatting. (Sometimes it's better to let a professional handle it LOL)

Thank you to my mother, LaFrancine Maria, for being there for me every step of the way, for making sure I keep everything in perspective, and for believing in everything I do. I LOVE YOU.

Last, and NEVER EVER least, THANK YOUUUUU to the best readers ever! You have made this Southern girl's dreams come true and I owe you everything! Yes, this is the last book for Aubrey & Andrew. Yes, I am known to change my mind but I think this one is sticking LOL. And no, no, no, I will not update their lives on my blog...just kidding. I totally will. I love you more than you'll ever know, and am grateful to have you aboard the F.L.Y. crew...

F.L.Y. (Fucking Love You)

Whit

39983127R00173